GREENWICHTOWN

GREENWICHTOWN

JOYCE PALMER

ST. MARTIN'S PRESS ✿ NEW YORK

www.stmartins.com

Design by Susan Walsh

ISBN 0-312-26597-2

First Edition: September 2001

10 9 8 7 6 5 4 3 2 1

To the memories of Fay

ACKNOWLEDGMENTS

Special thanks to the following people.

Ken for his love, support, and encouragement, especially when it was so hard to continue. Without him, I couldn't have done it.

Sunnypoo for all her love, help, sacrifices, and for always being there when I needed her.

Andre and Alecia for all the hugs, laughter, and purpose.

My wonderful professional and caring agent, Jean Naggar, for her commitment to my success.

My sharp editor, Diane Higgins, for her genuine belief in me, her positive input, and for making this book possible.

The Tarpon Springs Writers group for providing me with the warmth of a real family and constant encouragement.

GREENWICHTOWN

1

I WANT TO STOP crying but I can't. How can she do this to me? My god, my provider, my mother. Maybe she doesn't understand how I feel. I want to go with her, to help her sell tobacco, to help her call out, "Tobacco! Tobacco!" But she says that I can't go with her.

"Why not?" I ask.

"Cause the sun goin' be hot and the road goin' burn you feet, cause you no have no shoes," she replies.

I look at her bare dirty feet, callused from years of walking barefooted; her skirt that was once blue, but because of all its washings, the color has faded. Ma has only one and a half skirts: one, because it's the best one she has; half, because it's full of holes and banana stains. The half she wears most of the time.

Ma is wearing the broad-brimmed straw hat that she made herself. Her face is bony with hardly any meat on it. She has no front teeth, because they rotted from lack of brushing. We have no toothbrushes or toothpaste, because we can't afford them. Her hands are rough; her nails are jagged from tobacco farming.

"But Ma, you don't have no shoes either," I try to argue.

"Look! You can't come, and don't back-answer me, you hear?"

"Me coming with you!" I say in protest.

She stares at me, her eyes warning me not to follow her. I stare back, watching as she lets out a frustrated sigh, turns her back to me, and starts walking away. I decide to follow her, but I only take a half step for each one of hers, hoping that when she realizes that I am following her, it will be too far for her to send me back. But then she suddenly stops right in front of the budding hibiscus tree, breaks off a small twig, and starts heading toward me. Immediately I stop, digging my big toe into the brown dirt as she comes nearer with the twig in her right hand, while holding the basket of tobacco on her head with the other.

"Ma, me want come wit' you." I plead to her, and for a moment her eyes make me feel as if she will let me come with her. But then she raises the twig, and immediately I run back toward the house.

"Don't follow me!" are her last words as she leaves the yard. And then, as if suddenly remembering, she adds, "Me will bring back sweets fi you."

I must be about three or five years old; my sister Mavis told me so. I have sores all over my body; one on my forehead from a mosquito bite and several others on my bottom and on my legs from falling off sleighs. Ma says that I have bad skin, for every little scratch I receive turns into a sore instead of healing like it is supposed to. I walk back into the house where Julie lies sleeping, and shaking her awake I cry, "Julie, Ma leave me!"

"Hush ya, she soon come back," she says, as she hugs my sore-ridden body.

It is early morning, for the sun has just risen, and suddenly a pang of hunger reminds me that Ma didn't give us anything to eat before she left. She didn't have anything to eat either.

Our house is built of wood—rough pieces of wood. The roof is made of rusting zinc sheets, with tar covering the holes; but the roof leaks every time it rains. There isn't any tile or cement on the floor; it's just plain dirt. There are only two rooms, with the only furniture being two beds. The beds have no bases, just a big pillow on the dirt floor that we stuffed with dried banana leaves.

We built our kitchen from bamboo; there are four big bamboo posts placed rectangularly into the ground, and between them are smaller posts placed close together. We wove small pieces of bamboo between all the posts till we reached the top. On top we put more large posts to form the roof, then we covered the roof with coconut limbs. Inside the kitchen we cook our food, using wood for fuel and three stones for the pot to sit on. We have only two aluminum pots, five plastic bowls, four spoons, and five mugs, two of which were made from empty condensed milk cans. We have a toilet: a hole in the ground with a wooden box over it to sit on. There is bamboo all around it, forming the walls.

"Julie, you goin' make tea fi me?" I ask.

"We only have a little bit a sugar, and some green banana," Julie answers.

Julie is Ma's seventh child, and Mavis said that she is about eight years old. Me, I am the eighth and last. Clive, my brother, and Mavis, who is also my sister, live with us too and are still in bed sleeping. Mavis says that she is about twelve years old and that Clive is fourteen. My other two brothers and two sisters are grown and live someplace in the city.

Julie and I, we search for wood to make the fire, taking only the small twigs that we can carry. After finding the wood, we have to fetch water too. We get water from a spring a mile away from the house and carry it back in a small metallic paint bucket. While at the spring Julie says that I should wash my face, so that it looks cleaner. But I complain that the water is too cold, and I ask her what is the sense of washing my face now, when to-morrow I will have to wash it again? She tells me that if I wash my face with early morning spring water, it will give me the power to see spirits. But still I refuse, telling her that the water is too cold.

"Look, Fay! It not that cold," she says, washing her own face. Then I see her whole body trembling when the water touches her face, and I laugh, for I know that she is trying to trick me. But to make her feel better, I wipe the corners of my eyes with my dress and say, "Julie, look at me face, it clean now." But she only rolls her eyes toward the sky to show that she has given up on me and my dirty face.

For breakfast we make mint tea in the black pot and then roast a couple of green banana fingers in the fire, and sprinkle them with salt. We never have lunch, but when Ma comes home from selling tobacco, we will have dinner.

We make kites from the plastic bags that we find on the road, and for a tail we use a piece of fabric from the old curtain that hangs at the window. We have never flown our kites because we have no string to tie them to. Ma said that she would buy us some thread when she had some money, but that was a long time ago.

We make sleighs from coconut limbs. We take them up to the top of a hill not far from the house, sit on them, and slide to the bottom with dust covering our whole bodies. A lot of times going down the hill, the sleighs roll over with us, and we fall headlong at the bottom. Our hands and feet are scratched up, and at this point we quit and head for the river. The river is behind Mass T's property, behind the hill.

Mass T is a very old and kind man. He has four cows on his property, and sometimes he'll give Ma a whole bucket of milk, which becomes the day's meal. For breakfast we'll have a piece of bread (that's only if Ma sells any tobacco) and a large cup of hot cow's milk with sugar. For dinner Ma'll make a big pot of cornmeal porridge. In return for the milk, my brother Clive runs errands for Mass T, like fetching water and getting firewood. Mass T sells fresh cow's milk, and everyone buys milk from him. When Ma has some money we buy milk from him too, but Ma hardly has any money, so he gives us more than we buy. Other families trade yams, tomatoes, or whatever they have for milk. Everyone likes Mass T because even if someone doesn't have anything to trade he will let them have the milk.

At the river we wash the clothes we are wearing and bathe our bodies without soap. Then we walk home through Mass T's property, being careful not to get any cow ticks on us. Going home, all we can think about is dinner. What will Ma cook? A lot of times Ma has nothing to cook but the root of a yam or a lone roasted breadfruit. So, we always expect the worst, and on many occasions, we search for anything that can help with dinner.

Sometimes we go over a wooden bridge into a large banana plantation at the far end of the river, and steal maybe three dozen green bananas. On rare occasions, we find ripe ones that we eat immediately. Clive sometimes climbs coconut trees and picks young jelly coconuts, which we break open, drink the sweet, clear liquid, and eat the soft meat from inside. If there are any old dry coconuts on the tree, we take them home to Ma, and she makes a sauce called *rundun,* by boiling the coconut milk, till only the creamy part remains. Then dinner is boiled green bananas and *rundun.* Ma even makes her own cooking oil from coconuts. Our favorite time is mango season, for we can survive the whole day on ripe fleshy mangoes. Sometimes we race to see who can eat the most mangoes the fastest. Everyone's face becomes plastered with the sweet juices of mangoes, and our clothes get yellow stains all over them. Clive always wins, but Mavis says it is only because he is greedy, and the fact that I finish last means I am less greedy. But still I admire my brother's greediness, and when I am eating mangoes my only aspiration is to be like him.

Whenever it is ackee season, Clive climbs ackee trees and picks mature ackees; only the open ones with the yellow and black part exposed beneath the red ackee pod. Mavis says that ackee and salt fish are the national dish, but we can't afford to buy salt fish. So we cook ackee and boiled dumplings.

One day after Ma goes off to sell tobacco, all four of us— me, Julie, Mavis, and Clive—go hunting for birds. Clive has a beautiful slingshot that he made himself. He never lets us use it, but he does let us select stones for it. Today we are lucky: We go into the woods and there is this small bird sitting on a low branch. Immediately we stand still while Clive positions himself to shoot the bird. Unfortunately I am standing on top of an ant's nest without knowing it, so as Clive starts the slingshot I start screaming. The bird flies away.

"Wha' wrong wit' you?" Clive asks angrily.

"Ants bite me up!" I reply through my tears, while stamping my feet to get the ants off them. Mavis picks me up and carries me back to the house, while Julie and Clive continue looking for birds.

"Let me see you foot," Mavis commands as she puts me down on the large pillow filled with dried banana leaves. My feet are swollen and have big lumps where the ants attacked.

"Me goin' get some bush fi rub you foot. Me soon come back!" Mavis says and goes outside. She comes back with some sticky leaves that she rubs on my lumps, and to my surprise the lumps begin hurting less.

Soon after, Clive and Julie return home with grins on both their faces. As soon as we see the two birds they have brought home, we start grinning too. "How you manage catch them?" Mavis asks.

"After you and Fay gone, me and Julie see the same bird that did fly away, and me shoot at it again, and it drop out a' the tree," Clive proudly replies.

"Then when we a come back to the yard, me see one more

bird right in front of me, and me show Clive, and Clive shoot it," adds Julie. Even though the birds are small, we make a nice pot of soup with them, using yam, green bananas, pumpkin, coconut milk, and young leaves from the dasheen tree as we have seen Ma do.

We all fill our bellies with soup and just sit around waiting for Ma to come back from selling tobacco. Ma comes home, and we give her some soup and watch the expression on her face. She looks at us as if we are her mothers and we are feeding our child. We can see by the way she drinks the soup that she is pleased. Pleased that today she has something to eat that her children have provided. It isn't much, but it makes her feel like we share her burden of trying to provide for four children without much help. At this time I feel such contentment, sitting on the ground in the kitchen with Ma drinking our soup.

Ma has some money from her tobacco sales, and to show us her gratitude for the soup, she sends Clive to buy a can of sardines and a pound of flour, so we can have sardine and boiled dumplings for dinner. I love this meal, and I cherish each taste of the dumpling soaked in sardine gravy. We don't have sardine very often, as many times Ma comes home without selling a single piece of tobacco. We see the disappointment on her face and by the way she carries her still-loaded basket, slumped over like an old woman and dragging her dusty feet. Days like these we go to bed without dinner.

Today is Saturday. How do I know? Because Ma told me so. For us there is no time, no date. Only today I know it is Saturday because it is important.

There is an old lady. I don't know how old she is. She must be very old because she walks bent over with a stick. Her name is Miss Sissy, but everyone calls her Missy for short. She lives all by herself down the track from us. We never see her too often, but Ma fetches water and wood for her sometimes. Missy has a son who lives in the city, and very often he brings her bread, canned mackerel, rice, flour, and soap. Sometimes Missy will offer Ma some food after Ma has helped her, but Ma refuses, saying that we're okay, but we need the food. Ma says that she is not going to live off Miss Sissy. "Why not?" we ask.

Ma says, "Me don't want be no leech on nobody!" Sometimes we go and fetch water for Missy after Ma goes selling, even though she already has water, hoping that she will offer us the food that Ma normally refuses. She never does.

Today is Saturday, and Missy died three days ago. Ma cried, but we only cried because Ma was crying and not because Missy died. Normally when anyone dies, a nigh-night is kept for them. A nigh-night is a get-together feast for the dead, but the dead don't eat, only the living hungry people. A nigh-night is supposed to be kept every night after the person dies until the person is buried. Missy's nigh-night is different, for her son has money for only one good nigh-night because nigh-nights are expensive, as there'll be rum, fried fish, bread, bammy, goat-head soup, and plenty of food. Today is Saturday, and we are going to Missy's nigh-night.

When we go to the river to wash ourselves, Ma comes with us too. She takes the dirty clothes to wash, but there isn't much as we don't have much clothes, and none of us have any shoes. Mavis has the most clothes, four blouses and three skirts. Clive has one shirt, one pair of pants, an old T-shirt, and an old pair of shorts. Julie has one dress, one skirt, and two blouses. Me, I have the least amount of clothes. I have one beautiful dress with prints of flowers all over it and a broad waistband that ties into a bow at the back. I love the dress so much that I keep it folded up all the time. I never wear that dress, as I am afraid of getting banana stains on it. I get by, by wearing Julie's and Mavis's blouses that hang on my skinny body going down to my ankles, looking like an oversize dress. Mavis, Julie, and I have two pairs of underwear each but Clive doesn't have any. Today I will be wearing my beautiful dress to Missy's nigh-night.

Today we have soap. Ma has soap. She bought a bar of cake soap for the laundry, which we use to wash bodies with. She watches the bar of soap like a hawk. She doesn't buy cake soap very often, because we can't afford it.

I am in the process of bathing myself, when I find myself staring at the river so intently that I feel as if I'm hypnotized. A wonderful feeling has engulfed me, for I am in love with the river. I am afraid of it, yet I love the way the water runs around the big rocks. I love the rounded stones in it, where Ma puts the clothes to dry. I love the peace of the river. Peace? Yes. She never cries, she never hungers for food like us. She's always open, always free. Free to carry us away if we get in her current. I wish I could be a river. Does she feel us as we enter into her edge and wash ourselves? Does she love to see us come to her dirty and walk away feeling clean? Does she feel? I am standing there in a daze, naked but warm with the sunlight on my body. I listen to her speaking to me with her every gurgle, her every splash, her every whisper taking my thoughts flowing with her.

"Fay, what the hell you doin' wit' the soap? You no see that you goin' melt it down if you leave it in the water!" yells Ma's angry voice breaking my thought. By the time we leave the river, the sun is high in the sky and the ground is hot, but not too hot for us to walk home.

When we reach home, Ma combs my hair into plaits. I put on my dress, Mavis puts on her best skirt and blouse, Julie puts on her dress, Clive puts on his pants and shirt, and Ma puts on her skirt and blouse. There we are, all five of us, very dressed but with no shoes. We feel good, we are clean, and we are with Ma.

We arrive at Missy's yard, and everyone that knew Missy is there. The smell of fried fish fills the air, and everyone seems happy about the nigh-night although Missy is dead. The men are busy playing cards and dominoes, while the women sit talking idly about their day-to-day chores. I can think only of food, and food alone. I can't wait to sink my teeth into the deep-fried sprats that the women prepared with vinegar, pimento, and onions.

Soon I have eaten so much food that I think my belly is going to burst, but I am so happy. When it starts getting dark, the adults fill empty soft drink bottles with kerosene to make bottle lamps and stick pieces of tightly rolled newspaper into the mouths to form the wicks. Everyone is getting ready for the singing of the nigh-night songs. Ma loves to sing, and she leads the crowd into the singing of "Come By Ya, Me Lord." Mass T has brought his drum and somebody else has brought a tambourine. The whole place comes alive with the beating of the drum, the rattling of the tambourine, the harmonizing voices, the dancing, and the swaying. Everyone claps and sings, and some who do not know the words hum along with the tune. Some of the men are drunk from drinking white rum, and some of the women are drunk too, but they pretend to be sober. Later on everyone starts heading home with the drunken ones staggering with the flames on their torches swaying from side to side, as if the flames were drunk too. They sing all the way home, the same song over and over again. We go home down the track, and while Mavis and Clive walk beside Ma, who holds the bottle lamp, Julie and I try to catch fireflies. When we arrive home Ma looks sort of strange, as if there is a light inside her too.

The next day is Missy's funeral. Mavis tells me that it is Sunday. She says that Sunday comes after Saturday, and that Ma's friend is going to be buried. Just like yesterday we go to the river and wash ourselves, then we get dressed in the clothes from the day before and head for Missy's yard.

There are all these people dressed in black and white. Some

are wearing old clothes, some are wearing nice-looking clothes, and some people even have shoes on; nice shoes with heels. I guess that they must be rich people, not like me and my bare feet. Of course Missy is there too. She is lying in front of her doorstep in a coffin made of dark brown wood, coated with shiny varnish. She lies on a white fluffy fabric and has flowers around her head. She looks so different now; her face has ugly dark marks on it, and she appears to be sleeping.

Most of the people have wreaths with them, and the Reverend Dixon has a great big Bible with him. He is a fat man with a round face who always asks us, "Why don't you come to church?" And we always reply, "We goin' come next week." But we never go, as the truth is Ma doesn't like his church for it is too far away and she has already been baptized in the Church of Zion. At the Church of Zion people wrap their heads with turbans, get into the spirit, and roll all over the ground and speak in tongues. They say it is the language that the angels and spirits speak to them in. I never understand why they have to jerk so feverishly and roll on the ground to speak to the spirit, and I wonder, What does the spirit tell them? Ma goes there every week and she has her own robe that she keeps at the church, a long white one that goes all the way down to her ankles, with a red cord tied around it. Sometimes I go with her and watch the happenings of the church.

The Church of Zion is built of bamboo with a basin of flowers at the altar. The benches are also made of bamboo, and the roof is made of thatch. The leader is called Moses. He is a tall skinny man with long uncombed hair and a long beard, as he never cuts or combs them. He wears sandals all the time, and his toenails are so long they look like claws. Inside the church there are signs written in red paint on white fabric. The people beat drums and shake tambourines, and all the men and women including Ma wrap their heads with turbans despite the heat.

But still I like the Reverend Dixon; his clothes are always clean, and he always wears nice shoes. Today he is wearing his black suit with a white necktie, and a silver cross hangs from his neck. Missy's son is wearing black pants, a white shirt, a black tie, and he is one of those people wearing shoes.

The reverend makes a speech as we stand in the front part of Missy's yard, about Missy going to heaven, and that she will be in the arms of God. Now the crowd is crying, wiping tears, and blowing their noses. Then slowly they begin to sing "Amazing Grace." They sing a few more hymns, and then Missy's son and three men pick up the coffin and take it to the back of the yard, where a hole was already dug and cement already mixed. The crowd follows the coffin, and as they lower the coffin inside the hole, more crying begins. The men pour dirt and then cement over the hole, and put a tombstone with Missy's name and age on it, along with a white wooden cross. Then everyone puts their wreaths on top of the grave and all around it.

Finally we are going to eat, and all I can think about is the smell. The smell of curried goat, fried fish, fried dumplings, roasted breadfruit, rice and peas, and goat-head soup. Soon almost everyone is busy eating; those who aren't sitting on makeshift benches of flat rocks or tree stumps are sitting on the ground. Missy's son is sitting there looking all sad, but I am happy as I am about to have a feast. Mavis, Julie, Clive, and Ma join the food line while I sit on the ground and wait.

"Hey, Fay, wha' happen?" I turn around to face my good friend Stumpy, who despite being the same age as I am is a bit shorter.

"Nothin'," I say as he sits down beside me, wearing black pants, a white shirt, and like me he has no shoes. I have known Stumpy all my life, he lives with his mother and father in a small house next to Mass T's property. Stumpy's father plants tomatoes to sell at the market, and his mother is pregnant; and all that you need to find her with is her belly. Unlike Stumpy I have no father, and Mavis tells me that when I am older, she will tell me about him.

"You eat already?" I ask.

"Yes, cause me mother help share the food, and me the first one fi get," he replies.

"Ma gone fi food fi me," I say.

"Yesterday me help Papa fork up the ground fi plant more tomato. Him no make me use the fork, so me just use a piece a stick, him say him soon plant the seed them."

"You want some a me food when Ma come?" I ask.

"No, man, me belly full up," he says as he stands up and pushes his belly out.

"So wha' you a do tomorrow?" he continues.

"Me not doing nothin'," I reply.

"You want we go over plantation tomorrow?" I ask.

"Yeah, man, after me finish me tea, me will come over you yard."

"All right," I answer as Ma gives me a plate of food.

"Wha' happen, Stumpy?" Ma asks.

"Nothin', Miss Voy," Stumpy says as he heads toward his mother, who is drinking soup.

Just like in his church, the Reverend Dixon has a crowd around him. He is eating while he is preaching, about the good Lord this and the good Lord that, while the crowd utters an occasional "Praise the Lord!" between mouthfuls.

After the meal everyone just sits around talking, enjoying the get-together and secretly hoping for another funeral so that they can get another free meal. Afterwards everyone helps clean up the mess in Missy's yard and starts leaving, each expressing their sadness about Missy's death. We stay behind, for Missy's son is going to give Ma some of Missy's things. She didn't have anything much, but Ma will get her old wooden table and four beaten-up chairs, along with the two old dented black pots that Missy

cooked in. Ma also receives leftover fish, curried goat, and food
that Missy had in the house. Ma thanks Missy's son, and we head
home down the track. As soon as we're inside, I change into
Mavis's blouse; then I neatly fold my beautiful dress and put it
on the table.

The next day Ma works on her flower garden; she's got Joseph
coats, ten-o'clock flowers, creepers, potted plants, and many
other flowers that I don't know the names of. The garden makes
the house look prettier, with its neat rows of stones Ma has
collected and designed around the flowers. A couple yards away
are neat rows of tobacco plants. Ma has another smaller garden
next to the tobacco, where she plants tomatoes, pumpkin, and
anything else that can help to feed us.

Ma gives us leftover fried fish with roasted breadfruit and mint
tea for breakfast. Clive is still sleeping, Mavis is washing the few
dirty dishes, while Julie sits in the doorway twining her hair. I
am waiting for Stumpy so that we can go over to the plantation
to play. I don't know when he will come, or if his Pa will let
him come. When the sun is nearly high in the sky, he arrives.
"Wha' make you just come?" I ask, angry with him for being late,
yet relieved that he arrived.

"Me mother have fi go a river fi wash clothes, an' me go wit'
her fi help her," Stumpy answers.

"All right, me a go tell Ma say that me goin' wit' you," I tell
him, as I walk within shouting range of Ma.

"Maaa!" I yell.

"Wha' you want?" she asks, looking up from her gardening.

"Me an' Stumpy a go over plantation. Me not staying long," I
assure her.

"Make sure that you no get in no trouble, and make sure that
you come back by dinnertime.

"You hear me?" she continues.

"Yes, Ma," I reply as Stumpy and I go off to the banana plantation.

Near the plantation is a patch of land that is not cultivated. It is covered with tall grass that almost reaches our necks, and a couple of large trees here and there, under which a few wild dasheen trees grow. The ones under the shade of the large trees still have dazzling drips of dew on the leaves, and as soon as our eyes meet the small beads of dewdrops, we run toward them and carefully make them into a bigger droplet and drink the pure water off every single leaf. We have our own special mango tree that to us is a house: The limbs and branches are the roof, and the shady spot under the tree is the inside of our house. We collect leaves and place them on the ground to make our bed, and Stumpy gathers stones to build a fireplace. We don't cook anything as we have no matches and nothing to cook. We search for sucksops to eat and leaves to make plates with. This is our dollhouse: I am the mother and Stumpy is the father, while the children are made with sticks and have grass for hair. I tell the children what to do, while Stumpy pretends to be farming. We eat our sucksops, but soon our bellies begin to groan from hunger.

"Me hungry," I tell Stumpy.

"Me hungry too," he responds.

"You want we go over to the plantation fi look some ripe banana?" I ask.

"But wha' if the worker man them catch we?"

"We will run from them," I say as we start tidying our dollyhouse, removing all evidence that we were ever there. We walk through the bushes toward the plantation, being careful not to step on any sharp stones that might hurt our bare feet. Stumpy holds my hand while he uses his other hand to push the bushes out of our way.

We walk slowly, hoping to find some neglected banana tree

with ripe bananas on it. We reach the rusty fence made from old wire, and holes where some parts of the wire have rusted through. As far as our eyes can see are banana trees, with grooves cut in the soil to collect rainwater. Big green bunches of bananas hang from the large trees, while small banana trees are sprouting next to the large trunks. The trees go on and on in the ground that has the color of a ripe mango, and scattered weeds grow between them.

We hear the voices of men and when we get closer we can see them in the field talking. They have rolled the sleeves of their shirts up to their elbows, and sweat is running down their faces to their chests. Their faces are black and shiny from the sweat, and they have machetes dangling from their muscular arms. We're bending down behind a banana tree hiding from them, for if they should see us they would chase us away, or even beat us, for trying to steal their bananas. We scan the nearby trees for a bunch of ripe bananas, but sadly enough there aren't any. So with disappointment we crawl back through the fence, our bellies groaning louder and louder by the minute.

"So wha' we goin' do now?" I ask Stumpy.

"Me no know," he replies, and just as quickly he adds, "Oh, yes, this morning when me follow me mother go a river, me did see a whole heap a ripe almonds."

We walk back through the bushes, across the wooden bridge, and down the track through Mass T's property, and to the river. A few of the big almond tree branches hang over the water, casting a shadow over the rocks. I look at the river now; at the white foaming water running around the rocks and the clearness of the water where the current is less swift. I hear the soothing sound the water makes and I feel the gentle wind on my body that sways the branches of the almond tree. The bush is a deep dazzling green along the banks.

"Fay, wha' you doin'?" Stumpy asks.

"Nothin'," I reply, for every time that I come to the river, she casts her spell on me. She captures my thoughts, then she speaks to me, "Come to me, come to me my child," and I forget about my groaning stomach and my hunger. "Come into my beautiful waters," she urges. "Lie in me, stay with me," she continues. Every time that I am ready to go, someone always calls me, and my fear of the river returns.

"Make we put the almonds in a you frock," Stumpy says as I hold out the end of Mavis's blouse in front of me to make a pouch, holding it up so that the almonds won't fall out.

We head back to our mango tree, selecting round rocks to crack the almonds with to reveal the brown nuts. We eat the juicy flesh of the fresher ones, and now we are no longer hungry but sleepy. We fetch some more leaves and make a bed on the grass in the shade; then we lie down and look up through the branches at the blue sky with the puffy white clouds. We watch the sky for a while, both of us trying to spot a cloud that looks like an animal.

"Me see a donkey," Stumpy says. Before I can ask him where, he adds, "Right there on the small piece a cloud. Me even see the donkey ears!" I look at the cloud, but the ears look like horns.

"Me see a cow, a man cow!" I yell, watching Stumpy's face search for a cow. "Where?" he asks.

"Right beside the donkey," I reply with a big burst of laughter. Stumpy laughs and says, "You must be blind! That is no man cow! That is a donkey!" His laughter subsides, and while looking for more cloud animals, he says, "Fay, when me get big, me goin' build a big, big house. Then me goin' marry you an' make a big, big field."

"How you goin' marry me when me is taller than you?" I ask, laughing.

"Chow man, that no matter!" he says as he turns on his side facing me and closes his eyes.

I fall asleep too, and I dream about Stumpy and me. Stumpy is grown and his little dark face is now big and has a beard. He looks so handsome: His chest is broad like his father's. I see myself, and I am big too with breasts and all. I see us holding hands, and smiling as we walk toward our dollyhouse. I wake up smiling, but Stumpy is already awake, lying on his back looking up at the sky.

"Wha' make you a smile?" he asks, looking toward me.

"Nothin'," I reply, too ashamed to tell him about my dream.

"We better go home, cause me mother will start wondering where me is," he says.

"Me too," I tell him as I get up from our hard bed, my body aching from lying on the ground. We go through the bushes across the bridge, and through Mass T's property.

"Fay, look wha' me have fi you."

"Wha'?" I ask, puzzled.

I turn around, and Stumpy is handing me a red hibiscus flower.

"Thank you," I say as I put the flower in my plaited hair, bid him good-bye, and head home.

When I arrive everyone is inside the kitchen, and Ma is making dumplings. "Where you was?" Julie asks me.

"With Stumpy," I answer, taking my seat in the kitchen and waiting for dinner to be ready. Night comes, and with it the lullaby of nighttime insects; at bedtime I crawl on top of Ma, as the bed feels too lumpy for my aching body. I drift toward sleep with the sound of Ma's soft, buzzing snores and the flower flattened against my face and Ma's beating chest.

2

WE GET UP EARLY the next morning, as we know that Mass T is coming over with milk that will make our breakfast of cornmeal porridge. While we're drinking our porridge we hear, "Miss Voy! Miss Voooyyy!" and Ma goes outside to see who is calling her. "Jesus Christ, Flo, me so glad fi see you!" Ma says, and by this time Julie, Mavis, and Clive are at the doorway, but I remain seated with my bowl of porridge.

Flo is my sister, Ma's second or third child, although I have never seen her before. She is fat, and her complexion is a lot darker than Ma's. She is wearing shoes, a beautiful pair of blue jeans, and a red blouse. She has big ears that have shiny gold loop earrings hanging from them; her face is oval; her black shoulder-length hair has been straightened and has slight waves in it. A gold bangle dangles on her right hand, in which she is holding a heavy-looking black plastic bag. I imagine she must be very rich.

"Come inside! Come inside!" Ma urges her. She comes inside, looks at me drinking my porridge, then at our furniture, and finally settles her large behind into the chair next to mine.

"Fay, this is you sister Flo," Ma says. "Um, um," I respond as I lift up the spoonful of porridge.

"So how life, Miss Voy?" Flo asks.

"Boy! Life rough. Life hard wit' me," Ma replies.

"Me carry some food fi you," Flo announces as she opens the bag and starts piling the contents on the table. We glue our eyes to the food on the table, as we have never seen so much food in our house before. There are three cans of corned beef, two loaves of bread, four cans of sardines, two cans of condensed milk, a two-pound sack of sugar, and some funny-looking biscuits.

"Thanks, thanks—thank you." Ma stutters because she doesn't know what else to say.

"Wha' happen, Fay?" Flo asks me, cradling my chin with her fingers and delaying the spoonful of porridge to my mouth. I do not reply, but I smile as I think of the food on the table.

"Me think that me goin' take Fay back wit' me to town, for a short visit," Flo says.

"Wha' make you no take Julie wit' you instead, cause she is a bit older," Ma says, looking at me and then at Julie.

"Cause she not too pretty," Flo whispers, not loud enough for Julie who is standing at the doorway to hear. My face creases into a frown, for I think that my sister Julie is very pretty despite what this big, fat, rich, mean woman has said. Then I stop drinking my porridge; as I am hoping that Flo was just joking about taking me with her to town. But when I see Ma reaching for my beautiful dress and telling Flo that I have no shoes and that she will have to comb my hair, I know I will be going and start to cry.

"Hush ya, Fay, she only taking you for a short visit. And look at all them nice things that you goin' get when you go to town," Ma says, trying to comfort me.

"Like ice cream and dolly and nuff playthings," Flo adds. I stop crying; after all it will just be for a short visit, and I have no idea what ice cream is, but it sounds nice, and maybe I can bring back some for Ma, Julie, Mavis, and Clive. I finish my porridge, and we all head to the river so that I can bathe, as everyone will be coming to see us off at the bus stop.

Ma leaves my dress on top of the hill and puts a rock on it. While she bathes me, everyone else with the exception of Flo starts getting themselves washed too. After I am washed, I scramble up the hill to put on my dress. As I pick it up, I see the shimmer of the river's water below me. I let go of my dress and walk closer to the edge of the hill to get a better look at the sparkling water. I can hear the river whispering to me again in her soothing voice: "Come to me, my child, don't be afraid, come to me, my child." I can feel my body move as my legs start walking toward the water. The reality of standing at the edge of the riverbank has left me and is replaced by a powerful need to merge with the river and become part of her shimmering current. I take another step, and instead of feeling my foot landing on the hard ground, it lands on air, and now I feel my body falling into the river. I feel the sharp pains of bushes, branches, and rocks whipping my body. The side of my head collides with a rock, and I hear the thud of the encounter. Warm liquid runs down my face; suddenly I feel tired, and a voice within me whispers, "Sleep."

"Clive! Clive! Catch her! Quick!" Flo yells in horror, pointing and looking at my falling body.

Clive sees me and runs through the water to the rocky bank of the river and catches me just as I am about to land on a pointed tree stump. The side of my head above my eyebrow is bleeding from a small hole. I want to fall asleep but I can't, as Ma is wiping my head with the blouse she is wearing. She tears her skirt and ties it tightly around my forehead to stop the bleeding.

"Fay—you all right?" asks Ma with tears in her eyes.

"Um, um," I answer weakly as my head spins and throbs

with pain. Clive goes and gets my dress, for I still have to go to town with Flo, but all I want to do is close my eyes and sleep.

We have left the river, and Ma, Julie, Mavis, and Clive come with us to the bus stop. At a small shop Flo buys me a soda, two Band-Aids, and two pills. We wait a long time for the bus, and while I share my soda with Mavis, Julie, and Clive, I hear Flo and Ma speak.

"You know, you goin' have one less mouth to feed for a little while," says Flo.

"Me know; 'bout when you bringing Fay back?" Ma asks.

"Me don't know, 'bout a week," Flo replies. I wonder what "a week" means, so I ask Mavis. She says that for every night I must hold up one finger. Then, when I have all the fingers on one hand and one finger from the other hand, then that is a week. Then she holds up her fingers to show me what a week should look like and says that there are about six nights in a week.

The bus is finally arriving, and I hug Ma, Clive, Julie, and Mavis. Julie whispers in my ear that if Flo should ever give me rice for dinner, I should remember to leave at least one grain of rice on the plate instead of leaving the plate completely bare. Ma says that I should behave and listen to Flo and that she will see me soon. I get into the bus and wave good-bye, excited, as I have never been inside a bus before; there are seats where people can sit two together all the way down to the back. Flo sits down beside me, and as the bus starts to drive, I stand up to wave a last good-bye to my family. Then quickly I try to remember all the fingers that Mavis had shown me. But before I can fully remember, I hold up both hands with one thumb down, and I see Mavis's smile widen with satisfaction. I take her smile to mean that I did the week right with my fingers. As I watch their faces getting smaller with the distance, I feel like a hero, as neither Mavis, Clive, nor Julie has ever been on a bus.

We have reached a city. I don't know what city. We are waiting to get off the bus, and there are all these people with large bags; they are wearing good clothes and even have shoes. The women are waiting to get their loads off the top of the bus: bags of fruits and coconuts, large bundles of sugarcane and bananas. Most of the women are fat and are sweating from the heat and shouting, "No, no, not that one, the one behind it, in the flour bag!" to the man who is on top of the bus unloading their goods. There are so many people, so much food; everywhere there are people selling food, even children.

"Banana chips! Popcorn! Cheese biscuits!" they yell. There are men selling sky juice in small plastic bags filled with crushed ice, syrup, and a straw from ice-filled carts, their different-flavored syrups covered with bees. There are women cooking on the sidewalk over charcoal stoves and selling food, such as curried goat or stewed chicken with rice and peas in paper boxes. There is all this noise! Each voice is trying to be higher than the next one; and the smell of rotting garbage and of the stagnant water running along the sidewalk.

"Give me you hand," Flo says as she takes my hand. 'Me goin' to buy slippers fi you, cause you can't walk barefoot in town."

We walk toward the wooden stalls, where I see lots of vendors selling clothes, shoes, mugs, plates, pots, and so much other stuff. I can't take my eyes off the things. We stop at a woman vendor, and Flo buys a pair of black sandals for me. I have never worn shoes before. Oh, my goodness! The sensation of wearing shoes! I feel such joy because finally I fit in with the town people for I am wearing shoes. I can't take my eyes off my feet, and every step I take I look at my feet. I feel Flo tug my arm, and then she says, "When we reach home, you no fi call me Flo, you must call me Mamma."

"Um-um," I answer, although I don't know what to make of Flo's strange request.

"And me goin' change you name to Clara, cause one woman that live in the yard, she already name Fay," she adds, and I nod with suspicion, wondering if she has forgotten that I going back home to Ma in a week.

"Little boy, sell me a popcorn!" Flo commands a young light-skinned boy with bags of what must be popcorn. She pays him, then opens the bag, pours some brown-looking lumpy things into her hand, and gives me the bag. I watch her put her hand to her mouth and stuff the contents inside. Her mouth is so full that she can hardly chew. I take only a few of the lumps and put them in my mouth. The taste surprises me, for they are sweet and taste almost like lightly burned brown sugar. Soon I am stuffing my mouth just like Flo, and within minutes the bag is empty.

We take another bus, but this time we get off on a dusty road where broken-down houses made of old boards and zinc sheets line the street. The black faces of people busy doing nothing peer at us, while above our heads bald-neck vultures circle the cloudless blue sky. This is the main street. We walk off to another street where there are more houses, but most of these are made of concrete. Rusty zinc fences run around some of them, while others have concrete walls and the day's laundry announces itself on the line.

To my surprise there are children in the street playing barefooted: How can this be when this is the city? They stop playing and stare at me with curiosity as surely my face is that of a stranger. I stare back at them, and when one girl smiles at me, I smile back at her, wanting to join in their game of hopscotch. We keep walking up the street till we come to a two-story building, when Flo stops and proudly announces, "This is where me live." I slowly turn my head and stare at the square building.

It's got a rusty zinc fence around it like some of the other houses. The paint has peeled off to the point where it is difficult to tell what color it was painted, and there are large cracks in the concrete. Some of the windows are boarded up, while the rest of them have zinc sheets instead of glass panes. The building is on the corner of the street and has two entrances: two rusty zinc gates. Flo opens one of the gates and we enter a treeless, dusty yard, in the middle of which is a concrete sink with a rusty pipe. Flo digs into her pocket and comes out with a large key dangling from a shoelace and pushes open an unlocked door that leads to a hallway. Through the first door is the kitchen, where a kerosene stove sits on an old wooden table with three pots and several plates and utensils. The next door is the bathroom, with an old cracked bathtub, a toilet without a seat and no way of flushing it except by filling a bucket and pouring the water into the bowl. Part of the wall is covered with years of soap scum and old mildew, and a rusty paint bucket sits by the toilet.

She pushes the large key into the last door, and I jump at the loud click the lock makes as Flo pushes open the squeaking door. While holding the door open, she beckons for me to enter, and cautiously I do so. I look around the room with the bare lightbulb hanging from the sagging ceiling. All that's inside the room is a bed, a wooden chair, a makeshift closet covered with an old sheet, and a wooden ironing board leaning against the bare, green, and ugly-looking wall. The bed has no headboard and is covered with a flat gray sheet with faded coconut tree patterns, under which are cardboard boxes; I suppose that's where she keeps her clothes. I sit on the bed because my head has started throbbing again, as if someone is inside it banging away with a heavy piece of wood. Suddenly I feel dizzy, my eyes burn, and I feel my body slipping into sleep.

It's evening now, and I awake with a feeling of terror as I

don't know where I am. The bed doesn't feel as lumpy as
Ma's, it doesn't smell the same, and it doesn't make a crumbling
sound each time I turn. I jerk myself into a sitting position and
start to cry.

"Ma, Ma, Ma, Maaa!" I yell.

Flo rushes into the room and asks, "Wha' wrong wit' you?"
I can't answer because everything is wrong. I want my Ma. I
want to sit on her lap and lean my aching head against her
bosom. Then, when I remember that she is far away, I start to
cry even harder. "Me head hurting me," I say between gulps of
breath.

Flo leaves the room and comes back with a new Band-Aid,
two pills, a glass of hogwash that is made from sugar, water, and
limes, and a plate of food, saying. "Here is some good stew liver
and rice." She makes me take the two pills, changes my Band-
Aid, and tells me to eat the food and I'll feel better. The aroma
of the liver and rice is making me hungry. Slowly I taste it, and
pretty soon I am eagerly eating and Flo watches.

A man pushes the door open and walks in. He's got huge
shoulders and large hands, his hair needs to be cut, and he smells
like rotten fish. His brown pants are cut off at the knee, and he's
wearing a black short-sleeved shirt. His nose is broad and puffy,
and from red curious eyes he stares at me. "A who this?" he asks
as he sits on the chair.

"A me daughter," Flo replies. "She used to live in the country
wit' me mother." I look at Flo in amazement, for surely she is
mistaken about me being her daughter. She looks at me, her eyes
pleading with me not to say anything. He looks me over as if I
am some merchandise that he is thinking about buying and says,
"But how come she no look like you, and how come she so brown
when you so black, and how come you never tell me 'bout her
before?"

Flo laughs—a sad, fearful, nervous laugh—swallows, and says, "But wha' kind of question is that? Her father was very light skin. And since you complaining so much that me cannot have you child, me went and get her, just to prove to you that me very able of getting pregnant!" Before he can say anything else, Flo leaves the room and comes back with a large plate of food for him. When he takes it from her, I notice that he has a large malformed index finger on his right hand. Flo calls him Finger, before asking him if he wants some hogwash. After he finishes eating, he hands Flo some money and says to her, "Me no catch nothin' much last night." Finger is a fisherman. He owns a small boat and a small outboard engine that he uses to go fishing with. He has a pair of black shoes, but he walks around barefoot so his feet are callused and hard just like Ma's.

So far I have held up one hand of nights, and Flo still hasn't gotten me any of the ice cream she promised me. And I have been noticing that each time that Finger comes home the bed squeaks as he moves up and down on top of Flo. Every time before the bed squeaks, Flo always checks to see if I am sleeping. I have often wondered what he is doing. I guess it is something that Flo doesn't want me to know.

Flo says we are going down by the seaside to see Finger. I have no idea what a seaside is, but I am hoping that maybe this is where the ice cream is. There are small concrete sheds all along the seashore that the government built, but as the number of fishermen grew, many of them built their own sheds out of old wood and zinc sheets. Flo tells me that a lot of the fishermen and their families live in these sheds.

"Wha' happen, Flo?" some people say in greeting her, and a fat woman pushing an old cart with her baby in it alongside some parrot fish asks, along with her greeting, "But Flo, which part you get the little girl from?"

"A me daughter! She use to live in the country with me mother," Flo replies, but the woman looks incredulously at Flo and then at me, for I bear no resemblance to her at all. Sensing the woman's disbelief, Flo adds, "She look just like her father!" Before the fat woman can digest Flo's response, Flo looks in the cart and says, "You have such a sweet baby." The woman's face beams with pride, and while she tells Flo about her baby, I look at the water.

The foamy waves gently lap the sandy beach, brushing the hulls of the beached fishing boats and green sea grass that has grown on them. Large seabirds fight for the fish that accidentally fall from the nets the fishermen are cleaning. The not-so-lazy birds dive into the light blue water trying to catch their own fish. There are holes in the sand, where the fishermen dug to get crude gasoline for their lamps. Flo has brought a plastic bottle with her that she tells me to fill with this crude gasoline by using an empty drink box that is small enough to fit into the hole. I fill the bottle, and now I am dirty from sand and gasoline. Everyone seems dirty: dirty children, dirty mothers, and dirty men. It's not the kind of dirt that comes from needing to bathe, but the kind that accumulates from the circumstance of life. The kind that stays with you all the time. Seeing no signs of fresh water anywhere, I wash my hands at the edge of the sea as the surf caresses my ankles, and then I begin to pick up the small seashells. Flo sits in the shade from the overhang of a shed and waits for Finger to come in from the sea. In the air there is a funny smell, and Flo says that it is the smell of the ocean. We wait and wait, and now it is almost evening, then finally I see a boat on the horizon. "Flo, Finger coming!"

"How come you know that is him?" she asks, straining her eyes against the glare of the soon-setting sun. "It must be him, for we been waiting long enough!" I hear myself reply. To our relief it is Finger. As the boat comes closer he throws the line to Flo, then steps into the shallow water, and pushes the boat onto the sand. He smiles at me, lifts me up, and because he has been teaching me the alphabet, he says, "Clara, spell *cat* fi me." I stare at his face with the blotches of acne scars, his big nose, his brownish teeth, and I say, "C-A-T *cat!*" Now a rolling thunderlike laugh erupts from inside him. He squeezes me tightly, and although his shirt smells like fish, I cling to his big warm neck. He puts me on the ground and says, "When you learn to count you can help me count the money from the fish." And my lips widen with a smile at the thought of being able to count.

Flo steps inside the boat and helps him clean the net. Some of the fish are still alive and jump out of the boat. My job is to pick up the wriggling fish and throw them back into the boat. One slimy parrot fish keeps getting away from me, and after the third attempt to hold on to it, I watch if Finger or Flo is looking at me and quickly kick the fish toward the water. It swims away, and I decide that if any more fish fall out of the boat I will put them back in the water. But no more fish fall out of the boat, and by the time that Flo and Finger clean the net of all the fish, a crowd of fish vendors surrounds the boat, waving money from their hands ready to buy fish. When it is all done, Finger gives Flo some money and says that he will be home later. On the way home Flo stops at the shop and buys some rice, butter, seasoning, and some sugar, and she cooks stewed fish and rice for dinner.

There are two other families living inside the square building. There is Miss Ivy, who lives upstairs with her husband, Sammy. Her son, Vincent, lives in the two rooms behind us with his girlfriend, Princess, and their four children. There is a big fat ugly woman with heavy lips named Fay, who lives upstairs with her five children and no father for them. She is about forty years

old, and everyone calls her a whore, as different men always
come from upstairs. Flo says that she's the reason why she
changed my name from Fay to Clara.

The cut on the side of my head and my sores are healing, and
Flo has bought me some clothes. Finger has started showing me
how to write. He says that he is going to buy me a coloring book
and crayons and that by the time that he is finished with me, I
will be literate. I have no idea what *literate* means, and he tells
me that it means being able to read and write. Sometimes he
holds my hand with his rough callused hand to form letters. He
says that learning to write is only a lot of practice. Soon I am
also able to read the storybook he has bought me: *The Three Bears*.
He reads it to me so many times that I think I have the book
almost memorized.

Things are going well with Flo and Finger. Flo has bought a
table with four chairs, a portable fan, and a black-and-white TV
set. I watch it each time Flo turns it on. Every time I watch it
I am mesmerized by the screen and all these people that fit into
it. They are mostly white people with straight hair, nice clothes,
nice houses, nice foods, and big cars. I wonder how often they
have to paint their black skins to make them white. They speak
differently than we do, and Finger says that they are speaking
English: the same language that *The Three Bears* is written in. I
am sure they can't be real people and that they belong to a fantasy
world like the three bears in the story, who can talk.

Today is Sunday. Flo is inside the kitchen cooking rice and
peas and stewed chicken. Finger is sitting on the doorstep smoking his ganja cigarette, and I am sitting beside him coloring my
book with the wax crayons that he got me. Then all of a sudden
the voice of a man yelling, "Fudgie! Fugiiieee! Fudge Mannn!"
disturbs our calm Sunday.

Finger puts out his spliff by tapping the lighted part on the
step and asks, "Clara, you want a fudge?"

"Wha' is fudge?" I ask him.

"It taste almost like ice cream," he replies. My ears perk up to the sound of those words *ice cream,* even though I still have no idea what it is. Instantly I shake my head yes. Finger holds my hand, and we walk out to the street.

"Fudgie! Hold on!" he yells to the back of the man on the bicycle, which has a white plastic bucket and a cardboard box above the rear wheel. As if charged with electricity, the man turns around and starts peddling hurriedly toward us. He stops and parks his bicycle on the cracked sidewalk and says, "Me only have chocolate fudge, but me have chocolate and vanilla ice cream."

"Sell me three cone cream," Finger tells him, and then asks me, "Wha' flavor ice cream you want, vanilla or chocolate?" Having no idea what vanilla is, I reply, "Chocolate," watching as the fudge man opens up the bucket. Then I notice the smoke coming from the open bucket.

"The bucket on fire! The bucket burning!" I urgently yell, fearful of losing the ice cream I longed for. To my surprise both men burst out laughing.

"Is not fire, little girl, is the smoke from the dry ice," says the fudge man. He tears a piece of paper from inside the bucket, puts a smoking cube into it, and gives it to me. Hesitantly I take it, fascinated that smoke comes from such a thing. I touch it and to my surprise instead of being hot, it's very cold. Then the fudge man tells me that this is what keeps the ice cream frozen. "Me can eat it?" I ask, wondering what such a burning, freezing thing will taste like. "No! Don't eat it!" yell both men at the same time.

Fudgie gives me the first cone he fills and, unsure of how exactly to eat it, I just stare at it. "Clara, lick the ice cream, or else it going melt and start running down," Finger says. I obey him, extending my tongue to taste it. I close my eyes as the cold—then warm, sweet, mushy—feeling passes through my whole body. Then Finger pays him, and we head into the yard to give Flo her ice cream cone. I watch as she gobbles it up in big mouthfuls, but I slowly lick my ice cream, enjoying every taste.

Today is Tuesday. The sun burns bright against the blue cloudless sky. Flo is at the concrete sink rinsing clothes in the yellow plastic tub, while I sit at the doorway, trying to teach Fay's daughter Christine the letters of the alphabet. The zinc gate opens, and Boogu walks through it, his flip-flop slippers fanning the dirt as he walks. Because he is Finger's friend, his smiling face is always welcome, but on his face today there is no smile. So I ask, "Wha' happen, Boogu?" but he doesn't respond. He just ignores me, and as if in some kind of a trance, heads directly for Flo, who stops rinsing the clothes and stands up.

"Wha' happen, Boogu, how come you face look so sad?"

I can't see his face anymore, nor can I hear what he is saying. The next thing I hear is a scream from Flo that is so loud and so sorrowful that for a moment my heart stops. It starts pounding harder as Christine and I run toward them, wondering what on earth Boogu has done to Flo.

"Boogu, Flo, wha' happen?" I ask, panting with fear and feeling as if my heart will burst from beating too fast. Flo is slumped over the wet concrete sink, gripping the running water pipe and shaking it as if she wants to break it. She loudly sobs and doesn't answer me. I look to Boogu to find out what could be so wrong that would cause Flo to cry. Boogu puts his hand on my shoulder and says, "Clara, Finger gone. Finger dead!" I am standing there transfixed, not only by the large hand on my shoulder, but also because I am digging inside my head for anything that can help me make sense of what Boogu has just said. A blank expression covers my face; the hand on my shoulder shakes me and, thinking that I didn't hear him, Boogu repeats, "Clara, Finger not coming back. Him dead!"

I nod my head so that Boogu can realize I hear him and let go of my shoulder, and he does.

"Bwoy, Flo, me really . . . really very sorry," he says. Then looking back at Flo as if unsure about leaving, he walks away, his slippers loosening more dust with each step.

The thought of Finger not coming back and seeing Flo slumped on the wet concrete sink and crying has stricken the urgent need in me to sit on Ma's lap, lean my head on her bosom, and block this whole day from my memory as if it never happened. With each sob from Flo, my desire to be with Ma becomes stronger, and in a short time the feeling overpowers me. I start crying and blurt out, "Me want go home to Ma, one week already gone!" Christine looks at me with puzzlement on her face. Flo raises her head and glares at me with red, squinting eyes. In a flash she raises a fisted hand and punches me right in my face.

"Aeeeiiihhh!" I yell, feeling the force of the punch topple me to the ground. Christine must have looked at me again, for I hear Flo yelling at her, "Go home to you whoring mother!" My body hits the ground with a tremendous thud, dust flies into my eyes, and my head goes backward, hitting the ground with another thud, and then I can no longer feel my body.

3

MY BEING HAS TURNED into a soft, glowing orange light that pulsates gently with each flicker of my fading existence. I no longer feel pain, for I am beyond the realms of feeling. Lulling arms cover me with a soothing embrace, and I welcome the hug. I can see the body of a little girl whose limbs hang loosely as she is laid on a bed by a woman crying, "Clara, Clara, me no mean fi punch you!" She is gently slapping the face of the lifeless child, and slowly I am beginning to feel each slap. I fight this sense of feeling that has returned to me, and I grope for the peaceful arms that no longer hug me. The sensation of water on my face completely awakens my being, and now its light glows a bright, burning red, as I become the little girl on the bed. Pain fills my entire head, and Flo is crying as she wipes my face with a wet rag. I want to open my eyes but I can't, for one eye is swollen, and as hard as I try, only a sliver of light comes in. A terrible anger fills me, and tears flow down the side of my swollen face.

It's been days since I've been outside in the dusty yard. Flo says that Finger died at sea, while he was fishing. No nigh-night or funeral is made for him, and we haven't been to the seaside ever since. I don't understand how Finger could have died at sea, but Christine tells me that she overheard a woman talking with Fay about Finger, and they said something about a blowup and dynamite.

My face has healed, but with each day that passes, I miss Ma more and more. Ever since the day that Finger died, Flo has been acting strange. She has started drinking white rum that she dilutes with water. She no longer bathes herself and smells terrible. She doesn't comb my hair either, and my hair is now in knots. Flo has not cleaned the room and hasn't been cooking much. She stays in bed most of the time and is losing weight. Every day she sends me to the bar to buy rum, and the bartender woman asks me who is drinking all that rum. I want to tell her that it is Flo; I want to tell her how Flo is living, for she has a friendly face and gives me a candy after selling me the rum. I don't tell the bartender, for I am afraid of Flo. Soon Flo sells the television, the table and four chairs, and then the fan. After many times of sending me to the bar to buy rum, we are desperate for food and rent money.

Most times there are men in the bar when I go there to buy rum for Flo. Drunken men, who speak loudly about other people's business, about the life in the community, and sometimes I listen. They say that most of the people here are unwanted children who have grown up to have another generation of more unwanted children. They say that if by the age of eighteen a girl doesn't have a child, or even several children, the people say she is barren. This becomes a daily curse to a girl, whose sole purpose in life (they feel) is to have children. The drunken man is smoking a cigarette and after a gulp of his rum he says to the other men, "Me would not mind if me have a gal like that. Me Matilda have seven children, and she expecting right now! What me need is a mule gal!" The other men laugh and mimic, "Mule. Muleeee." Then another man makes donkey sounds, and this makes them laugh more. Now I know the reason why Flo took me to live with her. We still pretend that she is my mother, and I call her Mamma. I want to go home to Ma, and I wonder why Flo doesn't want to take me. I am afraid to mention it to her because I fear she might punch me again.

After she caught her daughter Christine sneaking food to me, Fay that lives upstairs has become concerned about Flo. She has gotten Flo to start bathing again after many bitter arguments to talk sense into her. And since we have no money Flo no longer sends me to the bar to buy rum. In order to get money to buy food, Flo turns to Miss Ivy's husband, Sammy, who has been eyeing her. Sammy gives Flo money and sneaks into our room one night a week while I stand guard outside.

I am starting basic school that Flo has to pay for every two weeks. The school is not too far from where we are living, and is kept inside a woman's house. Her name is Miss Little, a fat old lady with most of her hair turning gray. There are only three classes and two more teachers: Miss Byrd and Miss Wilson. The house has five bedrooms, three bathrooms, and a kitchen. I think Miss Little lives in two of the rooms. The floors are wood, the walls are a light blue with large posters of animals with the corresponding letters of the alphabet below them. The toilets are clean, they flush properly, and there is always toilet paper.

There are about twenty children in each class, and we sit around three square wooden tables. Most of the time we have porridge for lunch that Miss Little cooks in large pots while she is teaching class. Then the classroom will smell so sweet. "Excuse me, me have to stir the porridge," she will say and go off to the kitchen. I had no idea there could be so many types of porridge: rice porridge, oat porridge, cream of wheat porridge, pumpkin porridge, banana porridge, plantain porridge, and my favorite, whole-kernel corn porridge. The great thing about Miss Little's porridge is that in addition to putting nutmeg and cinnamon into it, she also puts in vanilla to give the porridge a rich smell. When she serves each bowl of porridge she always puts a spoon of sweet condensed milk on top of the already sweet porridge. Sometimes we have other food like rice and stewed meat, but mostly it is porridge. I love going to school. I am on top of my class as most of what Miss Little is teaching me I already learned from Finger. I wear a green-and-white plaid uniform, with white buttons all the way down the front like a dress, black shoes, and green socks. I have no schoolbag. I carry my one exercise book in my hand and my short piece of pencil in my pocket. In the back of my head I carry the fears of what tomorrow may bring me.

I think that Miss Ivy suspects that something is going on between Sammy and Flo. One night after Sammy has sneaked into our room, her huge bulk, which is twice the height and size of Flo, appears. Before I can say anything she breaks open our door and catches Sammy rubbing Flo's breasts. Immediately Miss Ivy starts yelling and beating Flo, and within minutes the doorway is filled with people.

"Wha' happenin'?" Vincent asks as he parts the crowd, and without a pause in her battering of Flo, Miss Ivy says, "This stinking gal trying to steal me husband." Then Vincent starts beating Flo too. Sammy tries to help her by pulling Vincent away from her, but Vincent shoves him against the wall. I try to pull Vincent off Flo, but he just throws me on the bed. Flo is helpless against the beating and is crying. "Helppp! Lord have mercy! Woooeee!" I have started crying too, as I don't know what else to do. Finally Fay from upstairs pulls Vincent away from Flo, and Sammy drags Miss Ivy outside, who is yelling. "Gal, I goin' kill you, 'bout you try take away me man, right under me nose!"

I look at Flo, whimpering and shivering in the corner. Her head is bleeding, and blood is running down her face and neck, and is beginning to soak her blouse. Her eyes are red, her face is swollen, and her injured lower lip hangs down like a drooped breast. She is crying softly, like a baby. Her clothes are torn, and she looks confused, ashamed, and in shock. I am shocked too. I wonder, How will I go to school now that Miss Ivy and her son have broken up this thing with Sammy? Looking at her, I cry harder from sympathy and from seeing the blood and tears. I get my old blouse and give it to her to hold against her head to stop the bleeding. She starts crying harder, with hysterical short sobs as if something inside her has broken. I cry too; I cry for her, I cry for me. I cry because I want Ma. I cry because it is the only thing that I can do.

Fay helps Flo get up and supports her to the bathroom. The crowd thins out as they head in the direction of Miss Ivy's voice, who is now cursing Sammy. Flo bathes herself, and I get some clothes from the cardboard box under the bed. She looks a bit better: Her head wound is not that severe, and her cut lip will heal in time.

Fay brings us mackerel and dumplings. I am surprised by this action, as I know that she does not have enough food for herself and her children, much less for us. I tell her, "Thanks," and she hands Flo two aspirin. "Don't worry, everything goin' be all right," she says and goes back upstairs to her five children.

Two days have passed since the beating, and Flo has not been outside for fear of Miss Ivy, nor have I been to school. On the third day, she leaves early in the morning and comes back that evening.

"We goin' move in the morning," Flo says in a whisper. She has found another room, on another street, and in the wee hours of the morning, we start moving out our few belongings. The mattress is heavy, and I am sweating despite the cool breeze blowing, and I hope that Miss Ivy doesn't know where we are moving to.

The new room is a bit larger and in much better shape than

the old one. The yard has concrete in some places, which lessens the dust, and unlike the other treeless yard, there is a coconut tree and a mango tree. Our room is separate from the other tenants' rooms and has three wooden steps leading to the door. This yard has an old concrete wall around it, with thin cracks like veins. A Rasta man and his girlfriend live in another building in the yard, and together they have six children. She is younger than Flo and must have been pregnant for most of her adult life. People call her children "do," "re," "mi" as their ages aren't far apart. Another tenant is Melissa, a thirty-looking woman, with four children. Of course there is a communal bathroom and kitchen, and a concrete sink.

It is morning. The shop doors should be opening soon. I am still tired, I am hungry, but I am relieved that we have moved from the violence of Miss Ivy. Flo goes to the shop and buys some chicken back, a pack of noodles, some flour, and makes a pot of soup.

Sammy still likes Flo, and despite the beating he comes here most every evening before he goes home to Miss Ivy. He probably tells her that he is doing overtime. So now we are surviving.

Many weeks have gone by, and Sammy has been sleeping with us at least one night a week. He never sleeps over on the same nights. Yesterday was Thursday, and he slept with us. On Friday morning, when Sammy is just about to sneak out of our room, we hear someone yell: "One house up the road on fire and burning down!"

"I wonder which house burnin' down?" Sammy says, before he leaves. As soon as he is gone Flo says, "Clara, put on your clothes, we a go look 'pon the fire." So I get dressed, and Flo and I follow the crowd leading to the square building on the corner that we used to live in.

A large crowd of people has gathered around the building. Being a child, I have a hard time seeing over all the adults. I try standing on my toes, but all I can see are the chests of people. Flo pushes through the crowd, pulling me behind her, and yells, "Watch it! Watch it! Let me through! Let me through!"

The square building is completely burned. The fire started the night before, and all that's left are the square concrete walls, blackened and cracked from the fire. There are puddles of water all over, and soot floating in the air. There is a fire truck and a police jeep with two policemen, even though this is not a gunshooting scene. The firemen are pulling out bodies; burned bodies, no longer people, just charred meat. Some I recognize as children's bodies, and I instantly recognize the huge charred remains of Miss Ivy.

Tears are forming in my eyes as the fireman carries out the body of Christine, Fay's daughter. She is severely burned except for a small part of her face. One of her small eyes is open, staring ahead. That was the same little eye that I had seen filled with laughter when we sometimes played together. I taught her the alphabet and how to spell her name. She used to sneak me some of her food when Flo was drinking rum. I can never forget those eyes. What did she do to deserve this kind of death?

"One of the children, them must was playing with matches," one onlooker comments.

What does the onlooker know? Nothing! Nothing of Sammy sleeping with Flo; nothing of Flo buying the gasoline at the gas station; nothing of her sneaking out of the room, when she thought that Sammy and I were sleeping; nothing of her muffled cries when she returned.

Sammy is standing at the front of the crowd, just staring at the pile of burned bodies and crying in babylike sobs. I am sure he still loves Miss Ivy. I imagine he can't stand the sight of his wife's body that burned to a crisp while he was with Flo. But most of all I guess that he can't stand the fact that everything he owned is gone. Just ashes.

A fireman touches his shoulder and asks, "You live here too, sir?"

"Yes, sir," Flo answers for Sammy, who just stands there, looking sad and crazed by his feelings of deceit and loss.

The policemen take their statements. They explain to Sammy that they are taking the bodies to the morgue and that he should come and claim those he is responsible for. A fireman asks the crowd if anyone knows any relatives of Fay and her five children. Silence answers him back. I stand there and watch as the police jeep pulls away with the burned bodies inside, and the fire truck follows the jeep. Now my face is soaked with tears as my mind falls deeper and deeper into darkness.

It has been months since the fire at the square building, and now Flo has Sammy all for herself. He lives with us all the time, and he gives Flo more money as he no longer has to share it with Miss Ivy. We are living better. Flo has bought a table with four chairs, and a fan. She buys some clothes for herself to look good for Sammy. We have dinner every night. Most times Flo buys chicken and some chicken back for dinner. And when she shares the food, I end up getting only a tiny piece of chicken and chicken back, but Sammy doesn't get any chicken back, he gets only chicken. This doesn't bother me one bit, as every time she does this, she gives me an extra piece of chicken back.

Things are going well till Sammy starts coming home later and later each evening from work. He comes home drunk, staggering and cursing at everything he comes in contact with, including me. Some nights he doesn't come home at all. He says that he is doing overtime, but he is giving Flo less and less money. He says the government is taking more and more taxes out of his pay. Flo asks him, "Then what the sense in doin' more work and gettin' less money?"

"Well, me goin' stop do all that overtime, cause a just waste a time," he chuckles.

I know exactly what is going on. I can see the signs. Sammy no longer looks at Flo with feeling in his eyes; he no longer likes the food that Flo prepares. All his actions verify the unbearable fact: *He has another woman!* Flo realizes this, as now their relationship has reached the point where they quarrel every day and he swears at me all the time. She decides something must be done. I agree with her, for if there is no Sammy, then there is no money, no food, no school. I have started hating Sammy; doesn't he realize how heavily we depend on him in order to survive? Doesn't he know that I need him in order to go to school? Doesn't he care? Flo and I are worried. She sits staring into space, at the wall, at the floral patterns of the sheet on the bed, with her hand under her cheek wondering what she is going to do.

The next morning Sammy leaves early, as he works far from where we live. We get dressed and head for the bus stop. We take an old bus, and after driving for a while I begin to see beautiful homes, all painted in pretty colors; like yellow, pink, green, blue, and white. There are no zinc fences around these homes, just nicely painted walls with lovely flowers around the sides. I guess this must be a rich neighborhood. Why can't I live here? I ask myself as I stare through the bus window at the big houses. The bus drives on and the scenery begins to change to shades of poverty: rusty zinc fences, shabbiness, children in ragged clothes, dusty streets, and that look of hopelessness on people's faces that I see every day.

Flo yells, "One stop, driver, at the next bus stop!" And we get off next to an abandoned gas station. We cross the street, turn on another road with old houses, and then stop in front of

a tire shop. On the street in front of the tire shop a puddle of
stagnant water has collected in a pothole, and next to it, its
source of bathroom sewage runs down the street.

On one side of the tire shop is a small track going down to
some houses. We walk along the track till we're in front of a
zinc fence with large flags flying on a stick; red flags, yellow flags,
and green flags. Across from the zinc fence are old graves, something of a small cemetery. There are bushes growing on top of
the tombstones, choking the graves. Flo pushes on the zinc gate,
and an eerie *Eeerrrkk* comes from it as she opens it up. We enter
into a yard with lots of different flowers, all arranged in a circle;
green flowers, red flowers, so many colors, so many varieties, so
beautiful yet so strange. In the middle of the circle is a tall table
with bottles of water on it and a small white wooden cross in
the middle.

A few feet away from the garden is a wooden church with old
benches, a large altar with an open Bible, and crosses everywhere.
A bare lightbulb hangs from the middle of the church's ceiling,
and there are paintings of Jesus Christ, all showing a beam of
light around his head. Behind the altar there is a painting of Jesus,
standing in a green pasture, holding a sheep in his arms, but in
this painting he doesn't have any circle of light around his head.
People are sitting on the long wooden benches inside.

An elderly woman with deep, squinting eyes comes up to us
and asks Flo, "You here to see the man?" Flo nods yes.

"Wait here," says the woman, who returns with a big red flag
on a piece of stick and two pieces of cloth. She holds the flag
high above her head and starts flogging the air all around us while
chanting a song that is unfamiliar to me. I am wondering, What
on earth is this woman doing? She tells Flo that we are being
purged of any evil spirits that have followed us. She says that
we're to join her in the final purging. We walk around this circle
of flowers and say,

*"The Lord is my shepherd, I shall not want. He maketh
me to lie down in green pastures; he leadeth me beside the
still waters. He restoreth my soul; he leadeth me in the
paths of righteousness for his name's sake. Yea, though I
walk through the valley of the shadow of death, I will
fear no evil; for thou art with me; thy rod and thy staff
they comfort me. Thou preparest a table before me in the
presence of mine enemies; thou anointest my head with oil;
my cup runneth over. Surely goodness and mercy shall follow me all the days of my life; and I will dwell in the
house of the Lord forever."*

We repeat this prayer three times, still walking around the
circle. Then the woman gives us the two pieces of cloth that she
takes from her pocket and tells us to put them on our heads.
She tells Flo that the next time we come here, we must bring
something to put over our heads as we cannot enter into the
church with our heads bare.

We enter the church and sit in the next empty spot on the
long bench, beside a skinny woman with a handkerchief on her
head. While we wait a man wearing a straw hat says, "Bwoy! Me
hear say that this man good, good." To no one in particular, just
to break the silence.

"Me hear the same thing that is why me come here wit' me
daughter," says the skinny woman. The man nods his head and,
quite sure that she has everyone's attention, the skinny woman
continues. "Me daughter bright, bright at her school. We live in
this yard with two other women, and the two a them have a
whole heap a pickney. Every single child that them have, them
worthless. Who no thief, a gunman; who no gunman, breed-up
and worthless; and the rest a them probably beg fi stay alive.
You see, when me daughter pass her exam fi be able to go high
school, the whole lot a them envy me. Them want me daughter

fi be worthless like fi them pickney. So them obeah me daughter and set demon fi follow her everywhere she go, even when she a go to school. From that, she start lookin' in a space, she don't want eat, she don't want do nothin'. And one night she wake up, and start to jumpin' up and down on the bed, and cry, 'Stop beating me! Stop beating me! Wooooeee!' And me ask her, who beatin' her? And she ask me if me no see the man that is beatin' her? Me no see nobody, so me start pray, and call 'pon the Lord. And the next mornin' when she wake up her whole body full a black-and-blue marks. So somebody must really did beat her." The skinny woman narrows her eyes to slits as she looks about the room, and everyone says, "Um, uh," in agreement. Satisfied that we all agree, she continues, "Now that me stop her from goin' to school, the whole lot a them in the yard glad. Me really lookin' hard fi some place else fi move to, out that yard. I only hope that the man can make her better."

I look at her daughter. She is wearing a pale blue dress with black shoes and a pink washrag on her head. She is so meager that I can almost count every bone on her face. Her eyes have fallen deep down into their sockets, and she is just staring into space, as if hypnotized into a state of unawareness. There is nothing frightening about her, just a dead emptiness glowing back at me from her sunken eyes. I slowly turn my head to look at the floor, as I am overwhelmed by the feeling to cry for this girl. As I start to cry, an old man walks into the room toward the altar. He walks with such purpose, such life, that a deafening silence fills the room. He claps his hands in front of his face and says, "Good morning, stand up, and let us pray." He waits until we are standing and begins:

> "Oh Lord, my God, have mercy on us today as we stand
> before you. Give me the strength to help all them people
> that have come from far and near. Dear Lord, grant me

the power to heal them troubled live and touch them heart
forever more, I pray in Jesus' name. Everyone join me:
Our Father, who art in heaven, Hallowed be thy name.
Thy kingdom come. Thy will be done in earth, as it is in
heaven. Give us this day our daily bread. And forgive us
our trespasses, as we forgive those who trespass against us.
Lead us not into temptation, but deliver us from evil. For
thine is the kingdom, and the power, and the glory, for-
ever and ever, amen."

Everyone opens their eyes and sits down. Then he starts writing down the names of all those who need his services: Each person will be served in the order in which they came. Flo and I are at number eleven. Everyone puts whatever they can afford into the basket that the flag lady brought and set down on the red concrete floor. This is the charge of the obeah man. The flag lady leaves with the basket of money and arrivee number one, and we wait. I'm bored, and my behind is starting to hurt from the hard bench, but soon the conversations start again. They talk about life in general; their day-to-day struggles in coping with people who are bad minded and envious; their failed attempts at outdistancing poverty. All of their stories are sad and make me feel like crying. I want to tell my story too, about missing Ma, Clive, Julie, Mavis, and Stumpy. The sad stories are getting softer as thoughts of Ma float through my head; the way she smelled of chocolate after pounding cocoa beans for hours and making them into small round balls to make hot chocolate. Now I can't hear the sad stories, for I am in the fields with Stumpy.

Suddenly Flo tugs my arm and says, "Come wit' me." We walk out of the church toward the back of the yard, where there is a small shed. This is the obeah man, his office. It's a small zinc shack with an old table and two old chairs inside. He sits there with three white candles that are lit, and he has a notebook and a pen. On the table there is a small mirror that reflects the candle flames. The white parts of his eyes are red, as if he has been crying or needs to sleep.

"Flo Higgins, come inside and sit down," he says. "And leave the child outside," meaning me. I stand outside and lean my body against the zinc hut so I can hear what they say.

"Me think that me man Sammy is keepin' another woman wit' me," Flo says. "Yes, is true, him cheatin' on you wit' a sort of a fat woman, her face round, she well built, and she have buff teeth, and she have light brown skin. Me can see that she want him all for herself." I peep through a hole in the zinc. Through this hole I can see him staring at the mirror at the candles' reflection. I am confused, for the obeah man just gave a perfect description of Miss Ivy. Maybe the obeah man is confused too. Confused or not, Flo asks him, "So what me must do fi get him back?"

"You must tie him to you, so that she can't take him away from you."

"So how me goin' tie him?" Flo asks.

"You must come back wit' some *pum-pum* hair from the two of you, and you must bring one a him dirty shirt, and a piece a parchment paper."

"A'right, Dada, me will come back when me get everything," Flo says. Quickly I move away from my peephole, wondering what the obeah man is going to do with the hair from Sammy's and Flo's private parts.

It is almost evening. We go home, and as usual Sammy comes home late and fights with Flo. He punches her, and she lands sprawled on the concrete outside. I pretend not to notice; after all, what can I do? Her face isn't bleeding but only doubled in size. Flo dares not fight back, for she is afraid of losing Sammy. I hope the obeah man will make it stop.

A few days have passed, and finally Flo has obtained all the
items necessary to make things better. She obtained the pubic
hair after Sammy had bounced up and down on her (I pretended
to be sleeping); the dirty shirt and parchment paper were easily
obtainable. Strangely enough, I feel that things will get better.

It is early morning, and Flo wakes me up. She tells me to go
bathe myself and put on my clothes. Sammy has already gone to
work. We have a piece of bread and some mint tea and set off
for the obeah man. As before, Flo stops the bus at the abandoned
gas station and we walk toward the tire shop. We arrive, and
the flag lady purges us around the circle of flowers. Happily we
sit down, as we are arrival number three. While we are sitting
and waiting more people arrive, and soon Dada enters the church
and starts the prayer. The flag lady arrives with the basket, and
now we are waiting for our turn.

Finally Dada tells Flo to come in and leave me outside, and
as before I go to my peephole.

"Me have him dirty shirt, the *pum-pum* hair, and the parchment
paper," Flo says. Dada examines the items and then says, "Me
goin' tie you and Sammy together, so that him cannot leave you.
Him goin' treat you better, and him goin' leave the other woman.
First me goin' tie you and him *pum-pum* hair together, so that
him always come back to you *pum-pum*. Then me goin' write you
and him name together on the parchment paper three times. And
them me goin' wrap the *pum-pum* hair in the parchment paper,
add some of me special power, and wrap it up in him dirty shirt,
and bury the whole thing in a the graveyard. And in couple days,
you just wait and see, things goin' be good."

I watch Dada, who seems to be making a knot with the pubic
hair. Then he writes something on the piece of paper, while he
chants in some strange-sounding words. As soon as he and Flo
head outside, I move away from the zinc and stare in the opposite
direction. "Wait fi me here, me soon come back," Flo says to

me, as she and Dada go across to the graveyard to bury the shirt. I watch them burying it, and when it is all covered with dirt, Dada says another prayer. Then Flo hands him some more money for the basket. As we leave the obeah man and head toward the bus stop, I can hardly wait to reach home, to see if any of this has worked.

4

A WHOLE YEAR HAS gone by, and Sammy and Flo are getting along; maybe the spell of the obeah man has worked. The place where Sammy works has closed down, and I am no longer going to school because we have no money. Sammy tries hard to find another job, but he is not able to find one. Now we're all going to bed without dinner. We can't even afford to buy chicken back. We are getting hungrier and hungrier with less and less food, and we are desperate. Flo has changed and instead of Sammy starting a quarrel, she's the one that starts it.

"Wha' you want me fi do? Every day me go out and look fi work, and me no find none.

"Wha' you want me fi do?" Sammy sobs, but Flo doesn't answer.

There is a man that makes pottery who Flo thinks will give her money. She walks funny every time she sees him, wiggling her behind so he notices her. Well, he does notice her, and pretty soon Flo is sneaking into his pottery shop when Sammy goes to look for work. The potter doesn't have a woman, so this is almost perfect for Flo. But how will she get rid of Sammy? I wonder, as the words of the obeah man float around in my head. "Me

goin' tie Sammy to you so that him can never leave you." Now
I worry if Dada will be able to untie this knot. I hope he can,
for Sammy won't leave us alone. He's always here watching Flo
instead of looking for work. Sometimes, if Sammy can find a
day's work, Flo will go to see the potter. He gives her money,
and she cooks something for us to eat. We eat the food and wash
the plates and pot so that Sammy doesn't know that we have
eaten. When Sammy arrives home, we act hungry. Then Flo tells
Sammy that we didn't eat anything all day and that our bellies
are hurting from hunger. Sammy believes Flo, and he gives her
every penny from his day's work. Flo cooks, and I am very happy
to eat again. Flo doesn't give me much food the second time as
some of it needs to be left over for breakfast tomorrow; chicken
back, boiled bananas, and dumplings.

Life goes on like this for a while, with Flo sneaking to see the
potter and Sammy not having a job. The potter doesn't come to
our yard to see Flo as he knows that Sammy lives with us. Today
is Saturday, the day on which the potter sells his pottery and
gives Flo money. He meets Flo at his workshop in the evenings;
I guess they bounce up and down there. Flo needs to go and see
the potter without Sammy knowing, but Sammy has been in the
yard all day. He has no money to give Flo so I haven't eaten all
morning. Flo tells Sammy that she is going to see her friend
Sophia, to see if she can borrow some money from her, to buy
something to cook for dinner. Sammy agrees, and Flo goes off
to see the potter, leaving us behind. After she has gone, Sammy
says, "Me think that me should go wit' her, so if Sophia no have
no money, me will try fi borrow some from Derick." My eyes
widen with fear, for if Sammy goes now and follows Flo, then
he will find her heading for the potter! I try to think of something
to say that will stop him, but my mind comes up with nothing
sensible. I tremble as Sammy puts on his shoes and leaves the
yard. I start to pray, "Dear God, please no make Sammy catch

Flo and the potter together. Dear God, please make Flo come home with some money, so that me can have somethin' to eat, and not go to bed without dinner again. I pray in Jesus' name. Amen." This is the best prayer I can manage. I hope that God answers it, or there will be a big fight between Sammy and Flo.

The sun has gone down and I am standing by the gate waiting for either Sammy or Flo to return. It is getting dark, and the mosquitoes have come out to feed on my skinny body. Every few seconds I slap myself where the mosquitoes have bitten me. There is a whole swarm of them above my head, and each one is buzzing a loud, annoying tune. I slap the mosquitoes to keep my mind off Flo and Sammy, for they seem to be gone a long time.

The last ray of daylight is disappearing, and I can see the outline of Sammy's body coming down the street. He has almost reached the gate, and he seems very angry. My heart begins to race as my pulse quickens, my palms sweat, and my head is throbbing. Flo is nowhere to be seen, and I try not to think about what might have happened to her. He pushes the gate open so forcefully it hits the wall. "That no good whorin' mother you have, me just catch her with a man! I goin' kill her wit' beatin' when me catch her!"

I start to cry, slowly sobbing with fear and now with hunger, as I know that I will not have any dinner tonight. It is getting darker and darker, and with the darkness, there're more mosquitoes. I slap at these insects that are biting me in order to survive. They need my blood in order to live, just like Flo and I need Sammy's or the potter's money. I have never thought about life that way before; maybe the hunger is getting to my head. I want to go inside the room away from the mosquitoes, but I am afraid that Sammy will beat me.

I stamp my feet, I slap myself, crying softly at the same time, as I do not want the other tenants to hear me or find out what's in store for Flo. It will be a disgrace when the other tenants find out that Flo is cheating on Sammy, because in the tenants' eyes, Sammy is a good man. He gave Flo money when he was working, and he comes home every night. It's just that being a good man is not enough to stop the pangs of hunger in our foodless stomachs. What is the good in being a good man when you can't even provide food for your woman? Good man or not, he is no longer of any value to Flo, since he can't give us what we need.

Sammy is still inside the room. I don't know what he is doing in there. The other tenants are also in their rooms but me, I am standing out here in the dark, being eaten by mosquitoes and wondering, Where is Flo? A slight breeze begins to blow and wearing my thin shorts and blouse, I am beginning to feel cold. People unaware of my gas pains from not eating are going up and down the street. I see the outline of a fat woman coming down the street. She rocks from side to side with each step, and slowly I realize that it is Sophia, Flo's friend. She comes nearer and I am stooping behind the wall so that she doesn't see me, for surely she will want to know what I am doing standing by the gate at this hour of the night by myself. She crosses the street and is now walking on the side I am on. I can see her bulk coming closer, and I hope she passes by without seeing me.

She reaches the gate and, to my surprise, pushes it open and sees me. "Clara, what you doin' behind the wall at this hours a night?"

"Nothin'," I answer, as I wish she wouldn't start questioning me. I notice for the first time that she has something in her hand. It looks like a box drink and something round. "Flo say that me fi give you this and find out where Sammy is," she says, handing me the box drink and a round bun with a piece of cheese in the middle. With gratitude to Flo, I eagerly bite into the bun, and happily, with my mouth full, I tell her, "Sammy inside the room."

"Me goin' try talk to him," Sophia says, as she heads toward our room. Within seconds I have eaten almost the whole bun, and just as I am gulping down the box drink, Sophia runs out of our room and starts yelling, "Help, woooeee! Lord Jesus! Somebody heeelllppp! Woooeee, Sammy dead!"

She keeps yelling, and the other tenants come out to see what all this noise is about. She runs up to me breathing heavily, and says, "Clara! Sammy dead, him kill himself!" I think she's just joking, as I swallow the last piece of bun and drain the last drop of the box drink. When Tony the Rasta Man comes out of our room and murmurs, "Him really dead bad," I realize that Sammy is dead. I have no feeling of sadness, only relief that he won't be able to beat Flo.

Sophia tells Tony the Rasta Man, "Run go call Flo, she over me yard, and tell her wha' happen to Sammy!" Tony rushes past me, and now more people are gathering in the yard. The crowd has blocked the doorway to our room. Slowly I walk toward them, hoping to close our door and get rid of all these nosy people. Why don't they mind their own business? I part the crowd and say, "Excuse me! Watch it, watch it, make me pass, excuse me," and make my way into the room.

The burned bodies from the square building did not prepare me for what I am looking at. Sammy has torn out the plaster from the ceiling, revealing the beams on which the roof is built. The room is filled with ceiling board, plaster, and white dust. On one of the beams Sammy is hanging by his neck, from a piece of the clothesline that he has doubled several times to give it strength. His neck is broken. His tongue hangs from the corner of his mouth, where a bubbly froth drips down on the bed. His eyes are wide open, staring at me. The chair he used to reach the beam lies on its side. My stomach churns noisily inside, and

I push past the bodies. I run outside and violently throw up the box drink and bun and cheese. I slump down beside the puddle of vomit, as my knees collapse with the weight of my body and my head spins with pain.

Tony returns with Flo. I can hear her voice as she parts the crowd and goes inside the room. Then I hear her screaming, a loud, shrilling "Aiiiaaaiiieee!" that rips through the darkness and penetrates the very fibers of my tormented head. She is crying, and Sophia is holding her so she doesn't fall down. I know that Flo wanted to get rid of Sammy, but I am sure that she didn't want to get rid of him like this.

"Wooeee, somebody go call the police fi me," she sobs. Tony goes to call the police while everyone waits in the yard, mumbling that they can't understand why anyone would want to kill himself.

"Me could never hang meself," says Tony's girlfriend.

"God not goin' allow him to enter heaven. Him goin' straight to hell," adds someone else.

Soon a police jeep pulls up with two policemen inside. They quickly part the crowd and analyze the hanging man. One starts to write in a small notebook, while the other one asks, "A who live in this room?"

"A . . . me . . . sir," Flo answers.

"Where was you when all this was happening? And who last see him before him kill himself?"

"A me, sir. Me not too long leave and did 'round Sophia yard, when Tony come call me and tell me say that Sammy hang himself."

"About what time that was?"

"Well . . . 'bout sometime after six a clock, sir," Flo replies.

"What him name?"

"Samuel Johnson."

"What date him born?"

"Me no too sure, sir, me think him born May 5, 1954, or 1957," Flo answers.

"What is the address here?"

To this Tony answers, "Seven Third Street, Kingston Thirteen."

"You have any idea why him would want fi hang himself?" the other policeman asks.

"Well, no, sir, is only that him lose him work, and life get hard."

This is sufficient for the policemen, who start taking down the body with Tony's help and put it in the back of the jeep. They tell Flo they are taking the body to the morgue and that she must go there tomorrow morning to claim the body. The jeep pulls away, and the crowd gradually thins out, till only Flo, Sophia, the other tenants, and me remain. With my head spinning and my stomach aching, I crawl to the doorstep, where I sit hugging my knees and slowly rocking back and forth.

The other tenants go back into their rooms so that Sophia can help Flo clean up the mess in our room. Sophia knows why Sammy killed himself. Sammy had caught the potter bouncing up and down on Flo, and when Flo and the potter saw Sammy, they both ran. Sammy ran after Flo, and Flo ran all the way to Sophia's yard to seek refuge. Sophia shielded Flo with her huge bulk, and when Sammy left, Flo told Sophia that Sammy had caught her with the potter. Then Flo asked Sophia to buy the box drink and bun and cheese and take it to me, for she knew that I was hungry, for I hadn't eaten since this morning.

Despite the fact that I am happy that Sammy is dead, I feel sorry for him. First his wife was burned to death while he was sleeping with Flo, and when he lost his job, he found Flo with another man. He didn't know that Flo had gone to an obeah man and cast a spell on him so that he would never be able to leave her. Rather than beat Flo, he felt it would be better if he killed himself and left Flo with the guilt of his death. As long as we live, Flo and I will never forget Sammy's open eyes and frothy mouth.

It is now late in the night. Flo and Sophia have cleaned the room. Flo changes the sheets and tells me to go to bed, and then asks Sophia to sleep with us tonight. I am still hungry and sick with gas. There is little room on the bed for me, and Flo is hanging off the edge, for Sophia has taken up most of the bed with her huge bulk. I try to fall asleep but I can't. Every time I close my eyes I see Sammy's face when he said he was going to kill Flo with beating when he caught her. I have overheard stories of women tying men, and the men beating the women to death when they wanted to be set free. I keep seeing Sammy's body suspended from the ceiling and the froth dripping on the bed. I am terrified of falling asleep, as I am afraid of Sammy's *duppy*: his evil spirit that can come back and harm the living that I overheard people talking about. I toss my head from side to side in the small place that I have between Flo and Sophia, trying to fall asleep. Tiredness takes over and I fall asleep. I start to dream. In my dream Sammy turns into a big black bull, and he has a long chain around his neck. Flo and I can hear him coming closer as the chain is dragging on the concrete: Clunk . . . Clunk . . . Clunk . . . Clunk! Flo and I are inside the room. We don't know what to do as he draws nearer. Sammy, the big black bull with red eyes, reaches our room and starts bucking at the door with his powerful long horns. With each buck there's a loud thud and the door shakes. Flo is holding on to me on the bed and saying the Lord's Prayer, but her prayer doesn't help. The door comes crashing down with the big black bull, who stops, digs his hooves in the floor, and charges at us. *"Aa-ahhhiiiaaa!"* I scream as I wake up dripping with cold sweat and trembling with fear from my nightmare.

"Clara, Clara, wha' happen to you?" Flo asks, springing up from the bed. I feel dizzy. My head is throbbing with pain, and I feel sick from hunger.

"Me dream say that Sammy come fi kill we," I mutter, unaware that I am crying. Sophia looks at me sadly, and I can feel the fear in Flo's eyes as she looks at me. We both know that she had tied Sammy to her at the obeah man. Does this tie extend beyond death? If so, we will have a lot of trouble from an angry *duppy*!

"You know we goin' have to get Sammy spirit out a the room," Sophia says.

"Me know," murmurs Flo. None of us want to sleep anymore; we just sit on the bed till we see the streak of daylight under the door, and Sophia goes home.

Flo and I go to the shop and buy some bread and some sugar to make breakfast. On the way back, we see some of the on-lookers who were in our yard last night. "Flo, me so sorry that you lose such a good man," a woman with straightened hair carrying a baby on her hip tells us, and Flo just nods. Then the shopkeeper gives us an extra piece of bread to show us his feelings. We go home and each have a piece of bread and a cup of mint tea for breakfast. While I bathe myself, Flo discusses Sammy's death with the other tenants, who are still in shock that he actually hanged himself. We get dressed in our good clothes and are sitting on the doorstep, waiting for Sophia to arrive. Today Flo has to go to the dead house and make arrangements for Sammy's body.

When Sophia arrives we go to the main road to get a bus to take us to the morgue. A bus arrives but is packed with people. As we force our way onto the bus, Flo asks a man sitting close to the door if he could hold me in his lap. The man nods yes, and I am glad that I don't have to stand all the way to the morgue. The bus sways from side to side as the driver is taking the corners too tightly, and with each pothole the bus goes over, the passengers cling to the overhead railing.

I am sitting on this man's lap. All of a sudden I feel this hard thing against my bottom. I pay no attention to it, just assuming that this man has a hard lap. Slowly, with each lurch of the bus, the man holds on to me. With each lurch his hard lap rubs against my bottom. His lap keeps rubbing me, and as the bus nears to downtown, the man makes one final lurch with the movement of the bus, and now my bottom feels wet. The bus stops, and Flo takes my hand, waiting for Sophia to come off the bus while I feel my behind. It is slightly wet, and I know there must be something wrong with a grown man peeing in his pants. I am never going to sit on a man's lap again.

We walk through the streets passing people selling cigarettes, housewares, clothes, cheese biscuits, banana chips, popcorn, patties, and so many other things. I stare at the things, especially the food, wishing I had some money to buy some. We reach the city morgue, which is behind the hospital. The windows need cleaning, the building needs paint, and above the entrance a sign reads CITY MORGUE. There are a few people going in and out of the morgue, and there is an attendant who gives out a number and benches where you sit and wait. When our number is called, a man comes out to take us to the body. The attendant looks at me trying to decide if I am old enough to see the body, and Flo says, "Is her father, she must see him." So we go inside, following the attendant to a room where there are large refrigerators. In the middle of the floor is a pile of bodies waiting to be sorted out. "Newcomers," says the attendant when he sees me staring at the pile of bodies. The attendant then asks Flo when the body was brought in. "A yesterday, and him was wearing a blue shirt and a khaki pants. Him was wearing shoes," Flo says, but that doesn't help, as all the bodies are naked. The attendant moves from refrigerator to refrigerator, asking Flo to take a good look before she says, "No, is not him." We can't find Sammy's body in the refrigerators, so the attendant goes back to the pile of bodies and starts removing body after body, making a new pile. At the bottom is Sammy's body. He has turned blue and black, and swelling has enlarged his face. The tag on his toe says, "Samuel Johnson, death by hanging, 7 Third Street, Kingston 13." I start to feel nauseous, and I can tell that Flo and Sophia feel the same way.

Now that we have found the body, we must decide what to do with it. Flo tells the attendant that she doesn't have much money to bury Sammy and that she doesn't know any of his family. The attendant tells her that she can have the body cremated for a little bit of money. This pleases Flo very much, because now she won't have to worry about the cost of a normal funeral.

"So you can take care a that fi me?" Flo asks the attendant.

"Yeah, man, me can do everything fi you, me can even get the death certificate fi you."

"So how much that goin' cost?"

"Me think that 'bout one hundred dollars will cover it."

"If me bring the money tomorrow, when you can do it?"

"If you bring the money tomorrow, then the next day you can get everythin'."

"A'right me will see you tomorrow, 'bout three o'clock in the afternoon."

"Yeah, man, just ask fi Winston tomorrow when you come," he replies, going back to the pile of bodies.

We leave the morgue and its horrible smell. We stop at a drugstore, where Sophia tells Flo the things she must buy to burn inside the room to get Sammy's spirit out. They buy candles, incense, oils, and strong-smelling powders. This time, going home, I do not sit on a man's lap, as I fear he might rub his hard lap against me. We arrive home, and Sophia leaves, after expressing how relieved she is that Flo won't have to stand the cost of a funeral.

Flo and I go to the shop to get something to cook for dinner. Even while she eats, Flo looks bothered by Sammy's death. Tony comes to the doorway and tells Flo that if she needs any help with anything, she's to let him know.

"Me goin' cremate Sammy body, and me don' have enough money; the only help me need right now is a loan. You can lend me some money?"

"Bwoy! Me wish me could, but me have only twenty dollar in me name. If you want it fi borrow, me will lend you. But you goin' have to pay me back by the end of the week, cause me goin' want it fi me food money."

"All right," says Flo, and Tony goes and gets the twenty dollars and gives it to her.

Dinner has finished. Flo leaves the yard and tells me that she will be back soon. I am sure she is going to see the potter to get some money from him for Sammy's cremation. I hope that she gets it, so we won't have to go back to the morgue. I also wonder about the obeah man. Will he be able to undo the knot that he tied between Sammy and Flo, and what will happen if he can't untie the knot? Will we be terrorized by Sammy's *duppy*? Will Sammy's spirit still bounce up and down on Flo? Will he hurt me? I wonder, remembering the story the skinny woman told at the obeah man about a *duppy* beating her daughter; about not being able to see or do anything about it. I also remember the look on the girl's face of total emptiness, as if someone had stolen her soul.

It's evening. The sun is disappearing in the sky. Instead of staying inside our room, I go toward the gate to look out at the street. That's all that everyone does here. People sit on the sidewalk in the evenings and chat about other people's business and greet each passerby by saying, "Wha' happen?" I stare at the people sitting on the sidewalk across the street. I know each of them. I know their children and their meager dogs. I know who is sleeping with whom, as I have heard Flo chatting about it with her friends. I look at them, at each one hanging on to nothing and waiting for some kind of a miracle to happen to change their horrible lives. I am glad they don't know why Sammy killed himself, for that would be the topic of their gossip this evening.

The children are running around playing games. I dare not join them as Flo says I can only stay inside the gate. Flo says that these children are hooligans, and she doesn't want me to mix with them. Yet sometimes she goes across the street and sits on the sidewalk and chit-chats with their parents. I lean on one foot, then the other. My hands hurt as they are on the wall with my head resting on top of them. Despite that, I am still standing there waiting for Flo to return; waiting like the people on the sidewalk for a miracle; a miracle of going back to Ma. I look across the street at these children and I feel sorry for them, for they don't know anything about wide-open spaces, tall grasses, and large trees. These children don't know about the free river that used to speak to me and cleaned me with her waters when I was dirty. They don't know about my longing for Ma, or my sadness in living with Flo. I want to play with them, for they look happy running about the sidewalk in their old clothes and bare feet. I want to tell these children about how Stumpy and I got almonds at the river and how we played under the mango tree.

One of the mothers slaps her child and tells her to sit down and shut up. Tears form in my eyes as I realize that all these children live the same way that I do. They get beaten by their parents. They look just as skinny and they seem to be looking for the same thing that I am looking for. A feeling of sanctuary. Don't cry, I tell myself. Sing! Sing the song that Ma used to sing, when she held me in her arms. I try to remember the song, but it is buried in my head with all my longings. Slowly a word comes, then another. Now the whole song comes back to me, the way that Ma used to sing it. I hug myself, as I softly sing.

> "Come we down!
> Come we go down!
> Come we down to Linstead market!
> Come we go down!
> Come we down!
> Fi go buy banana!
> You a-rock so! Me a-rock so! Wit' the bunch a banana!
> You a-rock so!
> Me a-rock so!
> Wit' the bunch a banana!"

Ma would rock me on her knees from side to side when she sang this song, imitating the rocking movements of women carrying large bunches of bananas on their head. I rock myself gently and pretend that Ma is rocking me in her lap. I sing the song several times, and now I feel better.

Finally Flo comes back, and I can see by the look on her face that she has gotten the money. We go to bed early, as I think that we are going to the obeah man tomorrow. I try not to think about Sammy. I tell myself that it is not Flo's fault why he killed himself. For if he had been able to provide for us, then Flo would not have to be sneaking to see the potter. It's his own fault, I decide. Besides, there is more space on the bed, and he has paved the way for the potter, so that I can start going to school again. Yet I feel sorry for Sammy's spirit, for what on earth is he going to tell Miss Ivy when he meets her in the world after death? I hope that she's happy to see him and not too harsh with him for cheating on her with Flo. That's my last thought as I drift off to sleep.

"Clara, wake up!"

"Um-um-um."

"Clara, me say that you fi get up!" Flo yells in my ear, making me to sit straight up in the bed wide awake. The dark heavy curtain at the only window blocks out any light, but by the light under the door, it looks like early morning. I slowly get off the bed, when Flo says, "Go tidy youself and put on them clothes."

"But wait till you cool off," she adds.

Flo makes some tea. There is no bread. We go to the bus stop, and just as I suspected, we are going to the obeah man. The bus comes and there are a lot of seats in it as most people aren't awake yet. As before we get off at the gas station. Flo pays the conductor, who yells to a woman wearing a brown dress at the bus stop. "You coming, lady?" The woman shakes her head no. And the conductor hits the side of the bus with his hand, telling the driver to drive on.

We arrive at the obeah man. We are the first ones there, for the flag lady is just opening the church door, and the place is empty. We are purged and we sit in the church, waiting for Dada to arrive. More people are arriving, and each of them sits next to the person who arrived before. Soon the church is full of nearly twenty people. Dada comes in as usual, holds his service, and prays. He takes down names, and the flag lady leaves with the basket. It's now Flo's turn to see Dada.

"Come inside, Flo Higgins, and leave the child outside," he says and I go to my peeping hole in the zinc shed wall.

"So how things with Sammy?" Dada asks Flo.

"Sammy dead. . . . Two night ago. . . . Him hang himself, in a me room. Today me goin' have to cremate the body, cause me can't afford fi bury him. And since me did tie him to me, me wonderin' what me must do fi get him spirit fi leave me?" Dada becomes silent and while looking in the mirror, he says, "Me can see that him catch you with a man. The man tall and skinny, and him work with clay." I am trembling with astonishment at Dada's statement. Flo doesn't say anything and by her silence, I know she feels ashamed. For here she is at the obeah man where she tied Sammy to her so that Sammy would leave the other woman. Then she is at the same obeah man, who knows that Sammy killed himself because he caught her with another man. If I were her, I would feel embarrassed too.

Still staring intensely at the mirror, Dada says, "Sammy die very sad, him soul no satisfy. Him still tie to you even at death, so is a lucky thing that you come back this soon fi see me. Cause on the third night him *duppy* would start haunting you. We goin' have to dig up the shirt, with the parchment paper and the *pum-pum* hair, and we goin' have to untie the knot and purge the whole thing before the body get burn. Me goin' get the things them over the graveyard. Take off you panty and put it 'pon the table till me come back." I move away from the peephole and quickly I turn my head in the opposite direction of the obeah man's office. He passes by me, without even looking in my direction. My eyes follow him to the graveyard, but then the flag lady passes, and I quickly direct my eyes to the ground.

Dada comes back with his shovel in one dirty hand and Sammy's old shirt in the other. Soon he's inside the shed. I go back to my peeping hole, thinking that Dada is going to bounce up and down on Flo in order to appease Sammy's spirit. Instead he starts undoing the knot in the *pum-pum* hair, and when it seems like he has completed this task, he tells Flo to spit on the parchment paper with the names written on it.

He takes her panty and wipes the saliva all over the paper with it.

"You won't be getting you panty back!" he tells Flo, and despite the sad look on Flo's face he commands, "Go outside!"

Flo can't see me peeping, for she is standing just outside the door. He rolls Sammy's shirt and Flo's panty together into a

small bundle and puts it on the ground all the way in the corner
of the shack. From his pocket, he takes out a bottle with some
green-looking liquid and pours it on the bundle while chanting
some funny song. He takes one of the burning candles and lights
the bundle in one quick movement. Now he begins to chant faster
and louder, while pounding harder on the table with his fist.
Then, as the last flicker of flame dies, his pounding and chanting stop.

His face is wet with sweat from the heat and, slumping down
in his chair, he angrily says, "Come inside, Flo Higgins!" and Flo
obeys.

"Look! Me just untie you and Sammy. Him won't be bothering
you. But as long as you live, you must never set back foot a me
place. Cause if you ever come back here, the spell goin' break,
and Sammy *duppy* goin' haunt you, fi the rest a you life!"

That's fine with me, I say to myself, moving away from the
peephole.

As we leave the obeah man and walk down the track, Flo
looks sad. Her eyes look down on the road, and her shoulders
look droopy. I don't know whether it's because of losing her
underwear, or the fact that for future problems, she will have to
find a new obeah man. The sun has risen. The tire shop is just
opening its old wooden doors as we head for the bus stop.

We go home. Flo cooks rice with butter. It is now afternoon,
and we are going to the morgue. We walk slowly along the
streets, as Flo wants to get there as close as possible to three
o'clock.

"Wha' time you have?" Flo asks the man selling watches.

"Ten to three. Wha' make you no buy a watch from me so
that you can know the time?"

"Me des. Me no have no money," Flo answers, increasing her
stride and pulling me along.

"Me lookin' fi Winston," Flo says upon arriving at the morgue.

"Me goin' call him fi you," the attendant says, leaving us sitting on the bench without a number. The familiar face of the man who told Flo yesterday that he will take care of her problem arrives and says, "You come 'bout Samuel Johnson, death by hanging. Right?" and Flo nods her head yes.

"Me have some good, good news fi you. You have the money?" Again Flo nods yes. "Me have everything ready fi you, me have him ashes ready, and me even have the death certificate." Flo opens her mouth wide with surprise. "Me soon come back," the attendant says, disappearing into the morgue. Within minutes he comes back with a piece of paper and something wrapped up in a black plastic bag and sealed with tape. "This is him death certificate," he says, handing the piece of paper to Flo. "And this is him ashes," he says as he hands the bag to Flo.

"Thanks. . . . Thank you," Flo says as she digs in her pocket for the money.

He quickly counts it. "If you want, you can buy a nice container fi put the ashes in, so that it no look that bad," he says, winking and smiling at Flo.

"Um-uh. Thank you," Flo says as we leave the morgue, relieved that we never have to come back.

Instead of going to the bus stop, we go to Lover's Park, a park on the edge of the sea where lovers are seen at all hours of the day. We walk wide of the young and old couples. "Wait right here," Flo tells me while she continues to the edge of the park. I watch her throw the taped-up plastic bag into the sea. Seconds later I see it bobbing between the white-crested waves.

We walk toward the bus stop with slow, heavy, dragging steps. As the bus starts driving toward home, I wonder about Sammy. Will this be the last of him?

5

A WHOLE MONTH HAS gone by, and the potter has moved in with us. He came with Flo one evening and slept the night. Then the nights became more frequent, till he showed up with his belongings. The potter's name is Patta. This is what everyone calls him, and I have no idea what his real name is.

I have started going to school—another school—again. It's a primary school that was built by the government. It's a series of square buildings with most of the windows missing because of being stolen. We sit on old benches with attached desks, and all over the dirty walls are pictures, writings, numbers, and posters. The government has started giving out textbooks, and so far I have been given a math and English book. Flo bought me a navy blue uniform, a new white blouse, and a pair of oversize brown shoes that go flop-flop with each step I make, despite the crinkled newspaper stuffed inside them. Flo has also sewn me a bag from the cloth of one of Sammy's trousers. I am grateful that I have something to carry my books and piece of pencil in.

My teacher's name is Mrs. Down, a woman with a fat, round face and small eyes that seem to fight fat to stay open. Her body looks as if heavy hands have pushed her body in from both ends. Her neck barely exists, her legs are short, and the extension of her body only happened sideways. Her fingers are fat and stubby, and she is always sweating. Most times she drags her stubby index finger across her forehead, and then she swings her hand to her side, landing sweat on the floor.

My classmates call me "Kick me, kill me." They have given me this name because my shoes are so much larger than my feet. They say that if I should kick any one of them by accident, the kick would produce instant death because my shoes are so B-I-G. Nevertheless I take the name without any bitterness at all. For every time they call me by the nickname, I laugh and even have a feeling of being really strong. I hate my big shoes, but I am happy that I don't have to walk to school barefooted. The only reason Flo bought me such large shoes is because she wants them to last me forever. Well, every lunchtime I take off my "Kick me, kill me" and socks and play dandy-shandy with the other girls. We divide into two teams, and we make a ball from an empty drink carton stuffed with paper. Two girls stand about twenty feet apart facing each other. They throw the ball and try to hit the girl between them. If the girl manages to get out of the way of ten balls, then all her teammates each wins an additional game. I like dandy-shandy, for many times I make so many tens that the other team loses.

My school is about a mile from where we live. Sometimes if we are late, Flo takes me through a shortcut, along a path right by the cesspool. Most days Flo doesn't have any money to give me to buy lunch. Luckily for students like me, the government sends a truck each day that supplies each child with a bun and a bag of milk. But the more fortunate children get lunch money from their parents to buy a patty and a box drink. While the poor children like me watch them with envy as they eat their delicious patties.

I have been made aware of the fact that Christmas is coming by my teacher, Mrs. Down. She says that we should celebrate the birth of Christ. She tells us about Santa Claus and even brings a picture of him to show us. He is a big-belly white man with a large white beard. He is wearing red-and-white clothes and lives in a place that is covered with ice. Santa Claus can sneak into children's rooms and give them *anything* that they ask for. I can't believe it when my teacher tells us that all children have to do is write a note to Santa Claus stating what they want, and they will get it. She tells the class that Santa travels on a sleigh with deer pulling it.

On Christmas Eve, after Flo has gone to the shop, I sit on the doorstep with a page from my exercise book and my small piece of pencil with the eraser long gone and, with my heart drumming, start to write a letter to Santa Claus.

"Dear Santa," I begin.

> You no know me, but me name is Clara, and me live at 7 Third Street, Kingston 13. Me sister Flo take me away from Ma, and me no see Ma since. Me no like living with Flo, and me is asking that you take me back to Ma on you cart, with you deer them. And when we reach where Ma live, me will go get a whole heap a grass, fi you deer them, cause them going be hungry, cause Ma live far, far from right here. If you can do that fi me then me no want nothing more fi Christmas, cause Ma is enough fi me, fi Christmas. If you no able fi carry me back to Ma, then you can give me some money, so that me can buy lunch when me go back to school. Thank you very much. And if me can ever do anything fi you, let me know. From Clara. By the way me real name is Fay.

I fold the letter so neatly and put it inside my old holey sock. It's now bedtime, and I carefully hang my sock on the doorknob and climb into bed. I have no trouble falling asleep as I know that Santa will only come while I am sleeping. I dream about waking up and being with Ma.

The next morning I wake up early with great eagerness. The sound of Patta snoring tells me that Santa couldn't take me back to Ma. So I figure that he has left me some money. "Me have fi go to toilet," I tell Flo, hoping to get to my sock as quickly as possible. "Carry the bottle lamp wit' you, the matches 'pon the table," Flo tells me as it is not fully morning yet. I quickly crawl over Patta and Flo, pick the lamp off the floor, and feel for the matches on the table. After lighting the lamp, I grab my sock from the doorknob and open the door. As I make my way to the toilet, I use my hand to shelter the lamp from the cool morning breeze that wants to blow out the flame. As soon as I close the toilet door, I dig into my sock expecting to find some money from Santa Claus, but my fingers feel the folded note and nothing else. I turn my sock inside out, and I see that the note is the same way I had left it, and there is nothing at all from Santa Claus. I read my note again, slumping down on the toilet, and my eyes fill up with tears. Why didn't Santa give me what I asked for? Is it because my sock has so many holes? Was it because I didn't write the note well enough? I try to think of more reasons, but each one makes me cry harder. I tear up the note and throw it in the toilet and decide that I am never going to believe in anything again. Then my hatred sprouts for my teacher, Mrs. Down, also known as Dumpy Down by her students, behind her back. After washing my face at the communal sink, I go back inside the room.

The holidays are long gone, and there is a jeepload of policemen with guns across the street. A thief lives there with his light-skinned girlfriend. They call him Spider, for his skin is very black. He robs the bread van, the chicken-back truck, and anything else that can be robbed. Gossip has it that he has several guns and a protective talisman he received from an obeah man; that no matter who he robs or what he does, no harm can come to him if he is wearing it. He wears only expensive clothes, and his girlfriend is loaded down with gold jewelry. He must not be wearing his talisman this morning, for five policemen with their long guns are rushing into his yard. The crowd grows, and Flo and I watch as they pull him out of his yard, barefooted and wearing only his underwear. His girlfriend is crying and yelling, "Leave him! Let him go! Let go me man!" But the police ignore her. They pull him to the middle of the street, and the crowd becomes silent. Then the silence is replaced with a loud *bang!* echoing a gunshot as the crowd runs for cover. Spider's body just falls onto the street, after the policeman shoots him in the head. Blood flows from his head.

"Nooo!" yells his girlfriend as she jumps on the policeman, knocking him to the ground in the blood. His gun falls, and she kicks him, punches him, and bites him. Then *bang!* sounds another shot, from another policeman who sees that his colleague is no match for this outraged woman. The bloody policeman pushes the dead woman off him, and his colleague helps him to his feet. As soon as the policeman stands up he grabs his gun and empties it into the dead body of Spider's girlfriend.

When the noise dies, a few heads pop up from behind walls to see the policemen throwing the bodies in the back of the jeep. They drive away with Spider's black, bloody feet dangling from the back. As soon as the jeep goes out of sight, the crowd gathers around the blood-covered spot. The crowd is angry and saddened by their helplessness against the police, who seem to have the power of death or life in their hands. "If me did have a gun me would shoot all a them police!" says a light-skinned man.

Spider and his girlfriend have no families nearby. So within minutes the tenants living in Spider's yard have started helping themselves to the belongings of the deceased. Soon the room is empty, and two women are fighting over a gold chain that belonged to Spider's girlfriend.

This is my life. My only escape is school, where I escape into learning mathematics, reading, and English. At school we read stories about happy people that are so strange and so foreign as my community would be without death. I am good in my lessons at school, for my lessons are all I have.

Flo is getting on well with Patta, and now she has started making pottery too. She works with Patta in a little shed next to the abandoned train line. Sometimes I watch Flo making pottery. It's a very hard job. First she has to find a clay spot. Then she has to loosen the dirt, using a big fork. She bags the dirt and carries it back on her head to the shed. She waters down the dirt and separates the stones from the clay, kneading it so that it is moldable. She makes vases and flowerpots, and they have to dry for a few days before being baked in the oven. The oven is a round bed of stacked stones with a hole underneath it for firewood. All the pottery is stacked on top of the oven and covered with old zinc and pieces of broken pottery. The oven burns the whole night, and the pottery comes out looking hard and tanned. Flo applies stain to the vases, then clear varnish, making them glisten in the sun. That is half the work, for now they have to walk in the hot sun from house to house in the rich neighborhoods to sell them.

Patta has started bringing me candies and sweet biscuits in return for putting his hand between my legs at night while Flo sleeps. I know that there is something wrong with it, but it feels nice, and I love getting candies and sweet biscuits, especially the ones that have vanilla cream between them. Now I rub myself. I rub between my legs, enjoying the little surges of current I get with each rub. Flo sees me doing it, and I tell her that Patta is the one who showed me how to do it. Flo lands me a powerful slap on my face. "No ever make nobody touch you down there!" she yells. "You hear me?"

I am crying, so I nod yes. Then, in a much louder voice she yells, "You must never, never, let nobody touch you down there!"

I can't imagine what's so bad with what Patta's doing. It's not like he is beating. But there must be something wrong with it, for Flo is packing Patta's things into a plastic bag. Now she is sitting on the doorstep, sharpening her machete. When she is done, she puts it by the door.

As soon as Patta arrives, Flo rushes toward him and starts slapping him with the sharpened machete. "Wha' the rass you feel up me pickney for?!" she yells at Patta, and the machete goes *slap, slap!* as it hits his body. Patta doesn't fight back. "A lie she tell!" Patta manages to say, but Flo is still slapping him all over his body with the machete. He finally gets away, and Flo gets his clothes and throws them in the street. "If me ever catch you ugly rass in a me yard again, I goin' chop up you rass! 'Bout you feel up me pickney!" Flo yells, as he picks up his belongings and walks away.

Flo walks back to our room huffing and puffing with anger, and I wonder if Patta will attack her at another time. And with him gone, how on earth are we going to survive?

6

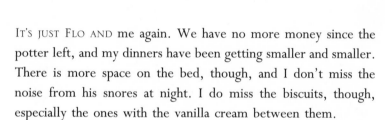

It's just Flo and me again. We have no more money since the potter left, and my dinners have been getting smaller and smaller. There is more space on the bed, though, and I don't miss the noise from his snores at night. I do miss the biscuits, though, especially the ones with the vanilla cream between them.

Flo decides that she is going to build her own shed to make pottery. She is going to build it along the abandoned train line, much farther down from where Patta has his shed. On both sides of the train line, people have made sheds to live in out of old boards. Flo says that these people are capturing land, and she is only going to capture a small piece, just big enough to make her pottery on. There are shed homes along the train line in clusters, and between the clusters are bushy unoccupied spaces. We haven't seen Patta since the incident, and Flo carries an ice pick with her in case he attacks her.

Instead of going to school today, I have to go with Flo to help her clear a patch of land for a shed. I love going to school, and I am sad that I am not going. It takes a lot of effort for me not to pout, and every few minutes I have to pull in my lips so that Flo doesn't see my pout. I am gathering bushes, and now my back is starting to hurt from bending so many times. I dare not complain for I know that if Flo doesn't make her pottery, we won't have any food. In one day we have cleared a big-enough spot for the shed and an oven. Flo sticks her machete into the ground, puts her hands on her hips, and surveys our achievement of a cleared spot of land. She seems pleased, but I'm not, for I know that we need wood and zinc to build a shed, and I have no idea where we're going to get them.

Halfway between night and morning, Flo wakes me up and tells me that we are going to get wood for the shed. I sigh with anger as I get up, dreading the encounter with the cool night air outside, and in the darkness of the night, I follow Flo toward the wharf. The wharf is a very large premises where ships dock to load and unload goods, which are stored in large warehouses. It is on the main road and a severely high cyclone fence with barbed wire on top of it separates the premises from the street. At the entrance is a guardhouse, and iron spikes run the full length of the big gate. Light shines from a utility pole illuminating the guardhouse and the wooden pallets on the concrete dock.

I am terribly cold as the sea breeze assaults my meager frame, for my thin old blouse and shorts provide no warmth. The street is empty, and inside the guardhouse we can see that the two guards are sleeping with guns attached to their waists. One of them is sitting on a chair with his feet on the desk and a hat pulled over his face. The other guard sits on a chair with his head on the desk, using his hat as a pillow.

Flo is staring at me as if she wants me to get the pallets. The gate doesn't go all the way to the ground, so there might be just enough space for my skinny body to get through if I lie flat on my belly. Flo reads my mind and whispers to me, "See if you can go under the gate and quietly push some pallet to me. And make sure that you no wake up none a the guard, else them will shoot we." I nod my head in agreement, but my body is filled with fear.

As soon as I lie on my stomach to slide under the gate, the breeze blows dust into my eyes. I have trouble seeing, I'm cold, and I'm terrified. I can feel my skin bruising from crawling on the rough asphalt, and now I am on the wharf's premises. I crouch on my knees, feeling the rough, hard surface beneath my flesh.

I swallow hard and rub my eyes to get rid of the dirt in them, but with each blink they only feel worse, as if someone is stabbing my eyes with a sharp knife. Concentrate! a voice in my head says, but I am trembling so hard that my teeth are chattering. If I make any sound, all the guard has to do is open his eyes and he will see me! I crawl toward the nearest pallet and try to lift it, but it is too heavy for me so I try to push it. As Flo watches, I push the pallet toward the gate while keeping an eye on the guards to see if they are waking up. I push slowly, gently, and the pallet makes a smooth *Eeerrr* as it gets closer to the gate. I can't push the pallet any farther as there is a lump in the asphalt. I push harder with all the force I can summon, hoping to get it over the lump. But to my surprise the pallet flips over on its side and comes down with a thud.

Instantly I run to the side of the guardhouse as the guards rush outside and start shooting up into the air. I am crying with the fear that they are going to shoot me. They are going to kill me! One of the guards sees me and drags me by the collar of my blouse under the light. "No shoot her, sir! She just a little pick-ney!" Flo cries from outside the gate.

"Wha' the rass you doing 'pon other people property at this hours a night, little gal? You know say that me could have shoot you?" I can't answer his question because my ears are ringing from the noise of the gunshots, and my teeth are still chattering.

"Let her go, sir, she is only a little pickney, she did just a-borrow one a you pallet them. Me sorry, sir, but times hard, and me really need some pallet fi build a shed fi make vase," Flo says, so pitifully that the mighty guard releases me from his grip. Will they call the police and put me and Flo in jail for trying to steal pallets?

A sigh comes from the other guard, as it is only a skinny child and a woman who have caused all this fuss, and not armed gunmen. I am still frightened, and to my and Flo's surprise the guard asks angrily, "Then why make you never just did ask we fi them?"

"Me did 'fraid that you wouldn't give me, sir," Flo meekly replies. I agree with Flo; they wouldn't have given us any of the pallets. They are only saying that because they are ashamed that they were sleeping when they were supposed to be guarding the place. There is a buzzing sound in my ears, and I am wondering if I will ever hear properly again. But I do hear the guard telling his coworker to open the gate and put some pallets outside. As soon as the gate opens, I quickly run outside, happy that they didn't shoot me.

I watch as the guard piles several pallets outside and says, "Look! make haste and carry them a you yard, and no sneak in a other people place again, for people will shoot you!" He locks the gate, then gives us a hard, dirty look. "Thank you, thank you very much, sir," Flo says several times, as we begin the task of carrying the pallets home.

We walk off, with Flo carrying three pallets on her head while I drag one behind me, with my arms hurting from the strain and my back threatening to break in two. I am sweating from this hard work, and the sweat feels cold against my skin. We stop to rest, and I flop down on a pallet, my body begging me to fall asleep.

"Come, me ready get up!" Flo tells me as she loads the pallets on her head. Reluctantly I obey and resume pulling the pallet.

We are almost home. It has seemed so far away, and I can hardly wait to collapse into the bed. As soon as Flo opens the door she tells me, "Go to bed," as she piles the pallets into the room and then leaves to get the rest of them.

It's morning, and I am not going to school today. Flo has decided that it is more important for me to help her build the shed than to go to school. I try not to show my disappointment. I hate helping Flo, and I want to go to school and get that free bun and bag of milk. I dare not protest. I have to keep my feelings to myself. I get up slowly after not getting enough sleep the night before. Flo makes some mint tea and starts separating the wood on the pallets. She packs into a bag her hammer and some nails, along with some salt, a pot, two spoons, two plastic bowls, and a jug of water, which I am carrying. On her head she carries a pile of wood, and she holds her machete in her right hand. We stop on the way at the shop, and Flo buys a pound of flour, a box of matches, and an ounce of butter.

We reach the spot that Flo had cleared two days earlier. She maps out where we are going to build the shed and starts nailing some of the wood together, while I pass her the nails. Then, with her machete and her bare hands, she digs four holes for the shed's foundation. She plants some boards in the dirt, and now I can see the formation of an outline. We are sweating from our toil and the heat of the sun, and now my stomach is starting to growl with hunger. We stop working, and Flo makes a fire to cook something. She kneads the flour, and as soon as the water in the pot starts boiling she puts in the dumplings.

Just as the fire is starting to go out, the dumplings are cooked. Flo gives me four dumplings and a spoon of butter; a raise from my normal share of only three dumplings. The butter melts rapidly into liquid in my bowl. I need not to be told to begin as I dig my spoon into the dumpling, dip it in the butter, and take a big bite out of it. I should really cut it into small pieces with the spoon, but I am too hungry to bother. She passes me a drink of water from the jug that washes the dumplings down into my stomach, and the comfort of a full belly washes over me, as I haven't eaten all morning. We sit resting for a while. I think about school, about playing dandy-shandy, and I am hoping that Flo sends me to school tomorrow, for surely she can finish the rest of the shed by herself. But where are we going to get zinc to cover the roof and a padlock for the door? She gets up off the ground, belches loudly, and brushes the dirt off her behind.

We work and sweat, making trips back to our room to get the rest of the wood. Now Flo has completed a square form by nailing boards onto the foundation, and she has even made a door. She will use a piece of old tire for a hinge, and the only things we need now are a roof and a lock. We rest again, and finally Flo packs up the bag and we head home.

The next day I still don't go to school, as we need to find a roof for the shed. Flo goes to see this rotten-teeth man who makes carts. He has large sheets of tin, and he looks like a madman with his dirty clothes, red eyes, and dirty beard. He spews froth from the corners of his mouth with every word he speaks. He smells bad, and I wonder if he doesn't know about soap and water. But he is the one with the tin sheets. Flo tells him, "Me goin' pay you as soon as me get some money." He rolls up the sheets of tin, ties it up with a piece of cord, and helps Flo to put it on her head. "That all right, just pay me when you have the money. Me know say that you not goin' run away wit' me money." Flo chuckles and replies, "You right 'bout that."

The top of the shed is not high, so Flo has no trouble nailing on the tin. She hinges the door using strips of old car tires, and now the shed is complete. Instead of packing up and going home, Flo decides to go look for clay. She doesn't want to go to the same place that Patta goes to, so that means she will have to start a new clay hole, hoping and praying that the soil has clay in it. We walk to a spot in the bushes and Flo starts chopping at the bushes with her machete while the insects and lizards run deeper into the bushes for cover. Flo loosens some dirt with her machete, picks it up, and rubs it in her hand. Yes! She has found clay! And now she is digging faster. It takes a long time for her to release enough dirt to fill the crocus bag that used to hold one hundred pounds of sugar. I trudge behind her as she wobbles back to the shed with the bag of clay on her head. She is going to need a lot of water to knead all this dirt, and I am praying that this task will not involve me.

"Clara, get up," Flo says, shaking me to life. As soon as she stops shaking me, I drift back to sleep. "Clara, get up, you goin' to school! Get up so that me can comb you hair." I instantly spring awake, as soon as I hear the word *school*. Flo has ironed my uniform and blouse. I clean and polish my "Kick me, kill me," and just the thought of not helping her brings a smile to my lips. She plaits my hair and makes black cornmeal porridge cause we have no money to buy milk. It doesn't taste bad, as she has put nutmeg and cinnamon in it. Porridge normally stays a long time in your stomach. She takes me to school. The eight o'clock bell is ringing, and quickly she says, "When school over, come over to the shed."

"Um-uh," I reply walking faster toward the school gate so as not to be late for class.

I reach my classroom, and right away some of my classmates ask me, "Clara, wha' make you never did come school?" Instead of saying that I was helping Flo to build a shed, I tell them, "Me did sick." I tell my teacher the same thing. I am ashamed of letting them know how poor I am: so poor that I don't even have lunch money, so poor that I don't know if I will have anything to eat when I get home.

Flo is set up very well with the shed. She has gotten two old drums, one that she stores water in and the other she uses as her workbench. Her tools are a piece of sponge, a few pieces of sticks, and a piece of rubber that she uses to smooth the clay.

I watch her work as she shapes a piece of clay into a vase. She makes leaves and flowers on the vases and gives them texture by stabbing the clay with a pointed stick. I don't do anything; I just watch her work, as I am afraid of getting clay on my uniform; not that the clay won't wash out, it's just that soap is expensive and I have to wear my uniform for two days before Flo washes it. When I go to school I am careful not to get my uniform dirty, but on the day that it gets washed, I get it all dirty while playing dandy-shandy.

Flo builds the oven by herself, and she has gathered enough wood for it without getting me involved. The oven is built out of rocks that are tightly packed together with clay between them, and old pieces of pipes supporting the base. She is getting all set to bake her pottery and that is why we are going to the shed this late in the evening. Flo has brought along some cardboard to make a bed on the ground. I help her pile the dried vases on top of the oven, being careful not to break them. I watch as she covers them and step back as she lights the fire under the oven.

I pull the cardboard far away from the heat and sit down as the flames intensify. I watch the flames dance. I remember watching other flames in Ma's kitchen as she made dumplings and told us stories about *duppies*. I miss Ma, and one day I plan on running away from Flo back to her.

Satisfied that the fire is going well enough, Flo lies beside me on the cardboard and tells me, "Go to sleep, cause we goin' have a whole heap a work tomorrow." I am not sleepy, but I close my eyes anyhow and listen to the sounds of the night creatures, making their own music in their own small world. I think they have a much better life than I do. They don't have to worry about going to school or selling vases to buy food; they don't think about where the rent money is coming from. They have a good, simple life. *Creik, creik, creeeiiikkk* comes the sound of a cricket as I drift off to sleep.

I can feel something crawling on my face. Half asleep, I brush at it and suddenly feel a stinging pain on my face. I jolt upright clutching my cheek and feeling the body of a large ant. I crush it between my fingers and then rub the spot where it bit me.

It's morning. I can see that the oven has finished burning and has cooled. Flo is lying beside me on the cardboard slightly snoring. She is dirty from loading the oven and tired from watching it all night. I watch her for a few seconds and then I shake her awake. "Wha'?! Wha' happen'?" she mutters, and by the confused look on her face I can tell that she doesn't know where she is. She rubs her eyes, and memory comes back into her head. She stands up and walks over to the oven. She looks pleased and smiles. Flo is happy she can make it on her own without a man. But I am not happy at all, for if there was a man around then I wouldn't have to stop school to do all this hard work.

We remove the pieces of tanned pottery from the oven, and Flo inspects them for cracks. We stack most of the vases inside the shed, leaving out those that we are going to carry home with us. Flo locks the door with a piece of rusty chain and a padlock that she borrowed from the man who makes carts. Flo carries four vases, two under her armpits and two in her hands, while I carry only one, cause that's all I can carry.

We stack the vases in the corner of our room where the pallets had once stood. Flo goes to the shop and asks the shopkeeper, "Barry, you have no empty box 'round the back that you can give me, fi carry some vase from 'round the shed?" The shopkeeper always has empty boxes, but today he only has small ones, which Flo has no choice but to accept. Now we have to make a lot of trips back and forth from the shed. This is something I am worried about, as some of my schoolmates live in my neighborhood and I don't want them to see me carrying a box with vases on my head. I am ashamed of Flo for being a potter, cause pottery is looked at as a dirty job; and now we are part of this dirty job. Potters are normally men who have dirty clay-soaked nails.

There is no certainty of Flo making a living this way. It is better for her to find a man who is a thief, for thieves have money; they are feared and respected and have guns. Flo cannot get a man who's a thief because thieves want nice-looking light-skinned gals. Flo is black, and by themselves her eyes, nose, mouth, and lips aren't ugly, but all put together on her face, they make her ugly.

I carry a box of vases on my head, feeling as if my head is being pushed into my neck by the sheer weight of the load, yet I do not complain. I know that despite my hatred for what I am doing, there will be no food if Flo doesn't make pottery. So I toil on.

It's the weekend. The vases have been stained and varnished, and now we are on a bus with a box of vases and flowerpots, going to the rich neighborhood. We pass lovely houses made out of concrete, painted, and with maintained grass. We see well-dressed people, who we hope will want to buy our vases. In the midst of a neighborhood with nicely painted houses, Flo yells, "Driver, me beg you let me off when you reach the big tree."

"Line up you bus fare," the conductor instructs Flo as the bus stops at the tree. " 'Ductor, help me down with the box a vase," Flo says as she pays him. He lifts the big box of vases and sets it down on the sidewalk. "Driver, drive!" the conductor yells, hitting the side of the bus with his hand.

Flo gives me a vase to carry in my hand. She puts the box on her head, and in her right hand she carries a flowerpot. I stare at these big houses. Everyone that lives here has to be rich, for there are cars in some of the driveways. Maybe someday I will live in one of these houses, I think to myself. Keep dreaming, the same voice from within replies.

Every house we pass, Flo yells, "Vase. Vase. Vaaassse. Who buy lovely vase?" I hold up the vase in my hand to our prospective buyers, who turn it around gracefully and hand it back to me. They say it is nice, but they have no need for it. We know we shouldn't be angry with them for not buying the vase, but I am. I put this sad pity-me look on my face and look them straight in the eye, but they still don't buy our vases. So we trot on and on, with our feet getting dirty and dirtier with each step from the dust.

We have been walking for almost two hours and haven't sold anything yet. To each woman Flo asks, "You buying this lovely vase, lovely lady?" She thinks if she calls them lovely then they might get swell headed and buy the vase. No such luck. They simply say no, and we walk down more streets. I peep into as many houses as possible. I can see that they have new furniture, curtains at the windows, color televisions, sofas, and chairs, but it's no good, for they still haven't bought any of our vases.

We must do something, cause we don't even have bus fare to go home, and it is too far to walk. My stomach is starting to groan noisily from emptiness. Frustrated, I walk up to this fat, well-fed man and say, "Sir, you want to buy this lovely vase for you lovely wife?" The man is taken aback by my directness, but jokingly he asks, "How come you know that me have a wife, little girl?"

"Me no know, sir, but if you no have a wife, then you must have a girlfriend." I am careful not to say "galfriend," for then he might think I am disrespectful. "Me sure say that you lady friend would like it if you buy her a vase." He smiles. Victory! He calls out, "Selma, come look 'pon them vase!" I am praying that this woman can see I am hungry and buy the vase and not save all her money for fancy clothes and shoes.

A woman with well-groomed straightened hair comes outside. She looks into my desperate eyes and in a soft voice asks, "How much is this one?" I have no idea, so I take a guess. "Ten dollars, ma'am," I reply. I should have said "madam." She turns the vase over in her hands and asks, "You have another like this?"

"Yes, ma'am," Flo answers, setting down her box and getting out another vase. "Don't you think that them will look good on top of the breakfront?" she asks the potbelly man. I have no idea what a breakfront is, but I'm sure that they will look good on it. Just give us the money! The woman goes inside, comes back out with twenty dollars and gives it to Flo. It turns out that the vases are only five dollars apiece. Flo feels very happy, and to show me that she is pleased, she buys two whole patties for me and a box drink. The sun beats on my back, and my feet are dirty from dust. We walk for a few more hours and sell more pottery; then as the sun starts to set, we sell the last piece.

7

❦

FLO AND I ARE surviving without the help of a man, and I'm still going to school. Then, just when Flo is becoming confident about her ability to survive on her own, the wings of change have started fluttering again. It's election time. I can feel the fear and anxiety in the air. Everywhere there is talk about "this party" and "that party." I don't know anything about the two parties, except that their colors are different, red party and green party. Each party has claimed its own territory and its own members. I didn't know about this division until the day after a truck loaded down with men, wearing red clothes and waving red pieces of cloth, rode through the neighborhood, shouting, "Red party! Red party!" over and over. The next day the division began. Then the men in the truck told all the adults where the lines were and who they had to vote for—the red party. Each day the sounds of gunshots echo in the neighborhood, echoing the death of some-body's father, somebody's brother, or somebody's mother.

We are living in the red-party zone. It doesn't matter if you like the red party or not, as long as you live in their territory, you're a member. There is a line drawn between each party's territories, the divider being the abandoned train line. No one crosses the line, or the other party will kill you. A woman who lives in the red-party area went to visit her mother, who happened to live in the green-party area, and she was stabbed several times. The stabbing was done by other women, who, like the men, established their own commitment to the green party.

Flo's pottery shop is in the green-party area, bordered by the train line. Since Flo's shop is in the green party's area, she has stopped making pottery, and now we have no money or food. I have stopped going to school, for school is in the green-party zone too. There are frequent attacks in our neighborhood from the green party. Every time we hear someone cry, "Them a come! Them a come!" the entire neighborhood takes to the streets and starts running toward the main road. I know who is coming. Men from the green party with their guns and their knives to kill us because we don't live in their zone. Some of the men in our red neighborhood have guns too, and instead of running they stand behind walls and fences and fight till one side runs out of bullets.

Flo and I are running along with a mob of people. I don't know where we are running to, for there is no place to run to, but we keep running just the same, as each one of us is trying to outrun the death that comes to claim us. We run till we're tired. We stop and I scan the crowd, mostly women and children. We wait, tired, thirsty, hungry, and scared. When the sun becomes softer in the sky, we head home, not knowing if this will be our last day alive.

We arrive home. There is a body here, a body there, blood here, and guts there. There is hardly any table scrap, and the meager dogs are feasting on the carcasses. They tear the flesh with fevered growls warning anyone who has the idea of stopping their well-deserved nourishment to stay away. Flo holds my hand. I close my eyes and walk with them closed, relying on Flo's pulling hand for direction. I open my eyes when I hear the familiar sound of our gate opening, and cautiously we enter our yard. The doors haven't been kicked open, and there are no bodies. Luckily Flo has some money. I don't know where or how she got it, and I don't care, cause all I can think about is eating something, anything. I am filled with gratitude when she cooks some dumpling and butter.

The people in our neighborhood leave their rooms at night and sleep in abandoned warehouses, used-to-be places of business that are on the main street near to the wharf. They are afraid that gunmen will come and shoot them while they sleep. Rather than sleep in the abandoned warehouses, we remove some of the wooden floorboards of our room and put some cardboard under the cellar. This is where we sleep now, under the cellar with chicken lice biting us all the time, their bites painfully pinching my skin. I kill as many as I can, squeezing the tiny insects between my fingers after they bite me.

One night while we are sleeping under the cellar, a group of gunmen come into our yard and kick open every door, including ours. We can hear them walking above us in our room. We dare not make a sound or they will start shooting under the cellar. I can feel Flo trembling beside me. One of them sits down on our bed, for I hear him say that our bed needs a firm mattress. As they leave one of the gunmen says, "Any gal me find me goin' screw her." We relax after they have gone and pray for the election to be over.

It is morning. There is a body in our yard. It is the body of Tony the Rasta Man. The gunmen have cut his throat, and he is lying in a pool of blood that surrounds his head, his back, and a small part of one of his thighs. The blood is starting to dry, and flies begin to land on his body. He had decided to stay behind so that no one would steal their belongings after his woman and children went to stay with relatives in the country. I want to cry but I can't, for the tears refuse to come.

Late in the evening the police come to pick up the body. The head on Tony's body is hanging by a small piece of flesh and as the policemen lift his body to put it in the jeep, the head falls off and rolls underneath the jeep. One policeman lies on his stomach to retrieve the head, and as soon as he throws it in the back of the jeep, they drive away, leaving behind the usual crowd of spectators.

The election has ended. The new prime minister has been put in place. Life tries to move on, leaving behind so many scarred and dead people. They mourn their fathers, brothers, mothers, lovers, and friends. Me, I mourn for my sanity. My turmoil in such a hostile world. I mourn for Stumpy, for peace, my river, and most of all, my Ma.

Months have passed and Flo continues making vases. I have gone back to school, and all we talk about is what happened during the election. One of my classmates, Shirley, never came back because she was killed during the election. Rather than play dandy-shandy with us, the boys play war, tying red and green strings on their arms and using sticks for guns. My school is not the same. We have no toilets as they were stolen. The teachers have gotten together their own money to install two toilets. The rest of the cubicles will have to wait on the government.

Our new teacher, Miss Twine, never came back after the election, so we have a new teacher, Mr. McCalla. He is tall with heavy lips, small eyes, and a small nose. Today is a sad day, as he is leaving, leaving us and the school for a better teaching job in a better neighborhood. I am crying, the whole class is crying. In a short time we have grown to love him. He takes such care with us, and doesn't beat us like the other teachers. He gives us hope and tries to instill values into our lives and tells us, "You are the future. You are the ones that are going to change the society in which we live. The only thing that will change our communities is *education!*" I want to change my life. I want to be educated. It's hard to get over losing Mr. McCalla, and every time I get sad by missing him, I think of what he said to the class, and it gives me hope. Now all I have to do is get educated. Our new teacher is a tall skinny woman with thick glasses and bulging eyes. She makes us miss Mr. McCalla with her boring, bad way of teaching, which she does in a voice that sounds like she has a permanent stuffed-up nose.

I am now ten years old. I am on top of my class, and now the opportunity for me to go to high school has arrived, the Common Entrance Exams. If you pass the exams, you can go to the high school of your choice. The exams include math, English, and mental ability. If I fail the exam, I can take it again two more times. If I fail all three times, then I will go on to a somewhat more practical secondary school. I study for my exams, and this excludes me from helping Flo with her pottery.

It is the morning of the exam. Flo tells me not to tell anyone that I am taking the exam, for they can go to an obeah man to ensure my failure. My uniform is beautifully pressed, my "Kick me, kill me" glisten with cleanliness, as Flo wants me to look very nice today. She tells me not to eat anything from anyone, for they might poison me out of envy.

"No make nobody touch you before the exam, and make sure that you pass." I nod my head to show that I understand as I go to take the exam that will determine my future.

I take Flo's advice and don't let anyone touch me before the exam. The examiners hand out the papers and announce, "You have two hours for this test, and when we say stop, you must stop, or else you will be disqualified. Any questions?"

No one says anything, and as soon as I hear "Begin," I start filling out the blanks of name, class, teacher, and date.

The day begins to pass slowly because I finished my test in

half the time and rechecked my answers. I keep my eyes on my wooden desk for fear of being disqualified. I follow each line in the old wood as I contemplate buying my great treat of a patty. Flo feels that this is a special day and gave me money to buy one.

The minutes drag on; as the last of the papers are collected, the entire room breathes a sigh of relief. After school I go to the shed, wondering if I have passed and what it will be like in high school.

Weeks go by, and Flo can hardly wait to buy the newspaper that announces the names of all those that have passed. The shop opens in half an hour, and Flo and I are already heading for the shop. There is a crowd of people at the shop door waiting to buy the newspaper too. The shop opens, and I am wondering, What will my name look like written in the newspaper?

As each person buys their newspaper they frantically search through schools for their children's name. I watch some faces fall because their child failed. One skinny woman sees her daughter's name, starts yelling with joy, "Woooeee! Woooeee, me daughter pass!" and begins running up and down the street.

Finally Flo gets her paper. My heart is pounding. Did I pass? I watch as Flo scans through the names under Merl Grove High School. I watch her slowly smile and then she shows it to me. CLARA MYRTLE, without a middle name.

8

HALF THE SUMMER IS gone, and today Flo and I are going to Merl Grove High School for new-student orientation. I see my will-be classmates along with their parents; most of them are rich, judging by their straightened hair, the way they are dressed in fashionable, new clothes and shoes, and their eagerness to shell out the money for the school fee. My school is all girls and is situated in an uptown neighborhood. We tour the school, and I notice that the buildings are well painted, and the grounds are maintained. There are two chemistry labs, two biology labs, a large sports field, lots and lots of classrooms, and, quite important, several watercoolers. The school grounds have a lot of fruit trees, and the toilets are all clean, and some have red hibiscus flowers painted on the walls.

People are not buying pottery anymore because they are saving up their money to buy back-to-school things for their children. This worries us, as now it is the end of summer holidays, and soon I will be starting high school. It's bad enough that the school has given Flo a bill for the school fee, but on top of that they have given her a long list of things that I will be needing: textbooks, special-colored shoes and socks, special-made uniforms, sports gear, and a whole pile of other things that I don't have. As a matter of fact we don't have anything. The money that Flo makes can barely feed us, much less buy all these things. Flo has started saving some money. So now instead of having chicken back and rice, we have dumplings and butter. So far she has managed to pay the school fee, buy the shoes, socks, uniform, and one textbook out of twelve.

On the first day of high school I am all decked out in my new uniform, and despite everything, I feel good. As Flo and I walk toward the bus stop, the people in the neighborhood smile at me with pride, at my great accomplishment of going to high school. Many of them have often wished the same for their own children, and because of that I raise my head slightly higher. I can see that Flo feels proud walking beside me, because her chest is pushed out like a rooster and each of her steps is planted with weight of a great purpose. She will be taking me to school every day until I understand how to get there on my own.

My class has thirty students. Every girl is wearing the same light blue, dress-looking uniform, and nice black leather shoes in all kinds of different styles; some are closed by laces, while some are closed by delicate designer buckles. Each of them has an expensive backpack, and their hair has all been straightened, which for me would cost a small fortune. They all have lunch money to buy the cooked lunches in the canteen: doughnuts, patties, meat loaf, milk, and so many other things that I can't possibly afford.

A few girls try to be friendly toward me. They ask, "Where do you live?" I am ashamed to tell them, so I try to think of someplace nicer, but as hard as I try, nowhere comes to mind, so softly I reply, "Greenwichtown." A cloud crosses their faces, as if my answer has just forecast rain. For the slum that I live in is known as a place that any sensible person would stay away from.

We are introduced to a different teacher for each subject. The teachers ask each student her name and what she would like to be when she grows up. The girl next to me wants to be something that I have never heard of, and the girl behind me wants to be a doctor. Now it's my turn. I have never really thought about what I would like to be when I grow up. For the idea of growing up has always been as remote as the moon to me. All I have ever wanted is to be with Ma, have enough food, and I would be happy. Not knowing what to say and looking at all these girls with their fancy hairdos, I imagine how great it would be if I were handed the small fortunes for doing their hair, and I say, "My name is Clara Myrtle, and when I grow up I would like to be a hairdresser." Disappointed murmurs fill the classroom. The teacher who will be teaching us French smiles to ease my embarrassment and, interrupting the murmurs, says, "Next student, please."

"My name is Patricia Connell, and I am aspiring to be an ophthalmologist." My mind goes blank, for I have no idea what that is.

"My name is Theresa Tomlinson, and when I grow up, I would like to be a teacher," says the next girl.

"Finally I have found someone who wants to be part of my profession," the teacher announces with a smile.

Then the last girl says, "My name is Simone Baker, and when I grow up, I want be a cosmetologist," and the bell rings, signaling break time. Later, in room number 22, Mrs. Buckle, our pleasingly plump, groomed, and short home-room teacher, gives us time tables, and tells us how much she looks forward to helping us succeed in high school.

School ends, and Flo is standing at the school gate, waiting on me. She stands there in her old clothes and sandals with the soles almost gone. She looks so poor compared with my teachers, who wear high-heel shoes and pretty clothes.

"How things go a school?" she asks me.

"All right," I answer, not daring to complain about all the things in the canteen that I could not afford to buy, and not daring to tell her how the other girls looked sadly at me when I said that I lived in Greenwichtown.

It's been two months since I have been going to high school, and I go by myself now. Flo goes and makes her pottery, and there is no man in her life yet. I am hoping and praying that one will appear soon, so I can get the rest of my textbooks and lunch money for school. Sometimes Flo gives me two slices of bread with butter and some lemonade to take to school. I eat by myself, as I don't want my classmates to see me eating this pitiful lunch when they eat patties and whatnots. I like going to high school, for it takes me out of the ghetto for a while, but at the same time it saddens me with the daily reminder of how much I do not have. For example, some girls buy cooked lunches every day at the canteen, which is normally beef, chicken, fish, or pork, served with rice and peas and salad. If I am lucky I may eat chicken once every two months.

After another school day ends, I go to the bus stop and head home in a packed bus. I get off at our street, and there is a madman, lying on the road with his big bundle of rubbish beside him. His hair is matted and glued together by dirt, and his nails look like claws. His face is blackened by dirt, and he seems to be sleeping. Knowing that madmen can attack people for no reason at all, I walk very quietly around him for fear of waking him up. As soon as I get passed his rotten-smelling body, he slowly gets up, sees me, and yells, "You whoring little slut! You think you better than me. Move you nasty, ugly rass!" I don't say anything, I just increase my stride, hoping for him to leave me alone. He gets up quickly and starts walking very fast toward me, all the while cursing me in the worst possible ways. "Me did screw you whorin', stinkin' mother so me could be you father! In fact me screw every big-pussy woman 'pon the island, so you no better than me!" I start to run, and my backpack bounces on my scared back. He runs after me, and when I look back I see him picking up stones from the side of the road; now he is hurling them at me! One barely misses my head as it swishes past my ear. "Help! Somebody help meee! Help!" I cry as the madman throws another stone at me. Luckily, a group of men standing at the corner see my dilemma and intercept the madman. They pick up rocks and throw them at him and yell, "Hey, stinkin' madman, go back down the road!" I look back, and I see the madman running in the opposite direction. I keep running just the same though my heart feels like it is going to stop from beating so hard. When I finally stop and try to catch my breath, I imagine all the terrible things the madman could have done to me. Strangle me, crack my head with a rock, poke my eyes out, bite me, or tear a piece of my flesh off, and then I think about how stupid the question was that the teachers had asked me: "What do you want to be when you grow up?"

Because I have hardly any textbooks high school has become hard, and it is difficult for me to do my homework. Sometimes when I try to borrow my classmates' textbooks, they insult me. "Why do you even bother coming to high school if you can't afford books?" one girl said. But there is one girl, though, who doesn't insult me; her name is Simone Baker, and she and I have become good friends, after she explained to me that a cosmetologist is the same thing as a hairdresser. I tell her about my neighborhood, the people, the shootings, the hunger, and the hopelessness that fill our lives. Simone tells me that she used to live the same way till her parents moved out of the ghetto. She also tells me that her father has moved to a foreign country. Simone has all her textbooks, and her mother always gives her lunch money. We sit together most every lunchtime, despite the fact that I seldom have any lunch. We help each other with our homework, and we talk about everything there is to talk about.

Today the sky looks like rain. It is early Sunday morning, and I am going to the communal toilet. After I finish and wipe my behind, I notice that there is blood coming from it. I wipe again, fearing that I have been poisoned! Then I realize that the blood is coming from my vagina. I pace around the toilet, thinking what to do. I know that I will have to tell Flo, for I will need pads. Uneasily I go to Flo and quietly say, "Me period start." She doesn't seem surprised or anything.

"Go get me old blue blouse, and bring me the knife!" she says. I do as I am told and watch as she cuts the old blouse into four pieces of cloth. "Draw down you panty," she says, and I pull my panty down around my ankles and watch as she folds up one piece of her blouse, and puts it between my legs.

"Pull up you panty. When it get soak with blood, you must change it, and wash it, and then pin it 'pon the clothesline." I nod my head, and she adds, "Make sure that you wash it clean, clean."

Despite knowing about menstruation from one of the school nurse's monthly classes, I feel uneasy about the cloth, for the school nurse never told us that we could use it; she had said pads. But I realize that no one will know what I have on beneath me.

I tell Simone that my period started, and she smiles and asks, "I wonder when mine goin' start?"

"You really want it fi start, when you goin' feel a whole heap a cramps, and pain?"

"Yes, me really want it fi start, cause when it start it mean that you turn woman." As we head for geography class we both laugh: Imagine that, me, a woman!

Some evenings on my way home from school, the men standing on the street corners go "Sceet, sceeetttt" at me as I walk by. They like schoolgirls, as they're cheaper to support for they live at home. I ignore them, hoping for Flo to find a man who will help take care of our needs.

Rather than yield to these men, I beg. Most evenings after school, I walk home passing a lot of well-to-do people. I'll walk up to a woman and say, "Excuse, ma'am, I have lost my bus fare; could you spare me a bus fare, please?" I say this sincerely, and sometimes I get enough to buy lunch for a few days at school. I thank them graciously and head for the nearest shop, where I buy something to eat and, rather than spend the money for a bus, I walk home.

9

THREE YEARS HAVE PASSED, and we have moved to Fifth Street. We have two small rooms, separated by a doorless partition in the back of the yard. A big ackee tree, which supplies the tenants with half the requirement of the island's national dish, hangs over the communal sink; the other half, of salted codfish, we cannot afford, but sometimes we do have stewed chicken back with ackees and boiled dumplings. It's October, and the ackee tree is changing its leaves. I slowly sweep the dried leaves, trying not to disturb a lot of dust from the ground.

The landlord, Mr. Royal, also lives in the yard, occupying two rooms. He is an old man with eyes that bulge out of his head like those of a frog, a down-bent nose, and thin lips. He is tall, with half of his head bald and the other half covered with low-cut soft gray hair. He has two children living with him, and they both have the same big bulging eyes. Their mother lives on another street with another man, for Mr. Royal used to beat her up all the time, so badly that she had to go to the hospital. The older is Donna; she is about twenty and has a small daughter. The younger child, Trevor, is the same age as me, and he acts like a girl. People call him "Sweets" even though he is not sweet looking. His nostrils flare up naturally like those of a donkey, and his lips are heavy and have the color of liver.

The only other tenant in the yard is Miss Pearly, who people call "Broomstick" behind her back. She is so skinny that with each step she takes, her bones look as if they will break. Her hair is black after many bottles of dye, and her eyes stare at you from deep within her head.

She has twelve children, but only two daughters live with her. Sandy, the older, got pregnant for a man that got life in prison for murder five years ago, while Cynthia has not yet succumbed to the disease of unwanted fatherless pregnancy. They both look like Miss Pearly.

Cynthia goes to school but is doing very poorly. How do I know? Because one day she left a book page with a math test on it in the communal toilet, for the future need of wiping her behind. She is a year older than me and just as poor, but you would never know it, as her whole family chips in to buy her school things. She is the only family member that hasn't dropped out of school yet.

Sweets and I are friends. I dare not tell him about Ma, but I tell him about my school, teachers, and other things of less meaning to me. I am afraid if I tell him that Flo is not my real mother and it somehow gets back to Flo, then she will beat me. He tells me about his family, about how cruel his sister is to him, and how to get back at her he pinches her one-year-old daughter, who hasn't learned to talk yet. He laughs as he says this and adds that when the little girl cries, he tells his sister that it must be a mosquito biting her.

"So, Sweets, you mother not comin' back?" I ask him.

"You mad? Me father say that if she come back, him goin' kill her." I shift my behind on the empty oil drum, for the rim is hurting my behind.

"When she did run 'way, Donna did have fi hide and bring

her clothes them to her, and if me father did ever know, him would beat Donna," he adds.

Mr. Royal looks like a harmless old man now. He is somewhat blind, and time has taken its toll on his body, wasting his muscles. Mr. Royal is also poor. He gets a pension from the banana company, but he still needs the rent he receives from the tenants. Each day he gives Sweets lunch money for school. I don't know how much, but sometimes I hear Sweets grumbling on his way to school, "What him think me can buy with this?"

Today is Sunday. I am around the back of the yard doing dishes. I have already swept the yard. As I am rinsing the last pot, I hear this hoarse, loud, woeful cry. Immediately I freeze, for it's the cry of war. I run toward the front of the yard, and Flo yells to me, "Where you think you goin'?" Her question of fear is left unanswered as all I can think about is seeing who is at war.

I reach the front of the gate, and almost everyone that lives on Fifth Street is standing there. Amid the crowd, sitting on the sidewalk, is Lucy, whose nickname is "Spongy," for people claim that she absorbs men, like a sponge does water. I look at her and cover my mouth in horror. Her face is severely burned. The burns start from her head and run down to her stomach in thin streaks, touching her first stretch mark and flowing down into the lines. Her eyes are still there, but her nose and lips have melted into her face, as if her flesh has been diluted. He upper arms are also burned. There is no more skin there, and all that can be seen is the red, swollen part of the underlying skin. There are deep craters of missing flesh here and there, getting smaller toward her wrists.

She was wearing black tights and a bright blue sleeveless blouse that ran the full length of her big hips. Most of her clothes lie in pieces beside her on the sidewalk. Her burned neck and drooped breasts still have bits of blue fabric hanging on the singed flesh. She is being showered with buckets, boxes, and cups of water from every direction.

"Bring more water!" shouts Michelle, as she dumps her last bucket of water on Spongy, drowning out her cries of pain.

"Somebody go get a car fi carry her a hospital!" someone else shouts, and several people take off running toward the main road.

Minutes later a white car pulls up with Sandy and Michelle in it. The crowd parts, and two tennants from next door, Baron and Donald, lift Spongy up and put her on the backseat. "Wooeee," she cries, as the car speeds away to the hospital.

After the car leaves there is silence. The kind of silence heard when you don't know what to say. A deadly silence, of grief, sympathy, hatred—and for me a silence of utter darkness. The darkness covers the very fibers of my existence in a thick layer of despair. The silence doesn't last long. "What a piece of wickedness!" says a woman, and the silence returns again. I stagger with each step, and when I reach the gate I hold on to it for support, and for the first time I notice that Flo is behind me. Cynthia, stepping over pools of water and pieces of fabric, crosses the street.

"Cynthia, wha' happen to Spongy?" Flo asks her.

"Marcia throw acid on Spongy, cause Spongy a sleep with her man. So when Spongy go to shop, Marcia wait 'pon her, and throw acid 'pon her. And when Spongy bawl out, everybody go fi water fi throw 'pon her."

Spongy has four children, whose father died after being shot by the police while he was robbing a store. That was three years ago, and Spongy was left alone to provide for her children. She has no job and no hopes of getting any, for there are no jobs. Her source of support is from men, any man, even somebody else's man. In this case Marcia's, who found out that Spongy was sleeping with her man and decided that the best way to keep her man is by pouring acid on Spongy. I feel sad for Spongy. How will her children survive now, with their mother burned and in the hospital? Now they will have to fend for themselves.

The crowd slowly disperses, and Flo and I head back to our rooms. My mind is reeling, thinking about Greenwichtown. I am repulsed by my daily life. There is always someone killing someone for something. What if, when I grow up, I end up like Spongy? I shiver at the thought.

I have thrown away the rinsing water from the dishes. Tomorrow is Monday, a school day, when I become part of a different world, a world where I experience things differently, through books. Yet each day I return home to a dark world. Where even though the sun is shining, all I see is darkness, my sad eyes seeing a sad world. Each day I hope that my life doesn't get snuffed out over some silly foolishness. The only hope I have is the powerful words left to me by a teacher. He said, "Only education can change your situation."

10

"ANYBODY HOME?" A VOICE asks at our door on a sunny Saturday morning. A voice sounding so strange to us that at the sound of it, Flo and I stop eating our breakfast of dry bread and mint tea.

"A who that?" Flo asks, sticking her head through the door.

"Good morning, ma'am, I am doing a house-to-house call, and I am wondering if you would be interested in speaking about God."

"Me eatin' right now," Flo answers.

"Okay, dear, I will come back in a little while, after you have finished your breakfast," replies the voice, and Flo comes back inside the room, pouting as if something is bothering her.

A short while later the woman comes back, not alone but with a white woman, a real white woman, in the flesh. Flo and I stare at her, for neither of us have ever seen a white person before, except on TV. No wonder she didn't speak patois. But this white woman must definitely be mad! For what in heaven's name is a white woman doing in Greenwichtown, where violence is rampant, muggings a way of life, and killings a means of expression?

She looks old. She has wrinkles all over. Her hair is a dirty white color and is pulled to the back of her head in a bun. She has blue eyes beneath hairless black pencil lines that are supposed to be eyebrows. Her nose is straight, pointing slightly upward, with tiny nostrils, and her lips are one thin line.

In Greenwichtown, we think that all white people are rich, as this is what we see on TV. They are always driving big cars, living in big houses with good food and beautiful clothes. But this white woman is wearing a simple old light blue blouse and a navy blue skirt. In her hand she has a bag, not a fancy bag like the people on TV, but a worn old brown schoolbag. The most shocking thing about her is that she is wearing plastic shoes. How on earth can a white woman be wearing plastic shoes?! For it is only extremely poor people like myself who wear plastic shoes. For wearing plastic shoes is only one step above going barefooted, and people compare it to wearing the rubber tires from a car.

The thin lines that are lips part and words come out of them. "My name is Sister Myriam. I am a Jehovah's Witness, and I am here to speak to you about God." Her voice sounds like the people on TV, and so different from the black woman, who adds, "And I am Sister Lindsey."

Despite Flo's shock at seeing a real white person, she recovers and says, "Me was just leavin' the yard. But if you want you can talk to me daughter, Clara, 'bout it." Flo turns to me. "Go get two chair fi them sit down on; me goin' down a Sophia yard." I do as I am told, getting the two chairs and getting the empty oil can for my seat. They sit on either side of me, and I swallow hard to hide my nervousness.

"Which school do you attend?" Sister Lindsey asks.

"I attend Merl Grove High School." I watch as Sister Lindsey's eyebrows arch upward, while the white woman's pencil lines for eyebrows move up toward her forehead, making it more wrinkled.

"What grade are you in?" Sister Myriam asks.

"I am in third form," I reply, and by this they can guess my age.

"Have you ever thought about Jehovah?" Sister Lindsey asks.

What kind of question is that? I pray to God every Thursday along with the rest of the school during devotion in the auditorium.

"No, I have not thought about God," I reply, anticipating that the next question would be: "What have you thought about him?" if I say that I have thought about God.

With my answer, Sister Myriam digs into her bag and pulls out a magazine, the *Watchtower*. "I am going to leave this with you to read, and when we come back, we can discuss it." I nod my head, and then she pulls out another book. I read the cover, *How Did Life Get Here? By Evolution or by Creation?* She starts reading from it.

I try listening to her as she reads theories of evolution versus the Bible's theory of Creation, but my mind drowns out her words. For what difference does it make to me or anyone else in Greenwichtown if life evolved or was created? For the truth is, whether created or evolved, life is a downright day-to-day misery for us. If God created me, then why didn't he make me white and rich like the people on TV? Who have so much and never hunger or worry about being able to afford to go to school. While if I evolved, then what have I evolved into? A child being raised by a sister, who doesn't know where her next meal is coming from. So once I was an ape, and now I am a piss-poor black girl with no guarantees of surviving so that I can continue to evolve. If I survive, will I eventually evolve to being white and rich, like the people on TV?

"What do you think about what Sister Myriam just read?" I don't realize that Sister Myriam has stopped reading. I repeat the question to myself: What do I think? "I think that we were created by God, in his own image," I reply. This I know from the Bible, for one of my subjects at school is religious education. I am afraid to tell them my thoughts.

I watch as Sister Myriam's thin lips part to a smile, revealing her long white teeth, and Sister Lindsey grins widely. Their faces beam expressions that a mother might show when a child finally realizes how to ask for the chamber pot. It's a look of deserved victory, for they both know that from now on everything will be easier.

Sister Myriam and Sister Lindsey prepare to leave. I wouldn't mind if they stayed longer, for I have nothing to do and nowhere to go: All I will do all day is study and read till it is dinnertime— if there is any dinner. Just as they are about to leave, Flo returns, and I am almost sure that she hasn't gone anywhere.

"You leavin' already?" she asks, acting to be surprised.

"Yes, but if it is okay with you we would like to come back and do some more Bible study with Clara," Sister Myriam says.

"Oh, yes, ma'am, you can come back anytime you want." A sigh of relief escapes from my lips, for now I'll have something to look forward to.

They come back the following Saturday. As soon as they arrive, Flo says that she was just leaving, and they give her an understanding smile. We talk about parts of the *Watchtower* I have read, and when we are finished, Sister Myriam says, "You should come visit our church and get to know Jehovah; we would really like to have you."

"I have no church clothes," I say, for I only have my school uniform, my old yard clothes, two panties, and one bra, which Flo bought for me only out of necessity when my high school's vice-principal said, "My job is to make you students into young ladies, and part of being a young lady is wearing a bra."

"If you have something to wear, will you come?" Sister Myriam asks.

"Yes!" I answer, happy at the thought of going somewhere, for the only places I go are school and the grocery shop, which is only two streets away. "But then you have to ask me mother," I add, meaning Flo. When they ask Flo, she says I can go.

Early Monday morning as I am getting ready for school, Sister Lindsey comes back by herself carrying a black plastic bag. She hands it to me with a smile. "I hope that they fit all right. I will pick you up at eight-thirty on Sunday to take you to church."

"Thanks," I say, as Flo pushes her head through the window.

"How are you doing today?" Sister Lindsey asks her as she leaves.

"Not too bad, not that bad at all," Flo replies.

Flo watches as I empty the contents of the plastic bag on the bed. There are two dresses, one yellow with buttons at the front, the other white with small purple flowers and a wide purple belt; two skirts, one gray, the other black and flared at the bottom; three blouses, two plain, while the other one is dark blue with butterflies of all colors embroidered on it. The shape of the blouse is like a butterfly, and the sleeves expand like wings when I raise my arms. The clothes all fit me and are fairly new.

"No tell nobody which part you get them poop-in-a clothes," Flo cautions me, for despite our and everybody else's poverty, wearing secondhand clothes is frowned upon. They are called "poop in a," which means that someone has worn them and has already farted in them. I nod my head. I am excited to go to church on Sunday with Sister Lindsey, for being a Christian can't be that bad, for my life has improved; already I have more clothes, which makes me very happy.

Like she said, Sister Lindsey arrives at eight-thirty on Sunday morning, ready to take me to church. I am dressed in the butterfly blouse, gray skirt, and my school shoes, having had a piece of bread and cup of mint tea. Her medium-size frame is dressed in a light pink dress with two frills at the bottom and white shoes with high heels. Her large white hat has a plastic bouquet at the side and in her hand she carries a black purse. She greets me with a warm smile.

I bid good-bye to Flo as I head through the back gate with Sister Lindsey, and to my great surprise she has a car! A small, cream-colored car that has a Volkswagen sign at the back and round, bulging headlights. The car is filled with other neighborhood children.

"Move close together, children," Sister Lindsey commands, and I watch as they squeeze together, managing to create a space big enough to fit a mosquito.

We drive through streets I never knew existed, passing broken-down places that look like my neighborhood, and other places that look the opposite of Greenwichtown. We stop in front of a small light yellow building with a new zinc roof and the words KINGDOM HALL OF JEHOVAH'S WITNESSES painted on it.

Everybody is already seated inside on wooden benches. When I enter the church I am perplexed, for there are no pictures of Jesus Christ, no statues of him nailed to the cross, and no words from the scriptures etched on the walls. This must be a new church; maybe they haven't gotten around to doing these things as yet.

Right away Sister Myriam joins us, wearing a plain green dress and the only hint of her being dressed up is the two black clips on the sides of her head. Sister Lindsey introduces me to the other people, who are all dressed in nice clothes, and I smile even though I notice that most of the women are wearing high-heel shoes while I'm wearing my plastic school shoes.

The clock on the wall behind the high desk where Elder Green is standing says it's almost nine-thirty. He tells us to join him in prayer, and starts the service with a hymn. As the music starts, the congregation begins singing a song I have never heard before, from a book. The hymn ends, and now the people take turns reading from the *Watchtower*. Elder Green asks questions about what was read, and several people raise their hands, hoping that Elder Green chooses them for the answer. But me, I keep my hands firmly clasped in my lap, wondering if there will be dinner today.

There is more singing, more discussion, and more prayer. The service ends, and everyone heads outside to chat with each other. I watch the faces of the people as they talk, and they look happy. Watching them, the world looks like a wonderful place, but it's so unreal. My world is not like that; it's full of pain, death, hunger, and violence. The only time I am happy is when I have food. I wonder if these people live in the same world with me.

Sister Lindsey touches my shoulder. "Would you like to stay for Bible-study class?" The thought of returning home and facing the possibility that there might be no dinner is enough reason for me to stay. It is only midday, and if Flo has any money to cook, she will wait till the shops are just about ready to close, so no one can see her buying chicken back, especially on Sunday. "Yes," I answer, hoping that there will be some food here, for the piece of bread and mint tea are long gone, and my stomach is starting to make noise.

The only ones staying behind are us children. Altogether there're ten of us. Sister Lindsey asks if we're hungry, and of course everyone replies with a loud "Yes, ma'am." She digs into her black purse and gives money to Fred, the largest boy in the class. "Go down to the shop and buy ten buns and ten bag juices." My stomach now leaps at the news of food. Sister Lindsey says that she will not start the class till after we've eaten, for she knows that we will not pay close attention without food in our bellies. We wait for Fred to return. We wait and wait and wait and still Fred does not return. Now we're all getting restless, and I can hear rumbling coming from other stomachs. Sister Lindsey raises her eyebrows with worry. "I wonder if anything has happened to Fred." Marvin, the boy sitting next to me, seems to know Fred, and says, "Ma'am, me can go and look fi him fi you." But Sister Lindsey says we will just wait some more.

"Wait here, I soon come back," she says, heading for the road and leaving us to worry, not about Fred but about the food that he should be bringing us. She comes back and says, "There will be no Bible-study class today. I am sorry I have no more money." Then she sends home four children who live within walking distance of the church. When Marvin gets up to go, she tells him to wait on her. Hearing her tell Marvin to wait brings looks of suspicion on the faces of the four children, for they must be wondering if this is some plot to outdo them out of the food.

"Can we wait some more ma'am?" one of them asks.

"No, it's best you go home," Sister Lindsey replies, and they leave with their faces adorned with suspicion and hunger.

Sister Lindsey, after locking the church doors, packs the rest of us into her tiny car, and tells me to use my lap as a seat for a smaller child. She drives down the road to all the shops, and we watch as she asks the shopkeepers if they have seen Fred. At the third shop we see the fat shopkeeper nodding his head positively to Sister Lindsey's question.

"Oh, yes, him was here not too long ago. Him was wearing a white stripe-looking shirt, right?"

Sister Lindsey swallows hard. "Yes."

"Ah, yes. Him did buy one small tub a ice cream, one bun and cheese, one chocolate milk, and one cupcake. And him even buy a plastic bag fi carry them in." Sister Lindsey comes back to the car, her face tense with disappointment. Now terrible thoughts run through my head. The thought of him stuffing his face with ice cream and that glorious food makes me boil with anger. What if Flo has no food when I go home?

Sister Lindsey delivers me home. I drag my feet as I open the back gate, sniffing the air for hints of cooked food.

"Good evenin'," I say as I enter the room. Flo is lying on the bed and seems to be sleeping; she doesn't answer. On the table lies my blue plastic bowl covered with the aluminum pot lid. I sniff around the edges, hoping for the smell of rice and peas, but there isn't any. I can surely tell that there is some stewed chicken back inside the bowl. I lift off the pot cover and my eyes beam with gladness, for there in my bowl is a heap of white rice (no peas) and a piece of chicken back. Suddenly all the angry thoughts in my head become grateful ones.

Months have passed, and I have become engrossed with my decision to become a Jehovah's Witness. I always go to Bible study, and I read the Bible that Sister Lindsey has given me. I even walk in the hot sun with members of the congregation claiming souls for Jehovah and try to sell magazines to people, most of whom don't have any money. I give them the magazine anyhow, hoping they'll read it, and using what little lunch money I have to pay for them.

My life in Greenwichtown now feels less harsh. I bear my hunger with dignity, putting other people's needs in front of my own. I live in a haze of thinking, doing, and saying the right things. I know Jehovah is watching all my actions, and all my rewards will come from him, and the more I suffer, the higher my rewards will be.

At school everyone notices the change in me. My classmates select me to be the class prefect, which I decline. But they insist. "Clara, you are such a good example, you study hard, and you get good grades," but still I calmly decline. I think only of Jehovah, and in thinking of him, I have become peaceful. Even the time when one girl calls me "a meager ghetto rat" I smile, telling her that Jehovah loves me and that I will pray for her.

Today is Friday. Flo has given me money to go to the drugstore to buy a jar of face cream for her. The drugstore is out of my school's way, and it takes me almost an hour to walk there for I have no bus fare. When I arrive, I hand the piece of paper to the druggist, and she goes to a shelf packed with different kinds of bottles, jars, and boxes. She comes back with a jar of cream and gives it to me. The words on the jar pledge to lighten the blackest of skins. It says that this cream is designed to give you a lighter-looking skin if used every day, and it should be kept away from children.

I collect the receipt and look at the change. It is enough to buy only one piece of candy, and as I walk I think about Flo. Why on earth is she trying to lighten her skin? Is this some desperate last measure to find a man who will support us? And how is she going to afford to buy this cream for life, when we can't afford to buy food?

Today at school the New Christian Choir asks for donations. I look at Flo's change, wondering if I should donate it, for I'm sure that Flo wouldn't be mad at my act of kindness. When the basket reaches me, I drop Flo's change into it.

When I reach home, I hand Flo the cream. She looks at it and then at the receipt.

"Where is me change?"

"Me donate it to the Christian Choir," I reply.

Her eyes flash with anger. "Wha' you mean by that?" she asks.

I ponder for a moment. "The change could only buy one sweet, and me drop it in the basket for the New Christian Choir," I say again, thinking she hadn't heard me the first time. I see her reaching for the mop stick, and despite my commitment to suf-

fering for a better life in heaven, I want to run. She swings the
mop stick in my direction. I duck down, and it barely misses me.

"Gal! When me send you fi buy something, me expect you fi
bring back me rass change!" she yells. "You know how hard me
have fi work fi me money!" This time she swings the mop stick
at me with greater force. I duck again to get out of the way of
it, but the stick hits me in the left eye. "Aiiieee, me eye! Me
blind! Me blind! Me eye!" I cry, holding my eye as my hand
begins to get wet with blood and pain seizes my head.

I remove my hand so that Flo can see that I am bleeding and
not swing the stick at me anymore. I hear the stick fall to the
floor. I stagger toward the communal sink and point my head
toward the sky, so that Jehovah can get a good look at my bleeding eye and multiply my blessings in heaven.

The more I wash away the blood, the more it flows. There is
a steady line of it washing down the sink. The blood won't stop.
Clasping my hand over my eye, I head toward the room to find
something to stop the bleeding. By the time I reach the room,
my hand is wet with blood again. It is running down my neck
and soaking into my school uniform.

"Make me see you eye!" When I remove my hand, Flo gasps.
She quickly rummages through my clothes, finds an old blouse,
and wraps my face in it.

The bleeding stops. I am now looking at the world through
one eye. Dinner is dumpling and butter. I can't eat, for my face
hurts when I chew, and my head is pounding. It's getting dark,
and I lie down to sleep. In the darkness, I whisper a prayer to
Jehovah to forgive Flo for she doesn't know what she is doing.
She is only attacking me because we have no money, and I'm
looking forward to going to heaven and never suffering again.

"Clara, wake up! Let me see you eye!" Flo says, shaking me
awake. She holds the candle close to my face, and I can feel the

heat from the flame. She looks under the bandage on my now-swollen-shut eye, and with awakeness comes pain. She moves away, blowing out the candle, and I try to fall back asleep. Not long after she wakes me yet again to look at my eye. I want to tell her to leave me alone. I want to tell her that I have forgiven her. I want to tell her that after forgiving her and praying for her, I deserve to sleep, but I don't say anything for I'm sure that Jehovah is seeing all my sufferings and multiplying my blessings more and more.

"Dear Jehovah, please let her, let me, rest," I silently pray.

The sound of water running at the communal sink tells me that it's morning, Saturday morning, the day Sister Lindsey comes and does Bible study with me. Flo's space on the bed is empty, and I can smell the aroma of mint tea boiling.

"Get up, make me see you eye," I hear her say, but when I try to raise my body, the pain in my head becomes so severe that I flop back down on the bed. Flo looks at my face and tries to remove the bandage, but it sticks to my flesh. Then she bathes my face with warm water.

"Me have fi go a toilet," I tell her.

"Use the chamber pot."

"Me have fi do-do," I tell her, for surely she couldn't possibly want me to use a potty.

"Me say that you fi use the pisspot!" she yells. The thought of using the chamber pot kills my urge, and I only pee.

Flo goes outside to empty the water that she used to wash my face with, and I quickly reach for the piece of mirror that she keeps behind the bed to see how badly my eye is damaged. My left eye bulges from my head like that of a frog. My brown skin has turned black, and my eyebrow is parted by a slanted cut. My eye is still swollen shut and there is yellow matter beneath my eyelid. I swallow hard, wondering if I will go blind.

Flo comes back in and gives me some tea and a piece of

bread. As I sip the tea I wonder how Flo will explain to Sister Lindsey what she did to my eye. After taking the cup from me, she says, "You must not go outside, not even if the house burnin' down!"

She locks the door and hangs a sheet over the window. "You better make sure that you keep quiet when the Bible woman come!" Now I wonder what to do. Is it better to disobey her and bear whatever pain she might inflict on me? After all, Jehovah is watching. Or should I just listen to her and lie to Sister Lindsey by pretending that no one is here?

Time goes by slowly, and I can feel that it is time for Sister Lindsey to arrive. Now she is knocking at the door.

"Clara, Clara!" she yells. Hearing no answer, she calls, "Flo, Flo, is anyone here? It's Sister Lindsey." Tears flow down my face. Flo is staring at me, daring me to make a sound. I want to call out, "Me is here, an' me want do Bible study wit' you." I want to show Sister Lindsey my injured eye and brag about the points I will get from Jehovah for my suffering. My tongue becomes heavy, and the knocking stops. Is she gone? Flo peeps through the keyhole and starts removing the clothes from the window, and I ask Jehovah, "How much longer must I suffer?"

11

I HAVEN'T GONE OUTSIDE in two weeks. I have heard Flo telling the other tenants that I am sick in bed with the flu. She insists that I tell everyone I walked into a door.

Today the postman brings a letter from my school, demanding to know why I have been absent for so many days. Flo tells me to write a letter explaining that my face collided with a door and that I will be going to school tomorrow. My eye has opened slightly and is showing only red. I can still see through it, but not very well. Flo buys Band-Aids to cover my cut and sends me off to school.

After my home-room teacher, Mrs. Buckle, reads the letter, she looks at me and says, "Clara, your injury doesn't look like you walked into a door. Are you sure that's what happened?" It kills me to lie, especially with Jehovah watching me.

"Me mother accidentally hit me in the eye," I say, for Flo won't know I have told the truth.

"What!" she says in shock, and the next thing I know, I am being led to the vice-principal's office.

Mrs. Larsen, the vice-principal, is dressed in a light green skirt suit. Her hair has been straightened, and her glasses are so far down on the tip of her long nose, they look like they will fall off. Mrs. Larsen is the most feared person in the school. She is fearless, and it is rumored that she is the last one to leave the school in the evenings. She is well liked and very funny. Mrs. Buckle tells her what happened to my eye. She lifts up the Band-Aid and looks at it. Now she is writing a letter to my mother, asking her to come see her as soon as possible. What am I going to do? If Flo finds out that I said that she hit me in the eye with a mop stick, then she is going to kill me! And if I don't bring Flo to school then the vice-principal will probably suspend me.

When I get home I don't show the letter to Flo; instead I keep it in my schoolbag. I decide to tell the vice-principal that my mother is extremely busy working and can't afford the time right now, and that she will come as soon as she can. But then again, I think about my mother, and, unlike Flo, I know that Ma would never hit me with mop stick. I pray that as time goes by and my eye heals, Mrs. Larsen will forget about wanting to see my mother. But I worry about Parents' Day, the only day when all parents must come to school to get an account of how their child is doing. Will Mrs. Larsen still remember about my eye by then? I'll leave it in Jehovah's hands.

Flo and I hide from Sister Lindsey every week, but she still keeps coming. Finally we stop, and Flo makes sure that she is there when Sister Lindsey arrives. "Where were you?" Sister Lindsey asks. "We did in the country visiting me sick mother," Flo replies, saving me from lying. "What happened to your eye?" Sister Lindsey asks, looking at me. "She walk right into a big mango tree branch." I cast my eyes to the ground when Sister Lindsey looks to me for confirmation. Then Flo chuckles and adds, "Sister Lindsey, me always tell her to look where she goin' when she walkin'. And look wha' happen cause she don't listen to me." Sister

Lindsey sits down, and the Bible study begins, but from the corner of my eyes I can see Flo giving me a warning look.

After Bible study Sister Lindsey tells me that in a few months the Jehovah's Witnesses will congregate together at the national stadium for their yearly convention. All the other Jehovah's Witnesses churches in Jamaica are going to be there. They use the stadium for this event, for not only are there the people from the congregations, who bring their family and friends, but also the friends who bring *their* families and friends. Sister Lindsey wants to take me to the three-day convention and asks Flo. "Yes, ma'am, she can go with you, cause me no see no harm in it."

The days are so hot that laundry dries in half the time. School is closed for summer holidays for another two months. Like the years before Flo has been given a list of things I'll be needing for the new term, which we cannot afford. My left eye has almost healed, and I can still see through it. The scar across my eyebrow is still there, and no hair grows on that spot.

It's Friday morning and Sister Lindsey has come to take me to the Jehovah's Witness convention. My whole body is excited; I have never been to the national stadium before. I see three fat women and a teenage boy in the car. He doesn't look at me when Sister Lindsey says, "Sister Gordon, Sister Black, Sister Hall, and Mark, this is Clara."

"Nice to meet you," I say, even though my body is being squeezed from both sides by the fat women.

We drive through Crossroads to get to the stadium. At the stadium I stare at the hugeness of the entire building. The stadium is packed full of convention people. All the people in the bleachers hold large umbrellas over their heads against the morning sun. They look like a painting of many colors under the cloudless sky. My seat is in the shaded part of the stadium. In the middle of the stadium is a large circular platform with mikes and huge speakers. Seeing the look on my face, Sister Lindsey takes my hand and tells me that she is going to show me all the other things that are part of the convention. There're a lot of food stalls selling anything from rice and beans and stew meat to biscuits, candy, and even coconuts. Instead of giving the vendors money, you give them coupons. Sister Lindsey gives me some coupons and tells me that they are to last me for the full three days.

As soon as we're seated and the convention begins, my stomach starts growling for food. I go out to the stalls. I buy some rice and peas and stew chicken. Then I think, Why not try the fish and bammy? The cake with the icing tempts me, so I buy a slice too. A man in a straw hat asks, "You want buy one doughnut, little girl?" I have never been able to afford to buy jelly doughnuts at the school canteen, so I tell him yes. After eating all the food my belly feels stiff, and I figure some good goat-head soup could get rid of the stiffness.

"I would like to welcome Elder Sanders and his congregation all the way from the Parish of Westmoreland," blares the voice from the loud speakers when I reach the ice cream stalls. The smiling woman hands me a cone with two scoops of chocolate ice cream, and my anxious tongue licks it. I walk slowly back toward our seat, and now my stomach feels like a battle is going on inside it. I quickly shove the last piece of cone in my mouth and rush toward the toilets. I hardly make it to the toilet bowl before my stomach erupts like a volcano. When I finish puking, my stomach is empty, my eyes tear, but I feel better. With the last of my coupons, I buy a coconut and my stomach welcomes the soothing drink. All the coupons Sister Lindsey gave me are gone, and this is only the first day of the convention.

At lunchtime the following day, Sister Lindsey says, "Let's go get our lunch now, Clara, for I really could use some food."

"Um-uh, um . . . ," I stumble, thinking of what to tell her. I'm ashamed of what I have done. "Me think that me will wait till later," I manage to say.

"I think you mean that you will wait till I give you some more coupons." I swallow hard, my eyes wide with surprise. "I know that you spent all your coupons, for with all the time you spent at the food stalls, how could you possibly have any left?"

"Me sorry, Sister Lindsey, but me never been to a place with so much food before, and it was like the food was calling me. But me have a slice a bread in me bag, me can eat it later on," I add, remembering the piece of bread from breakfast that I took with me this morning.

She sighs and touches my shoulder. "Look, Clara, me understand, me can only hope that you can learn by this."

"Me will, Sister Lindsey," I assure her, for I have learned since yesterday, when I threw up. She digs in her purse. "Here are some more coupons. I trust that you will do the right thing."

"Oh, yes, Sister Lindsey." My eyes beam with gratitude, and now we lunch.

Summer ends. A new school term is about to begin, and Flo is struggling to buy the things I need to go back to school in the fourth form. I return to school hoping to get by, by borrowing other students' textbooks. Simone's mother has been to foreign and back. On Tuesday, Simone shows up at school with a brand new backpack and a pair of size eight leather shoes, which she hands to me.

"Me goodness, Simone! How you know me size?"

"You know that you have the habit a taking you foot out a you plastic shoes in a class?"

I nod.

"Well, one day, me look inside, and me see the big size eight. So when me mother say she goin' to foreign, me tell her that she must bring a shoes and a backpack fi me friend Clara, for she say that things cheaper in foreign."

I hug her so tightly that she says that she can't breathe, and I gladly say good-bye to my plastic shoes.

"Try them on," she urges, watching as I put my feet inside my leather shoes. They fit perfectly, and now she helps me move my books from my old backpack that's full of patches and holes into my new one.

Simone and I remain close friends, and sometimes her mother sends me a slice of sweet potato pudding. I have tried converting Simone to becoming a Jehovah's Witness by inviting her to my church, but she tells me that she goes to a Church of God located near to her home. I persist and she says, "Look Clara! As far me see it, there is only one heaven and only one hell. So when the two a we die, we goin' meet up inside the same heaven, even if we religion different! Cause all we prayin' to the same God!"

The next week in religious education class, we discuss the different religions of ancient times. We end up on the subject of who belongs to what religion. My teacher, Mrs. Able, is rather dull, but in this particular discussion, she comes alive and even raises her voice. Her hair is unstraightened and pulled to the side of her head by a brown plastic clip. Her lower jaw protrudes downward, and I can see from her overbite and jutting front teeth that she sucked her thumb as a child. Her nose is broad and slightly flat, but she has big beautiful brown eyes and long lashes.

Mrs. Able makes it quite clear that she belongs to a Seventh-Day Adventist church. She says they don't eat pork and that she uses the rhythm method as her form of birth control. The whole class is wide-eyed. Seeing the look of shock on our faces, she goes on to say that Seventh-Day Adventists don't do any work after sunset on Fridays. She tells us that she has seven children and that she is making sure that they follow in her footsteps. Now I know why there are so many lumps pushing at her stockings: Her legs are covered with varicose veins from all those pregnancies, and even though she is wearing a bra, I can bet that her breasts have passed their *elasticity limit*. (I learned that if an object once stretched does not return to its original shape, then it has been stretched past its elasticity limit.)

The class is delighted to see this other side of our normally calm, sheeplike teacher. She's a good teacher, actually one of our favorites, for she will let us carry on with our chatting and then in her sweet voice she'll say, "That's enough, class. Let's carry on with the lesson." She always speaks with such grace and sits with a perfect posture.

Getting on the wave of the discussion, one girl gets up and says, "I'm a Mormon, and that is the right religion!" She seems quite proud of what she has just said till the whole class asks, "What's a Mormon?" She looks at the class as if we're stupid, ignorant people, but then she realizes that we all passed the Common Entrance Exam and made it to high school. "It's the Church of Latter-day Saints," she explains.

Annoyed by her look, or maybe it's just my brain adjusting to this idea, I blurt out, "You are so wrong! The right religion is being a Jehovah's Witness!" The class erupts with laughter at my boldness, and I smile at my outburst. Then Simone says, "Look! It don't matter what religion you are, for we all pray to the same God, and we are going to the same hell and heaven!"

Now the girl with glasses asks, "Then if there is only one God, then how come there are so many religions? And besides how does any one of you know that you belong to the right religion? For there is only one true religion, it's being a Catholic!" The class roars with such laughter that some eyes are showing signs of tears from laughing too much. Now our beloved Mrs. Able says, "That's enough, class; let's continue with the lesson."

Despite all the laughter I wonder why there are so many religions. And what happens if when I die God sends me to hell for belonging to the wrong religion? Now a river of doubt is flowing through my head, for my teacher and all the other students feel just as strongly about their religion as I do, and I know we can't all be right. "Dear God," I pray, "please remove all these doubts from my head."

My doubts continue to grow, and all the barricades that I have built around me fall away piece by piece. A large part of it collapses for Sister Lindsey is sick in the hospital with a bad heart.

I go to visit her in my school uniform, and who I see lying on the bed is no longer Sister Lindsey but a woman with tubes coming from all parts of her. She is sleeping, and the big fat nurse warns me, "Make sure you don't wake up the patient." I sit by her bed and hold her hand, and I pray to Jehovah to please bless Sister Lindsey and make her get better. I leave the hospital with tears in my eyes and my heart filled with worry.

A few weeks later Sister Lindsey dies. I tell myself that she is in heaven with Jehovah, but that does not comfort me. The congregation wants me to go to the funeral, but I can't. I don't think that I can bear the sight of seeing her being put in a box and cemented over forever. I want to remember her the way she was with the round smiling face and kind eyes.

Now I don't want to go to church anymore, for every time I go there, I think of Sister Lindsey, and tears appear in my eyes. I can feel my faith slowly dissolving. Why didn't God listen to my prayer to make Sister Lindsey better? Is this God's way of telling me that my religion is wrong?

I haven't been to church in almost three weeks. Sister Myriam comes to visit me, and she seems to have more wrinkles since the last time I saw her. It is Sunday morning, and I meet her at the front gate on my way back from the grocery shop.

"Clara, why have you stopped coming to church? Is it because you have no clothes or any bus fare? Is something wrong?" I want to tell her about praying to God and how he disappointed me. I want to ask her how come there are so many other religions, and how does she know that she is in the right one? I swallow hard and lie.

"Me mother say that me must stop comin' to church! And that if she ever catch me with any more Jehovah's Witness, she goin' kill me with beatin'!"

Sister Myriam's face crinkles to a frown. "Look, Clara, maybe we can put you up to live with one of the sisters. Surely there must be something we can do!"

"Me don't want to live with no sister," I say angrily, and her blue eyes become wet. "Tell you what, Sister Myriam, as soon as me get big, and live on me own, me will try and come back to church."

She grabs my hand. "All right, Clara, we will pray for you."

"Thanks." I walk into the yard feeling her eyes following me, as if I'm about to walk over the edge of a cliff.

12

MONTHS HAVE PASSED. FLO sends me to the shop to buy a pound of chicken back and a pound of flour. I hate buying chicken back, so I always wait till the shop empties out before saying anything to the shopkeeper. The last person leaves the shop, and just as I finish saying, "One pound a chicken back and one pound a flour," I hear someone call my name. I spin around and see a face I haven't seen in years.

"Sharon, wha' happen?" I haven't seen Sharon since we were in primary school because she was sent away to live with one of her aunts. Sharon's mother died when she was a baby, and since then she's been shifted from family member to family member. She is a year older than I am and looks mature. She has boobs, a big behind, and the flared nose that earned her the nickname "Skirtnose."

"Nothin'," she responds.

Seeing that I am still surprised at her being back in Greenwichtown, she tells me, "Me auntie that me did live with send me fi come live with this auntie that live 'pon Fifth Street."

"So you still goin' to school?" I ask, afraid that she might have contracted the disease of unwanted pregnancy.

"Of course me still goin' to school!"

"Which school you goin' to?"

"Me did pass me Common Entrance Exam, me going to Alpha High School," she proudly replies.

"Which form you in?"

"Me in fifth form."

"Which subjects you doin'?"

"Well, me doing math, bio, chemistry, physics, English, and Spanish."

"My! My! We doin' almost the same subject, the only difference is that me doin' French."

"You know say that, me still have me textbook them from fourth form. If you want me can give you them. Me woulda give me cousin them, but him have all a him book them already. By the way, if you want, me can help you study." I need textbooks even if they are not the same ones that I use in school.

"Which part 'pon Fifth Street you live?" I ask.

"Look all the way down the road, you see one black gate, 'pon you right-hand side?"

"Yeah, man, me see it. Me live just cross the street from it," I tell her, not knowing that she is related to Mr. and Mrs. Brown and their son, who wears glasses.

She smiles with contentment. "Come check me Saturday, me will look fi the book them by then."

"All right." I smile and take my goods from the shopkeeper.

I tell Flo about seeing Sharon, about her offer to help me with my studying, and her kindness in giving me her textbooks. Flo feels relieved that I am getting some free books, and anyone that has made it to high school is considered good company.

Flo hasn't found a man yet, and now she sells soap powder on the sidewalks of downtown Kingston. She has long gone selling, and I get ready to go to Sharon's yard, putting on my overworn blue plastic slippers, my old yard dress, and combing my hair in corn rows.

I cross the street, to the black gate. "Sharon, Sha-*ronnn*!" She sticks her head through the front door. "Come 'round the back! The dog won't bite you!" I do as she tells me and head toward the back of the yard. As I am turning the corner, I bump into a boy wearing glasses that I have seen many times on my way from the grocery shop, who rudely asks me, "Wha' you want?"

Sharon reaches the back of the yard just in time. "Is none a you damn business wha' she want, Four-eye!" She says this just as rudely as he had spoken to me, and now I begin to feel uncomfortable.

I follow her inside. "A the house me cleaning; me auntie and me uncle gone a work; only me and Four-eye is here." I can see that she is indeed cleaning and that they are not as poor as I am. They even have a refrigerator. The house has three small bedrooms, a kitchen, bathroom, and a living and dining area in one. She takes me to her room, and the wooden floor shines with cleanness. They have new furniture, and I am really amazed at how much they have.

The bed is made with a floral sheet. She has a dresser and a chest, of the same dark brown color, in the room. On top of the dresser is a pile of books, and next to the dresser is a chair. "See the book them there, help youself," she says. Then she goes by the door and yells, "Hey, four-eye boy! You not goin' clean you room before Auntie come?"

"Go die a bush, pudding-face gal!" comes back the answer from the boy with glasses.

"Tell Auntie fi go die in bush when she come!" Sharon yells back at him. With this he walks across the hall into his room. "Him is so lazy, you see." I do not say anything, for I do not want to be caught up in the middle of a quarrel.

I look through the books and to my great fortune, I find two books that I am using at school, a math and a biology book. I take all the books anyway, and Sharon searches for a plastic bag to put them in. She tells me that she has to wash her clothes when she finishes cleaning the house, and that I can study with her next week if I want to. "All right," I tell her, before I head home with my new books.

When Flo comes home I show them to her, but she only looks at their covers cause she can't read very well. Whenever I am absent from school, I'm the one that writes the notes. She always looks at the notes with admiration.

When the next Saturday arrives and Flo leaves to go selling, I eagerly clean our two rooms and go across the street to Sharon's yard. I call at the gate. Sharon has finished cleaning and is watching television, with Four-eye sitting beside her. I sit down and start watching cartoons too. After the cartoons, another show comes on, and then another one after that. We watch television till it's almost evening, and then Four-eye tells Sharon that she should start dinner. She curses him, and angrily he turns to me and says, "Hey, gal, why you don't go home to you yard and make Sharon do her work. You no see say that a evening now!"

"Move you ugly blind-eye behind, and go 'way!" Sharon yells. She tells me to ignore him, and that the reason why he is so rude is because he is half blind. She tells me that we are definitely going to study next week. I tell her, "All right," and as I am leaving the yard, I meet an older woman.

"Good evening, ma'am."

"Good evening," she responds, and I go home.

The same week at school the vice-principal, Mrs. Larsen, who also teaches me physics, starts a breakfast program. For only twenty-five cents each have-not student can get a roll, some scrambled eggs, and a big cup of tea with milk in it. Even I can afford that, although I will have to reach school much earlier in the mornings. On top of that she has started a lunch program, where for another twenty-five cents, each poor student can buy a cooked meal, and not only that, she will give it to you on credit if you don't have the money. Even if I have to walk to school on an empty stomach, I know that there will be food when I get there.

It's Saturday again, and I am at the black gate calling Sharon. She doesn't answer, so I push open the gate and walk around to the back. "Sharon!" The back door opens, and I see Four-eye's head come through the opening. "Sharon gone 'round the road, she say that she soon come back." Then, seeing the disappointment on my face, he adds, "If you want, you can wait fi her inside."

"All right." I enter the clean house.

"If you want you can watch TV but no turn it up too high, for me studin' fi me test Monday." I do not care to watch television, so I ask him, "Wha' subject you studying?"

"Me studying biology." He is not rude to me today, so I figure that I can help him study.

"You want me help you till Sharon come?" He ponders the idea and then answers, "Um-uh."

I follow him into his room, which is the same size as Sharon's. The walls are painted light blue. The bed has no headboard and is made with a sheet patterned in vertical lines.

There is a dresser with a black belt hanging from the side, and a small table with one chair beside it. The open window sports white curtains that flutter gently with the breeze. Under the table is a black leather backpack that says "Steve Brown."

"Me have fi study from me notes them," he says, looking at the floor as he speaks. He is in the same grade as I am, but at another high school. In little more than a year we will graduate.

"All right, so what you want me fi do?" I ask him.

"Just look 'pon me notes them, and make up questions fi asks me," he says, slumping down on the bed.

He hands me his biology notebook, and when I open up the first page, his neat handwriting stares back at me. After reading his notes for a while, I ask, "What are chromosomes?"

"They are rodlike structures, in living cells, that contain the DNA of the organism," he answers.

"Not bad," I tell him. "So what is DNA?"

"It stands for deoxyribonucleic acid, and it controls the structure, purpose, and other genetic information of each cell, during reproduction."

It is almost evening, I have asked him everything in his notebook, and Sharon has not yet returned. "Tell Sharon say that me will see her next Saturday." I leave for home.

Next Saturday comes, and all week long I thought about Steve and his test. As usual, I go inside the black gate and call Sharon. Instead of Sharon opening the door, Steve does. "Wha' happen to Sharon?" I ask him, hoping that she is there.

"She gone 'round the road fi look fi her boyfriend," he replies. My face droops. Just what I need. I have found someone to study with, and she has to find a boyfriend! Seeing my thoughts showing on my face, he says, "Come inside; we can study till she come." I figure that Sharon would not let me down so many times in a row, so I follow him inside.

"Me want study math," I announce, wanting specifically to do some difficult equations and to see how good this fellow is at math. I search in my backpack for my blue notebook. I flip through to the page where I have started on equations. "Get you pen and book ready, we goin' do equations." I pick the hard ones. Steve is not good at math, certainly not at equations, for he has come up with the wrong answers to all four equations. "When you takin' you exams, what kind of math you doin', general or basic?" I ask him, hoping for his sake that he is doing basic math.

"Me going to be doin' basic math," he says proudly, as if one should feel grateful that he is doing any math at all. He speaks with his eyes glued to the floor.

"Steve, how come you never look at me when me talking to you?" I ask him, and with that he lifts his head and looks right at me. I look back into his brown eyes, behind the thick glasses that distort them. In them I see the deep-rooted loneliness of life longing to be filled with laughter. He smiles coyly, but his eyes gleam with sadness that burns me. For a brief moment I feel like part of him. I can't bear to look into his eyes anymore. He must be feeling something too, for he sharply turns his head and looks down at the floor.

"Wha' wrong with you eyes?"

"Me nearsighted." I should have known, for I have covered nearsightedness in biology class.

I go back to the equations, and now he doesn't look at the floor anymore. I try to point out where he has messed up, but I am finding it difficult to explain his errors with him looking right at me. I continue with my explanation on the equation, and he still doesn't get it.

"Boy! You head tough like rock stone," I tell him, trying to divert his eyes from me, but he finds this flattering. He laughs, revealing perfect white teeth between full lips. I look at him and start laughing too. It feels good to laugh, so good that I do not want to stop. So good that we keep laughing.

At last our laughter subsides. He looks at me from the bed, our faces inches apart. His brown eyes are fixed on me. He touches my lips with his finger, and now I feel the softness of his lips that have replaced it. I feel the gentle warmth of his breath, and I press my lips closer to the source.

Then just as slowly as he began, we pull apart, leaving me

feeling dizzy, almost drunken from the effect of the kiss. We are speechless. The silence is unbearable, and I must speak. I must break this moment that has clutched me at my most indefensible part. My heart is beating so hard that I think it's going to burst.

"Ah, aahh, Steve," I stutter. I can't think of what to say. What can I say? He pulls me toward him again, covering my mouth with his lips. His tongue parts my lips, and a tingling energy passes through me. Then a feeling of warmth engulfs me and spreads through my entire existence. He lets go of me, gently, slowly. He doesn't say anything. I don't say anything either. What could we possibly say?

I start gathering up my things. I am frightened; actually, I am terrified of what I am feeling. With my heart pounding and my body trembling, I quickly float across the street to my yard. As soon as I reach the room, I flop down on the bed. I wish I had someone to talk to. Maybe I can talk to God, for he has seen what has just happened and he must be aware of the storm that is building inside me.

I get up when Flo comes home from selling and bangs on the door. She hands me a black plastic bag and says, "Go scale them two fish." I take the bag and peer inside at the silver-looking fish, as she hands me the knife.

The sun is dying over the horizon. In the distance I hear a big boom box playing, signaling the start of a dance two streets away. The sound of the music strengthens when I reach the far corner of the yard to throw away the fish belly. As I drain the water from the pot, I can hear the swift silence before the new song plays, and now it has started.

Up until now, I've learned to live without love

I cannot believe the words of the song. It echoes everything I am feeling. I rise with every note, for I feel as if that song was written especially for me. It will be our song. I feel so alive now, standing there with the two fish in the pot and my hands the odor of fish belly.

Flo fries the sprats and serves them with boiled dumplings and green bananas, but despite my hunger, I have no appetite, for who needs food when there is love?

Monday comes, and I can barely wait to tell Simone about Saturday. At lunchtime after buying lunch from the lunch program, I see her.

"Simone, guess wha' happen this weekend?"

"Somebody else get shot?"

"No, I think I'm in love!"

"Wha'!" she exclaims. "Tell me more! Tell me more!"

"Well, you know that four-eye boy, that me did tell you 'bout that was so rude to me." I pause for her answer. She nods yes.

"Well," I continue, "me go over a him yard fi study with him cousin, and him cousin gone look fi her boyfriend, and so me decide fi do some equations with him, and the next thing me know is that we end up kissing."

"How it happen?"

"It just happen."

"Well, how did it feel?"

"It was the best thing I have felt in my entire life."

13

🐃

GOING ACROSS THE STREET to Sharon's yard has become a weekly ritual. As soon I get there, I study with Steve, for Sharon is hardly there anymore on Saturdays. One time I bumped into her as she was leaving, and she looked happy. She told me that she is glad I am studying with Steve. She no longer calls him Four-eye because they no longer quarrel.

On this Saturday Steve and I have solved only one math problem, for we have been kissing most of the time. Steve undresses me out of my old yard dress, leaving me only in my panties. I am not wearing a bra for I have only one, and it's hanging on the clothesline at my yard because I washed it this morning.

He stares at my skinny body, then drops his shorts on the floor. I gape at him, and he pulls me to him, kissing my neck and making me shiver. He kisses me roughly, impatiently, so I ask him, "Steve, wha' about protection?" I know about contraceptives and pregnancy from biology class. I watch as he reaches into a drawer and pulls out a condom.

"Steve, you must be gentle, for it is me first time. Is your first time too?" He nods yes, as he eases me down on the bed.

He climbs on top of me, kissing me hungrily, and I open up

to him. I have difficulty receiving him, and my feelings of desire have turned to pure agony. Tears begin to flow down my face as pain grips my loin.

"Steve, Steve, stop. Steve, please, please, stop!"

He stops, kisses my tear-dripped face, and holds me tightly against him. I feel relief as he pulls away from me and sits on the edge of the bed. I try to sit up but I can't, for the lower half of my body hurts. I look at the sheet and notice blood. "Steve, wha' you goin' do 'bout that?" For his mother does his laundry.

"Don't worry 'bout that." He helps me to my feet and hugs me against his erection.

Despite my pain, I still ache for him, and when he asks, "You want try again?" I answer "Yes." When it is over, he collapses on me with satisfaction, but all I am feeling is pain and relief that it has ended. After that, the other times become more bearable and pleasureful.

It is now Saturday morning again. I am teasing Steve about his watercolor painting that has a grade C on it. He tells me that it was supposed to be a picture of the bottom of the ocean. The fish look funny because their heads are twice as big as their bodies. I am laughing at how ugly his art is, and he is trying to get the sheet of paper from my hand that I am holding high in the air. Now he starts wrestling with me for it. I love wrestling with him. His fingers, his unfocused eyes, and his childlike manner make me feel like a little girl again. I love to struggle against him and surrender, tired and helpless, toward his hungry lips. Now I feel free, complete, inhibited by nothing.

We become closer with each kiss, and each expression of desire becomes more intense. We pause; we touch again, each of us wondering if this is real. This feeling of totalness, of love, lusts, or whatsoever it is called. He wants me, and I want him more. He lets go of my captive hands, which clutch at him. He eases up, just to look at me. This is not a dream, I am here, we are both here. Then he falls back on me with gentle ease. He knows I am in no hurry. I will wait for him. My heart beats fast. I do have a heart. I only hope that it can cope with this pressure inside it. He unbuttons the buttons on my old yellow church-looking dress, revealing my young but ripe breasts. He kisses them slowly, and I hold his head as my nipples harden. He pulls my dress off and I am mesmerized by him. He has captured me. I feel like clay in his hands, and each mold produces beautiful yearnings. Yes, mold me.

He pulls off his T-shirt, baring his lean, hairless brown chest. He drops his shorts to the floor, and I stare at the big bulge in his briefs. He sheathes himself, before falling back on me. He kisses me deeply, almost violently, and we pause again only long enough to catch a molecule of air.

He reaches for my girly breasts, and I moan with satisfaction. He knows that I am ready for him, but he teases me, to the point where I struggle with him to have him. He likes the strug-gle. He wins; he always wins. Then his hunger intensifies, and I open up to him.

He enters me with gentle force, and we shudder in relief as our bodies merge. I moan as we move to the same beat. We dance, we climb, we reach, and our hearts beat faster with our rapid steps. Our heat rises, and just as I am about to explode into a million happy pieces, he stops, and we start dancing again.

I groan in approval for our maddened passion to last longer. We are drenched in sweet-smelling sweat and I can feel the pressure building as his tempo increases. We have now become one being with the same goal, of not letting this feeling end. Our song plays in my head. "I feel you inside my soul. . . ."

Our bodies glisten. We dance with quick steps to the fast beat. He covers my lips with uncontrollable kisses, and with his final lurch inside me I float off into the heavens. We lie motionless, enjoying our state of total happiness. Then he kisses me, a slow, soft kiss, before rolling on his back and pulling me to lie on his hairless chest.

Being with Steve has become like a drug. The more I am with him, the more I want to be with him. We try to see each other during the week if time permits it. I am no longer bothered by surroundings of death, violence, and hopelessness. I live in a cocoon bubbling with the joys of being in love.

Even at school I think about him. I daydream in class of our next encounter. School now seems unimportant. Everything is unimportant. I no longer take my lessons seriously; I hardly study, and as a result, my grades have taken a deep dive. Mrs. Larsen, who's the vice-principal and my physics teacher, tells me to come see her in her office after school. Normally I would be terrified of such a request but my insulation of love prevents me from being scared.

I enter into her small office. "Sit down, Myrtle." One of her trademarks is calling everyone by their surname. I sit down. "Myrtle, what exactly is happening to you that is so drastically affecting your performance at school? Your grades have gotten so poor." I want to blurt out, "I am so happy, I'm in love! I'm in love! The world is a wonderful place!" But all I say is, "I promise that my grades will get better." I hope this satisfies her, for no one wants the vice-principal on their back, for once she gets on, she never gets off. She will even keep you after school if she has to. She adjusts her spectacles. "You better make sure!" Her words sound threatening, and my fear of her returns, but as soon as I leave her office, I go back to my cocoon. Who needs school when there is love? But the thought of her going after me is enough to persuade me to work on my grades.

On Saturday, after we have studied a bit, Steve tells me that we should skip school on a Friday and go to the movies. He tells me that he will start saving his lunch money and I should do the same thing for two weeks. We arrange to meet at the park in downtown Kingston at precisely nine o'clock. On Friday morning I wait in the park after making careful plans not to go anywhere near the market gate, for that is where Flo sells her soap. I have been waiting for more than an hour, and I am wondering if Steve is going to make it. It is now eight-thirty and downtown is becoming crowded. At the stoplight, with a horde of people crossing, I spot Steve, and my heart leaps as I wave to him. He smiles his coy smile as he waves back. As soon as he reaches me, he asks, "How much money you have?"

"Me have two dollar," I reply, not adding that I owe the vice-principal for many lunches.

"Me have fifteen dollars." He sees the look of shock on my face.

"Me tell me father say that me going have fi do extra lesson and buy book fi exam preparation, and him give me the money." I smile lovingly at my lying partner, who smiles back and asks, "Where is the bathroom?"

"Follow me." We head toward the public toilets, where most cubicles are missing bowls and some have no doors. The stench of waste fills the air, and dirt floats on the walls. I quickly change into a dress, take off my navy blue socks, and carefully put them in my backpack. I walk out looking for signs of familiar faces, as I wait for Steve near the male bathrooms. Steve comes out, having changed from his full khaki school uniform to gray shorts and a black T-shirt.

"You ever go to the amusement park?" Of course I haven't been to one, so I shake my head no.

"Come," he says, taking my hand. "We goin' to Spanishtown."

We get on the bus. The conductor demands, "Bus fare!" and Steve pays for me. We get off in Spanishtown at the big amusement park. He buys the tickets for us to get in. There are so many children and parents and so many things to get on that I stare at in amazement. He pulls me toward the big spinning wheel. "We goin' on this first." I am not too sure that I want to ride on that thing that is spinning so high off the ground, but I do not object.

We strap ourselves to the seats of the large wheel, and he holds my hand for I am sure that the terror is showing on my face. As the wheel rotates I feel like I'm going to throw up. He screams with each revolution, and I start screaming too. Soon the feeling of nausea passes, and I'm enjoying each loud outcry that I make. We scream together, and it feels exciting to be out of control.

We get off the big wheel and Steve pulls me toward the bumper cars. He buys me cotton candy, which I devour rapidly. He pulls me toward the wishing well, and when it's my turn I pull out a multicolored cube puzzle. When it's his turn, he pulls out a pair of glasses with a big red nose attached to it. He puts it on my face and everyone, including him, is laughing at me. I bet I must look really funny, but I don't care, for when everyone laughs at me, I feel as if I am giving them some of the joy I am feeling.

My stomach starts to growl. "Steve, me hungry."

"All right." We head toward the food stand. We buy patties and box drinks and then we buy ice cream. I push the last piece of cone into my mouth, and he says, "Come, we going to the show."

We go the big theater in Crossroads. He pays for our tickets and gets me popcorn, my first movie popcorn. The lights dim, the Bruce Lee movie starts, and he kisses me. The movie continues, and every time Bruce Lee beats up the bad guys, the theater yells, "Yes! Yes! Yes!" with every kick and every blow that lands on them. When the other guys start beating up Bruce

Lee, the crowd yells, "No! No! No!" with every blow that Bruce
Lee receives. I feel alive yelling along with the audience.

It is now evening. If I had gone to school, I would have been
home already, but I figure I can tell Flo that I stayed behind at
school, in the library, to work on a project. I can even make up
the name of it: "The Evolution of Homo Sapiens." I am sure she
will not understand a word of it.

We change back to our school clothes and bid each other good-
bye, saying that we will see each other tomorrow. When Saturday
arrives Flo goes to sell her soap powder, and I eagerly start
cleaning the two rooms, with great anticipation of going to
Steve's house.

14

THE WHOLE ISLAND IS on storm alert. A hurricane that has been brewing in the Caribbean Sea is heading directly for Jamaica. The radio and television urge people to make preparations, to stock up on canned food, water, batteries, medicine, matches, candles, and everything else that can add to survival.

Schools have been closed, and no one goes to work. The entire neighborhood echoes the sounds of owners and tenants hammering. Windows are nailed shut, large stones are put on roofs, and water is collected and stored. Food is scarce, and everything else that one needs to survive the storm has risen in price. There is a charge of excitement in the community, as people rush about gathering things for the great event. Flo has bought four pounds of flour, two cans of mackerel, one bread, and two pounds of sugar. This is our total storm supply. Now the entire island anxiously awaits the storm's dreaded arrival.

The night darkens. The wind howls like a wounded, angry dog. Rain pours with venomous rage, and thunder roars so loudly that our two rooms rattle with each rumble. Sounds of roofs and trees being ripped apart and crashing against buildings add to our fear. Stones of rain pound our roof, and I am afraid that the water is going to stab holes through the zinc. Water has started coming in under the door, despite the sheet that Flo has stuffed under the opening. We are huddled on the bed, silently praying, and that's when we hear an earsplitting thud from the roof. We jump off the bed, standing in ankle-deep water, as the noise of gushing water comes from inside the other room. We dart toward the sound and, looking up, we see part of a limb from the ackee tree protruding through the roof. There is a large hole there, and water is pouring down the limb like a waterfall, filling up the room with water.

Flo pulls the sheet from under the door, so that the water drains out, but only more water comes in. Panic stricken, I wade my way back toward the bed, but now the bed is covered with water.

"Quick, climb 'pon the table!" Flo pulls the table to the next room, knocking over the chairs. The candle gets wet, and the light goes out. We climb on the table, wet, cold, and trembling, listening as the untamed assault continues and the water keeps rising higher.

Thoughts of drowning float through my head as the water reaches the tabletop, but now the wind is quieting down and the rain is losing some of its strength. Is it over? Or is it just getting started?

We stay huddled on the table, and now I can feel the water moving away from my wet behind. As Flo stands on the table, the wonderful arrival of daylight comes from beneath the door. Now I can see our buoyant belongings floating around in the water.

Flo wades through the water and tries to open the door, but branches and leaves come through the doorway. The whole yard is flooded, the ackee tree has toppled over, crushing the communal sink and resting on our roof. The rain continues to fall. "You all right, Flo?" the concerned voice of Mr. Royal yells.

"The ackee tree drop 'pon the roof, and me flood out!" Flo yells back.

"But you still alive!" As the day progresses and the risen water subsides, voices yell back and forth, and people start emerging from their rooms.

Greenwichtown looked terrible before, but now it looks worse. Most trees have fallen over, and some houses are completely gone, with only signs of their foundations remaining. Debris is everywhere. Fallen electric poles strew their wires over the streets. A large fallen mango tree makes a natural bridge across the street. The rusty zinc fence around my yard no longer exists, and more zincs are missing from other roofs in the yard. I feel so grateful to be alive.

Flo and I hear that some of the warehouses down by the wharf have suffered damage, and most of the people who live in Greenwichtown are going down there to steal anything they can.

"You goin' down there?" Cynthia asks Flo after telling us about the looting.

"Yes, wait for me. Me goin' get a bag." Flo and Cynthia leave the yard to take part in this justifiable robbery.

I stand at my gate thinking about Steve as familiar faces pass on the street, running to and fro with stolen merchandise. I hear a woman say to her friend that even the warehouses that aren't damaged are being broken into and stolen from. Some people carry cases of bar soap on their head, and two men are struggling with a refrigerator. Two women are fighting each other for stolen goods.

The coldness of my society confronts me. A desperate collection of people with only the sheer determination to survive by whatsoever means they can. They share the same dream of wealth, happiness, and a good life, but most people that are born here never get out, for they have no place to get out to.

I have a way out. I am going to high school. In a couple of

years, I will have a decent job. I am in love. I will have Steve as my husband, two beautiful children, and have my own house, in a nice neighborhood away from Greenwichtown.

Flo comes back with syrup, lotion, soap, shampoo, and a whole lot of other things that we never buy. The other tenants have stuff too, canned corned beef, tuna, and even radios. They share their things with Flo, and so we have corned beef and rice for dinner. The sound of laughter rings out from next door as the entire community is happy to get the loot.

It's been two days since the storm, and I haven't seen Steve since. I have heard that the entire island is shut down and hospitals are being flooded with injured people. I want to go across the street to see Sharon and Steve, so as evening comes around I tell Flo, "Me goin' over Sharon yard." She doesn't respond, meaning yes. After all, Flo thinks that Sharon is good company to keep.

I have never been to their yard with his parents being there. So as I reach the black gate, instead of waltzing around the back, I yell, "Sharon, Sharon!"

"Me comin'." She and Steve come to the gate.

Steve smiles at me.

"Me hear say that one man hand chop off with a piece a zinc, as him a come out a him house in the storm," Sharon says.

"Which part that happen?" I ask her.

" 'Round 'pon Third Street." We chat for a while, and she announces, "Me goin' round the road; me will see you later." Steve and I are alone by the wall, and night starts falling. "Me goin' home. Me don't want me mother wondering where me is. Is night a'ready." He pulls me to him and under the blanket of darkness, he kisses me. "Make we do it right here behind the wall."

"You must be losin' you mind," I tell him before planting a big wet kiss on his lips. I bid him good-bye and go home.

All of Greenwichtown has remained without electricity for quite some time. As a result of the many lootings, the army and the police force make a curfew in an attempt to recover some of the stolen items from these "rass thief" as the police put it.

Since the police are not successful in recovering any of the loot, they arrest a few men, hoping the arrestees will squeal on the guilty. The men do not say anything for they know that the police will probably keep the recovered loot for themselves. Among those arrested is David, the father of Donna's daughter. He was beaten so badly by the police that, after his release, he fainted and was taken to the hospital, where he died from internal bleeding. Donna's daughter has joined the long list of fatherless children.

It's been months since the storm and our schools have reopened. Flo still sells her soap, and Steve's parents have returned to work. The electrical poles are repaired by the power company. Those who had legal electrical connections are reconnected. Those who don't pay for their electricity simply come out with a long bamboo pole and make their own *bandulo* connections.

At school we are way behind our expected schedules, so now we do a lot of extra lessons and a lot of overtime, to catch up. We are even going to school on Saturdays, so Steve and I rarely see each other. After months of drilling our heads and stretching our minds, we are where we would have been without the storm. Since classes have lessened, Steve and I are finally home on a Saturday. Flo has long gone selling, and expanded her business to include bleach powder and cake soap.

I have waited so long to be with Steve. I call Sharon, but she doesn't answer. Steve's welcoming voice says, "Come 'round the back." As soon as I enter the house, he pulls me to him with one powerful swing of his arm. He covers my mouth with impatient kisses, and I respond in the same starved manner. He leads me to his room. We pull at each other's clothes. As soon as we are completely naked, he pulls me down on top of him, and then rolls over to be on top of me. He is eager to enter me.

"Steve, what 'bout protection?"

"Me run out, me no have any. We goin' use the rhythm method." He covers my mouth with his full lips. I have seen my religious teacher with a lot of children after practicing this method of birth control. Before I can voice my objection, he pins my hands over my head and penetrates me.

15

IT'S BEEN A MONTH since that Saturday, and my period is late. Steve and I had made love many times after that, and upon my insistence we used condoms. I am sitting on a very crowded bus sandwiched between a big fat woman and a tall man who stinks of cigarette smoke, on my way to the drugstore, to pick up the result of a pregnancy test that had cost Steve two whole weeks' lunch money. I get off the bus and start toward the drugstore with worry. I do something that I haven't done in a long time. I pray. "God, please make the pregnancy test negative."

I enter the drugstore, and there are only a few customers. I give the girl at the counter my receipt. She smiles. "Is that all you want?" I nod yes, taking the white envelope, and shaking as I head toward the park. My mind races back to last month, to the practice of the rhythm method. Was I in my safe zone or not? Being with Steve comes to mind sharply, but my safe zone dates are a confusing blur. In biology class I learned about reproduction, and I am afraid that my egg has been fused by one of Steve's spermatozoa.

I scan the park for a seat. If I open up this envelope and it is bad news, I probably will faint. I flop down on the concrete bench without even checking to see if it is dirty or not. Who cares if my uniform gets soiled?

With trembling fingers and a lump in my throat, I tear at the envelope. I pull out the pink piece of paper and read the bold black letters:

POSITIVELY PREGNANT.

My head throbs, my heart races, and my face wets with tears. My goodness! What have I done? What will I do? I could have an abortion! The thought of an abortion makes me sick. How can I think of killing the child growing inside me that was made from such passionate mergings?

But if I don't have an abortion Flo will probably kill me for getting pregnant! I won't be able to finish high school or graduate. I will not be able to take the Caribbean Examination Council exams, the C.X.C.s, or get a good job. I will never get out of Greenwichtown! But abortions are illegal, and anything that is illegal costs a lot of money. Where will I get the money from? Will I be able to get an abortion without Flo or anyone else knowing?

I cannot bear the thought of killing an unborn child. A child that Steve and I created out of love. I could move in with Steve, after all; he does have his own room, and if we take out the dresser there just might be enough space for a crib. But if I have the baby I would have to give up all my hopes and dreams of getting out of Greenwichtown! I must find a way to have an abortion.

When Saturday comes I cross the street to tell Steve the bad news. Sharon has gone to see her boyfriend again. When I tell him, "Steve, the test come back positive," he just stares at me, wide-eyed, with a worried look on his face. "Wha' we goin' do now?" "Me no know." I know what I have to do, so I tell him. "Steve, me goin' have a abortion. Me goin' find out how much it goin' cost, so from now on you better start saving up you lunch money. And if you can get money from you father you better get it." Tears well up in my eyes. He holds me to comfort me, but now he's getting aroused. He tells me, "Since you pregnant a'ready make we do it without a condom." Anger overcomes me, for sex is the farthest thing from my mind. Here I am with my life in shambles, and he wants to have sex! The same sex that has put my life in shambles to start with. It's the first time that I have been angry with him, and with the anger comes another flood of tears. "Steve, me damn well pregnant, and all you can think 'bout is you damn self! You better make sure that you get the damn money fi me get rid a me belly, else it goin' be hell between me and you! Me will see you Tuesday." I storm out of his yard, and he calls, "Clara! Clara!" after me as I rush home to cry. I cry because I never thought that my life would turn out like this. I never dreamed that I would one day be destroying my own created life form! I hate just thinking about it, for I really want to have my baby. I want to get married to Steve and, most important, I want to get out of Greenwichtown. I am sure that the guilt of killing my unborn child will haunt me for the rest of my life.

On Monday I go to school. I tell Simone the sad news, and she is shocked. "Clara, with all the methods of contraception we do in biology class, you get pregnant! How could you be so careless?" I agree with her: How could I have been so careless? So now the tears are forming again. When Simone sees that I am crying, she holds me. "Don't cry, child. Things not that bad. Besides, look on the bright side, at least you know that you not barren." I smile at her stupid statement, for right now I wish I were infertile.

"So wha' you goin' to do?"

"Me goin' have fi get rid a it."

A frown crosses her face. "But Clara, God will sin you bad, bad. You can't do that." God, thought I, had created me so that unprotected sex from insane passion would create pregnancy. I am not worried about God sinning me! I am worried that Flo is going to physically kill me.

"Me will have fi do it, for me won't be able fi graduate, me won't be able fi find a job, and me won't be able to leave Greenwichtown."

"Wha' Steve say when you tell him?"

"Him no say nothin', him only did want fi have sex despite me predicament."

"Well, child, if me can help you me will. But by the way, if you change you mind, me want to be the godmother." I laugh through my tear-soaked face at such an offer from my fifteen-year-old friend.

The whole week I go to several doctors, asking them if they do abortions, and how much it will cost. None of them do abortions, except for one doctor, who has a big bald shiny spot on his head. When he tells me how much it will cost, I almost faint at the price. I can't afford not even a fifth of what he wants. In desperation, I ask him, "Isn't there a cheaper way?"

"Look, young lady, if I should give you pills to expel the zygote, and they don't work, then I will have to scrape the lining of your uterus and give it a good flushing." I guess that justifies the price, but heavens know that there is no way that I can come up with such a large sum of money.

On Tuesday I cross the street to see Steve to tell him how much it will cost, but when I arrive, there is nobody home. I head home with my teeth clenched in anger. Steve's mother is coming down the street just as I am going home, and I pretend not to see her by looking at the sidewalk. I'm afraid that she might be able to tell that I have been fused by her son.

On Saturday after Flo leaves the yard, I cross the street and call Sharon, who tells me to come inside. A frown crosses Steve's face upon seeing me, and immediately I am angry again, for I'm the one that should be frowning. Fighting my anger, I tell him how much the abortion will cost. Sharon hears this. "Clara, you gone up?" By Steve's and my reaction, she could see that I have been fused. "Me God! Wha' the two a you goin' do?

"Me no know," I reply, for all three of us know there is no way that we can come up with that much money.

Time is flying by at a much faster rate these days. I am now two months pregnant. As my disease of pregnancy progresses, my entire body is changing. I can't keep down my twenty-five-cent breakfasts, and each morning I throw up in the communal bathroom before showering. I try to keep my nausea from Flo by eating slowly, but I still have to fight with each swallow. On top of that, I am salivating all the time like a leaking reservoir. I buy candy to eat so that I swallow some of it during my classes. But as soon as each class ends, I go to the bathroom to spit.

One of my classmates has observed the change in my behavior. Her name is Alecia, and at lunchtime, as Simone and I sit together, she confronts me. "Clara, you pregnant?" I look at Simone, who is looking angrily at Alecia for asking such a rude question. I want to tell her no, but the pressure of keeping it hidden is hard to withstand. "Yes," I tell her, feeling my eyes fill up with tears. "Me get rape by a wicked gunman, and him say that him will shoot me and set fire to me house if me tell anybody 'bout it." Alecia is shocked. She has no concept of what my life is like in the ghetto. I can't tell her the truth about being in love, having sex regularly, and the one time that I used the rhythm method I got fused, for she would feel that I brought it on myself.

"Why you no go to the police?" Alecia asks. Only a child from uptown, that can afford the luxury of cooked lunches, doughnuts, and milk, would make such a stupid statement, for ghetto people hardly go to the police except when a body needs collecting.

"Don't worry 'bout it, me will deal with me problem myself," I tell her.

The entire class now knows about my pregnancy and my alleged rape. Steve is no longer happy to see me when I go to his yard. We quarrel all the time now, and I tell him that it is his fault I am pregnant. He tells me, "A no my fault, why make you never take the pill?"

"The *pill*?" I ask in disbelief. "You damn well know that me can hardly afford lunch, much more fi buy damn pill!"

"Look! Me can't help you! A your problem, and you better find a way fi deal with it youself." I can't believe what I am hearing.

"And stop bothering me with it!" he adds.

How can he say this to me? When my whole future is dying partly because of him. My eyes flash red with anger.

"Look, when you did want fuck me, me wasn't bothering, right?"

He comes toward me, maybe to hold me. But in anger I lift my leg and kick him so hard in his crotch that he crumples to the floor in pain, and I hasten back to my yard to cry.

My head throbs from crying. Look what falling in love has done to me. As I'm crying, the song that I had proclaimed as "our song" starts playing in my head: "Up until now I've learned to live without love." The words stab me in mockery. I hate that song. I hate those words that had put me in such a blissful cocoon. I feel so stupid, I want to die.

The more I think about it, the more it makes sense. I wonder what would be the best way to kill myself? I want it to be quick, painless, and easy. I think of the note I will write to Steve.

> Dear Steve, I gave you my heart, and now in my time
> of trouble (caused by you) you have abandoned me.
> I feel so sorry that I ever met such a horrible person

as you. I can only hope that with me killing myself, you will always feel guilty. For you will be the cause of my death, and I hope that it will haunt you for the rest of your life.

Clara.

I think of a note for Flo too.

Dear Flo, my life with you has been a living hell. I never wanted to live with you, and leave Ma. But the fact is that I am pregnant! I have been having sex regularly under your watchful eye. Look on the bright side. There will be more space on the bed with me gone. By the way if you should see Ma again, tell her I love her, and that I will see her in heaven.

Sign Fay Myrtle.

I think about Sammy's death, but I don't think that I have enough courage for that. Then the idea hits me: I can jump off the bridge into the gully near my school.

16

TODAY IS MONDAY. I have left Flo's note in the sheets, hoping she will find it when she makes the bed. I have gone to the post office and mailed Steve's letter to him. Instead of getting off the bus after the bridge that runs across the gully, I get off before it. I walk toward the deep gully, made of large slabs of concrete, between which plants struggle to grow. When it rains very hard, the gully becomes a river of muddy water. I'm at the railing looking down into the ravine where I will end my life.

I stare down into the gully. I see the body of a dead dog with most of its body covered with black, baldneck vultures. My stomach is starting to turn, and now I feel nauseous. I throw up over the railing, watching the greenish liquid land at the bottom, and smelling the sourness of it. I feel better now, but I am still alive.

I can't kill myself where there is a dead dog and vultures. I cross the street and stand at the other railing. Just as I have mustered enough courage to climb up on top of it, I hear a voice calling, "Clara, Clara, wait fi me!" Why now? It's the voice of Alecia, the girl from uptown, the one that suggested I go to the police about my alleged rape. I can still jump!

Climb up and jump! I urge my body, but it refuses to move for I am horrified of dying. So now my terrified fused frame turns around and waves in recognition of her call. She reaches me and smiles.

"How come you comin' to school so early?" I ask, for all the students that come early are the poor ones that cannot afford the glorious breakfast that is supposed to be served at home—students like me.

"Me mother have a meetin' at the office, and she have to get there early, so she can prepare for the meetin', so me tell her fi drop me a school early. But she drive the wrong way, and it would take up too much time fi she drop me a the school gate, so she drop me off below the bridge."

"So how come you reach school so early?"

"Me come early so that me can buy breakfast."

"So, Clara, what you goin' do 'bout you rape and pregnancy?"

"Me goin' take care a it!" I do not want to discuss my life with Alecia. She gets the message and changes the conversation by asking what is served at the breakfast program. I tell her what is served. She doesn't buy any. She has had breakfast at home.

I must certainly jump this evening. I have already left Flo my note and sent Steve his, so I must do it! I must be brave. Simone is absent from school today, so I can't say good-bye to her. I hope that she doesn't take it too hard. I fight to control my nausea and spitting through my classes. I can hardly wait for evening so that I can get on with my death. I wonder what Flo will think when she reads my note. Will she be able to read it? How on earth is she going to explain my death to Ma? Does Ma remember the small skinny child that used to sit on her lap and lay her head on her chest? Surely she must remember me. Then, like a big heavy rock, it hits me. Why can't I run away from Flo and go live with Ma? I don't know where Ma lives! Well, I could travel the whole island till I find her. It is settled. I will return to Ma.

As the school day ends, I no longer think about that gully with vultures. I think about Ma, finding Ma, living with Ma, and suddenly I don't want to die anymore. But I need my few belongings, and I am going to need money!

The school bell rings, ending another school day. Instead of taking the bus home, I decide to walk. I decide that I will beg for money. I ask many well-dressed people to spare me a bus fare, for I have lost mine. Normally I would be ashamed of being seen begging in my school uniform, but today I couldn't care less, for today will be my last day of school.

I figure that Flo must have found my note by now. I figure that she should be worried, if she could read it. I cannot go home and face her, for just the part about me having sex would be enough for her to kill me. But I need my things because I don't want to go around the island looking for Ma in my school uniform!

I must face Flo and whatever confrontation that lies ahead. I don't want to be afraid of her. Why should I be afraid of her? If she should hit me, I will hit her right back. After all, I have been initiated into womanhood by my pregnancy. I am a woman now; I should start thinking like one. If she ever lays another finger on me, I will tell the entire Greenwichtown about her not being my mother and that she is infertile. I will tell them about her setting the square building on fire so she could kill Sammy's wife and get him for herself. I will tell them that the reason that Sammy killed himself was because he caught her with the potter. Yes, it is going to be war if she hits me! After all, I am going to be a mother, and I have to be strong for my child.

These thoughts run through my head as I walk along the street sucking on the ice from my bag juice. I have gotten fifteen dollars from my beggings, and to celebrate I bought a bag juice. As a matter of fact, I am going to demand that Flo tell me where Ma lives. Who does she think she is, beating me all those years? The nerve of her! I huff upon reaching my yard gate.

This will be my last day coming through this gate, I think, pushing it open. I walk through it and I can see that our door is open. Flo is at the communal sink rinsing and wringing wet clothes. I do not say my normal "Good evening." Instead I brace myself for her attack. When she raises her head and says, "Wha' happen to you manners, gal! You no know say that you fi tell people good evening when you come home from school?" I swallow hard, wondering if she hasn't seen my note. Didn't she read the part about me having sex regularly, and that I am pregnant? Why isn't she attacking me? Is she waiting for me to turn my back and then attack me from behind? My heart is thumping. "Good evening," I say, expecting her to say something, but she only goes back to rinsing the clothes.

I dread going into the room and being cornered with no place to run. If I don't go into the room, I will at least have the chance to run away to Ma, even if I have to go without my belongings. With her back toward me, I take quick steps into the room. I figure I can at least get to my yard dress and run back outside before she gets me. I dart into the second room and to my surprise the bed has not been made all day. I search the unmade bed for my note. I pull at the old sheets and I feel a rustle against my hand. Thank goodness, I have found it. I let out a breath of relief, for now I know that Flo won't attack me, for she doesn't know that I have been fused by the four-eyed creature across the street. I am so grateful; now I can improve my plans of finding Ma.

I tear the note to shreds and put it inside my backpack. I even make the bed. Flo is just about finished hanging the clothes on the line.

"Go 'round Miss Mumpsy shop, and buy one pound a chicken

back, pound a flour, and one onion." I gladly take the money
from her. This is the first time that I have ever been happy to
go to the shop and buy chicken back. As I am walking along the
street to the shop, Steve turns the corner and heads in my
direction.

I stare at him, for he looks so undisturbed and relaxed, while I
nearly killed myself this morning. The anger boils in my gut. I
want to hit him. I want to beat his brains to a pulp. I cross to
the other side of the street in case I should give way to my anger.
He passes me on the other side of the street without even looking
at me, as if I am a stranger. Shouldn't he ask me how I am doing?
How I am coping, with being fused by him? Suddenly I feel that
I should really have killed myself this morning. I wonder how he
will feel when he gets my letter. I hope it makes him feel horrible. He goes into his yard and closes the black gate.

The unmistakable loudness of a boom box blasts its way across
Greenwichtown, advertising the start of a dance. After cooking
dinner, Flo gets all dressed up and says that she is going to the
dance. I figure that this is all I need to complete my plans. I can
pack my things and take whatever money Flo has from her soap
sales and run away to Ma tonight.

As night falls and Flo leaves, I wait before packing my sparse
belongings into my schoolbag. I search the two rooms till I find
twenty dollars under the mattress. I take only ten. I take Flo's
red blouse too, for with me gone she will be able to buy more
clothes. I leave my schoolbooks, as I don't think that I will be
needing those. I am all set to go, but guilt makes me feel that I
should write Flo a note. A simple one that she will have no
trouble reading. I grab my notebook and rip a page out of it.
"Dear Flo," I begin. "I have gone to live with Ma. Sign, Fay
Myrtle." I put the note on the bed and lie down beside it, just
to wait some more till the nightly gossipers go to bed.

I fall asleep while waiting. I jolt awake without knowing how long I have slept. Flo hasn't returned. With fear and anxiety, I open the latch on the window and climb out, for Flo has locked me inside the room and taken the key with her. I push the window back in so it appears to be closed. Shiny stars above my troubled head seem to be winking at me. I feel cool. The air has a charge of electricity to it, or is it me? My eyes adjust quickly to the dark, and I can make out the outline of the square communal sink. I walk toward the board gate that separates the front of the yard from the back. I stop and listen for voices, any indication of the sidewalkers' nightly discourses. There is no sound except the distinct music from the dance. My heart is beating fast. I am a scared, pregnant thief. I should have left in the morning, when it is safer.

I reach the front of the gate, and there isn't a soul on the entire street. Just me, all alone on the street in the ghetto, in the wee hours of the morning. What if someone sees me? Who cares, as long as it's not Flo. The soft glow of the streetlights makes me uncomfortable. They make me feel so visible, so vulnerable. I head for the bus stop and figure that I will wait there till the first bus comes. If only I had a watch, so that I could know what time it is. This is going to be a piece of cake, I reassure myself, but the thought of cake makes me nauseous.

I will go through every street, to every country district, till I find Ma. I will tell Ma about the many times that Flo has beaten me and how horrible my life with her has been. I will tell her about falling in love, and then, softly, I will break the part about being pregnant. I bet she is going to be happy to have a grandchild! A little girl, perhaps. I continue comforting myself as I walk down the street, for I'll have to go to the end of the road and turn at the corner in order to get to the main road.

I rub my eyes, for I feel that they are fooling me. My heart leaps as I stare at the figure at the end of the street. Clad in dark clothes, the figure has stopped dead in the middle of the street, illuminated by the streetlight. I can see that the figure is Flo!

She has seen me! That's why she has stopped in the middle of the road. I can turn and start running in the opposite direction. I have the money and I have my belongings, but I am terrified. All my nerve of battle has dissolved into my bowels and has been replaced with the cold, unyielding fear that she has embedded in me. I am just standing there, frozen in my steps, by Flo's lone figure. How will I explain why I am on the mean streets of Greenwichtown in the wee hours of the morning with my belongings? I tell my body, Run! But it doesn't budge. My muscles have tensed into one big mass that refuses to carry out my commands. Instead of running like I am supposed to, I just stand there as Flo comes closer and closer. Soon she is at an arm's reach in front of me. "Clara, where you goin'?" The question sounds like a threat. Who the hell does she think she is, trying to threaten me? the frightened voice in my head says, trying to summon courage.

"Me goin' to live with Ma," my squeaky voice says. I had hoped that my voice would be firm, and fearless, against her. Suddenly a powerful pain knocks me and my belongings sprawling to the ground. I hold my hurting jaw, realizing that Flo has landed me a powerful punch to my face. I want to get up and hit her back, but I just hold my face and sob, thinking that my jaw is broken. I want to confess to her that I had fallen in love, that I am pregnant, and that I had almost killed myself this morning. I want her to hold me and tell me that everything is going to be all right, for I am all alone.

My bag is only a few feet away from me, I can still grab it and run, but she is towering over me. I am afraid that she is going to hit me again, but instead she just backs away from me as if to get a better look. She comes close again. "You a breed, you pregnant?" I do not answer, and in my silence I confirm it.

Flo cuts the silence. "All the sacrifice that me make fi send you a school, and get education, a the thanks this? You come bring in belly 'pon me! And now you want fi go put you belly 'pon Ma! You think that Ma can support you and you belly? Ma can't even feed herself, wha' make you think that me take you from Ma? Cause none of Ma pickney them can't read nor write, and out a all eight a them, you a the only one that get the chance fi go a school! High school at that! And you gone breed, and want burden Ma with you belly?" I have started crying harder, for I had never thought about it that way. I never realized that I was the only one of Ma's children to get to high school, and that I represented all their hopes. I was thinking that Ma was going to be proud of me. What is there for her to be proud of? My failure? My stupidity?

"So who is the father?"

I whisper, "Steve."

"Which Steve?"

"Sharon cousin."

"You mean the four-eye boy?"

I nod yes.

"Me rass clath!" she curses. "You couldn't find somebody better fi breed for? Somebody that working, and can mind the pickney?" Flo shakes her head in disbelief while I cry sitting on the cold asphalt. I cry because my jaw is hurting. I cry because I'm pregnant.

After Flo realizes that shaking her head won't do anything, she looks at me. "Get up off a the road and go in a the yard." My feeble, fused frame obeys her. I pick up my bag and walk toward the yard, with Flo following behind me. When I walk past Steve's yard, I wish that I had never set foot in it.

I go through the back gate, and Flo opens the door. She tells me to go to bed. With my throbbing jaw, I lie down on the note that I had left her. Flo sits in the chair holding her head, and is crying, soft, pain-filled tears. I close my eyes, trying to fall asleep, for sleep would prevent me from hearing Flo's hurtful sobs. Yet I am afraid of falling asleep, for Flo might actually kill me while I am sleeping.

17

IT IS MORNING. I can hear the water running at the communal sink. I can hear the voices of the other tenants as they chat with one another. I can hear Flo's voice telling me, "Get up, we goin' across the road." Why on earth are we going across the street? I walk behind Flo as she stops at the black gate, the same black gate that I have passed through so many times. She yells, "Miss Brown, Miss Brown!" This is early in the morning. The sleep-bitten face of Steve's mother sticks through the front door.

"Yes?"

"Miss Brown, me have fi talk to you," Flo says.

"Come 'round the back." I walk behind Flo, to the back of Steve's yard. My legs are slowly bending closer and closer to the ground with each step.

We see Mr. Brown sitting on a block of wood that came from a mango tree that had fallen during the storm, shining his shoes. He is very tall. He has the same lean muscular body that belongs to his son, and looks just like Steve, except that he doesn't wear glasses. I should say "Good morning." I should say something, but Flo chops in.

"Good morning, Mr. Brown, me come fi talk to you and Miss Brown." He doesn't look up from the shined shoes that he is still shining.

" 'Bout wha'?"

"Me want you son present too."

That's when he looks up from his shiny shoes. "Steve! Steve!" Mrs. Brown and Steve reach the back of the yard at the same time. Steve gives me a reproachful look. I look at him boiling with anger, and his eyes go to the ground. Flo looks straight at Steve. "You son breed me daughter, and me want know wha' you goin' do 'bout it?" There is silence. The kind that threatens to choke the root of my fused existence. I want the Browns to say, "Don't worry 'bout a thing," and hug me as the new family member, but the silence is stabbed with cruel words.

"You really come a me yard this early morning, fi come tell me that? How come you so sure that a him do it?" Mr. Brown says. I can't believe what I am hearing. I am waiting for Steve to say, "I am the father, I'm in love with her, and we will get married as soon as we are old enough." But instead he just stands there as his father goes on to call me a whore, a slut, and a worthless piece of trash with bad upbringing. I stare at Steve in total shock as the tears flow down my face. Why doesn't he say something?

Flo is boiling with anger, for she never expected any of this. Neither did I. Mrs. Brown says that she can't be sure that it is her son that got me pregnant. She tells Flo that she is not buying any cat in any bag.

"So wha' she goin' do fi baby clothes and all that?" Flo asks.

"She can use newspaper fi wrap up the baby fi all I care!" Mr. Brown responds. I cry harder, wishing that I had killed myself. Flo yells, "You think you blind-eye son better than me daughter? Move you ugly stinkin' rass!" And with that Flo pulls my arm and yanks me out of Steve's yard.

Some inquisitive people pop up their heads to see what all the noise is about. On seeing the heads, Flo yells louder. " 'Bout you not buying any cat in any bag! You not goin' see this damn cat when it born! You set a shit!" Mrs. Brown sticks her head around the corner and yells, "Move from me gate with you whoring daughter! I never did tell her fi come over me yard and spread her legs!"

Flo is fuming. When we reach home she collapses on the bed, and looks at the ceiling. "Lord, wha' me do fi deserve this?" All the while shaking her head, as if this is some nightmare. She sees me watching her with my tear-stained face. "Put on you clothes, we going to you school fi tell them that you not comin' back." I swallow hard, wipe my eyes, and look for something decent to put on. As soon as she goes to bathe herself, I quickly replace the ten dollars that I stole from her last night.

We are at my high school. Flo finds her way to Mrs. Larsen's office, who is chatting chirpily on the phone till she sees me, clad in civilian clothes and with a parent. She ends her conversation.

"Good morning. Please come in and have a seat." Her office is very small, and Flo has difficulty settling into the chair.

"What can I do for you?" she asks in that kind, caring voice of hers.

Flo bites her lip. "Well, ma'am, Clara pregnant, and she goin' to have to stop comin' to school. That is what me come fi tell you."

Mrs. Larsen looks at me, and she shakes her head. "Myrtle, how can you get pregnant when there are all these contraceptives? When your exams are in June? When you have your life ahead of you?"

I can't answer any of those questions. What am I going to say? That I fell in love?

"Myrtle, have you done a pregnancy test?" Flo's eyes widen with hope, but close when I answer yes. A shadow crosses Mrs. Larsen's face as she sighs with disappointment, and I feel like crying again. Then, as if injected by a needle of hope, her face comes alive with a beam of light as she says, "Well, Myrtle, you have your exams in June. There is a place by the name of the Women's Center, where you can continue to go to school, and you can do your exams there. It is free. They will give you lunch. It is a school for pregnant teenagers."

I almost fall out of the chair with hope, for I had no idea that such a place existed. If I pass my exams, then I will be able to get a job. Mrs. Larsen smiles and asks Flo, "Do you know where Trafalgar Road is?" She sees that neither of us know. "Tell you what, I will give you a ride in my car." She gets on the phone and tells somebody that she is going out for a while.

We follow her to her car, and she asks me, "Myrtle, have you studied the chapter on light rays as it relates to tinting?" Opening up the car door, I shake my head no. Thinking here I am in the soup, and she is concerned about the principles of tinting!

"Don't worry, Myrtle, I will give you a hint. There is going to be a chapter on tinting, as it relates to light rays, added to your curriculum." I smile at her, she smiles back, and more tears well up in my eyes.

She drives us to the Women's Center and tells us where to get a bus to get back to Half Way Tree Road. As she is leaving, she pulls me to the side. "Myrtle, here is my telephone number. If you ever need anything, just call me." My heart weeps in appreciation of her kindness, but all that comes from my lips is a confession. "I lied to my class about being raped by a gunman. Tell them it is not true. Tell them I will miss them." She hugs me like her own child. "Myrtle, we are all going to miss you too. Myrtle, you have a good head. I am begging you, Myrtle, please, *please,* pass those exams, for God knows that you are going to need them."

She leaves in her purple-tinted car, and Flo and I just stand there, staring at the well-kept building, painted in blue and white. I read the word "Administration," and Flo follows me into the building.

A cheerful young woman greets us. "May I help you?"

"I am here to attend the center."

"Okay. Please have a seat and fill out these forms, and I will be right with you," she says, handing the forms that request my name, address, school, grade, date of birth, subjects, and a whole lot of other things pertaining to my education and my pregnancy.

Another young woman shows us around the premises, and then she introduces me to my fellow pregnant classmates. One girl looks as if she is almost due, while the rest of them are in different stages of pregnancy. She tells us that I am given lunch free of charge four days a week, with the exception of Fridays, and that the center has a nursery. She says that there are students who bring their babies to the center, for they have no one to leave them with.

As Flo and I leave, her face loses its frown. Maybe it is because I can still do my exams. Or maybe it is because she is going to be a grandmother/aunt, of a little baby girl, perhaps?

My body is changing again. I am now sick all the time, with headaches and nausea, and I am having constant nightmares. My body is enlarging. I am getting fat. It has been two months since I have been going to the center, and in a few months I will be taking my exams. I don't know if I will be able to do exams in this state, but I am hoping to feel better by then.

My classmates are chirpy people, despite their pregnancy. There are eight girls in the class. They are mostly like me, poverty-stricken girls that had fallen in love and are babyfatherless in every aspect of the word. We all want to change our lives and make a good future for our offspring. We collect money from one another on Thursdays, for two people to cook and carry the food, normally curried chicken back and rice for all of us, on Fridays. We choose baby names and make plans for our future.

18

TWO MORE MONTHS HAVE passed. I am now six months pregnant, and I'm no longer going to the center. I have done my exams, and like all my pregnant friends, I am waiting to see the results. In all this time I haven't been in Steve's yard. Sharon has gone to live with another aunt. I have seen Steve many times on the street, but we just pass each other like complete strangers.

Today is Tuesday, and I am on my way to get my exam results. I feel worried. How many out of the six subjects did I pass? I get off the bus at my high school gate, with my somewhat large belly hanging over my waistband. I briskly walk toward the main building, hoping to quickly get my results and ease my mind.

The receptionist looks disapprovingly at my pregnant form and dryly asks for my name and my receipt before leaving. She returns, hands me a large sealed white envelope, and then, ignoring me, she goes back to her papers. I quickly march through the school gate for I will open up the envelope at the bus stop.

"You comin', baby mother?" the conductor asks as a bus slows to a stop. I shake my head no. The bus drives on. I rip apart the envelope with trembling fingers and pull out the thick sheet of paper. I skip the top of the page, with my name and date of birth on it, and run my eyes down all six subjects. They all have the same GRADE IV, except for chemistry, which has a GRADE V! I grab onto the side of the bus stop for support as tears flood my face and my pregnant body convulses. I have failed all six subjects. Another bus stops. "Baby mother, wha' happen to you, that you cryin'?" the conductor asks me. I ignore him and wipe my eyes and gripping my envelope of failure, I enter the bus. I flop down on an empty seat, and my mind races back to the days when I took my exams.

I was sick when I took my exams and having nightmares. I had hoped I would pass at least four of the subjects, but deep down I knew that I couldn't cope with the stress of academics along with such a pain-filled pregnancy. Now that I have failed, I fear I will never escape the abyss of unstoppable poverty.

I tell Flo about my failure, and she cries, not only for my failure but for the money that she has lost. For every cent that she had scrimped and saved to pay for my exams has been wasted on me. I have let her down by becoming pregnant and now by failing my exams, and with a child on the way, we have no money for retaking the exams.

It is nine o'clock. I am at the clinic for my first prenatal care visit. There are two nurses and about thirty poor, pregnant, chatting women. I take a number and wait for the nurse to call my name. It's almost two o'clock, and I still haven't seen the nurse yet.

Finally my turn arrives. I am weighed, my blood pressure is taken, my blood is drawn, and my chart is created, with information regarding my pregnancy. I lie with my dress pulled up, baring my abdomen that looks like a pumpkin, except for the color. It is time for the nurse to listen to the baby's heartbeat.

The nurse listens twice with her stethoscope, and now she is listening all over my belly. I am becoming worried that she cannot find any heartbeat. "Don't move! Me soon come back!" she tells me, and goes into the next cubicle. I can hear her. "Nurse Jones, come listen to this!" I fear that the baby I am carrying inside me is dead. Now both nurses are listening to my belly.

"Are you hearin' the same thing that I am hearing?"

"Yep," Nurse Jones answers.

"Wha' you hearing?" I brace myself for the bad news.

"We are hearing dual heartbeats." My mind races with questions. Does that mean I have some kind of a monster growing inside me?

"Wha' you mean by dual heartbeat?" I search their faces for an answer.

"It could mean that you have two babies inside you."

"Are they attached? Are they deformed?"

"We don't know, we will have to give you a letter to take to Jubilee Hospital, for a ultrasound, and then they will know if they are attached."

I rub my big belly, and it moves in response to my touch. The nurses laugh, trying to divert my worries.

I go home. On top of all my problems, I am going to be blessed with a two-hearted baby. Maybe my child has developed abnormally because of me. Maybe a baby needs a happy mother, with a happy father, in order to grow right. I tell Flo about what the nurses told me and she isn't in the least bit concerned that I might have a malformed child. She is only worried that she will have to buy double supplies for two newborns. But all this is only supposition. I may have only one child inside me who happens to have a spare heart.

I get on a bus and go downtown to Jubilee Hospital with my letter from Nurse Jones. The hospital is a square building painted off-white, and has about four floors. Flo has given me twenty dollars for the ultrasound, along with two fried dumplings stuffed with callaloo, a dark green leafy vegetable, and money for a bag juice.

My name is called, and I walk into the office of the male doctor. His office is clean, with diagrams of embryos, the reproductive system, and pictures of happy babies hanging on the wall. He has kind eyes, a broad nose, and thin lips. "Miss Myrtle, I am Doctor Lawrence. Please sit down so that I can examine you, before we proceed with the ultrasound."

His voice is so comforting. He takes my blood pressure, weighs me, looks at my eyelids, and listens to my heart.

"Change into the green robe on the bed and remove your underwear. Then lie down on the bed with your legs up. You can change behind the screen."

I do as I am told, but I feel very funny about exposing my private parts to a man that I don't even know. I put my legs up but keep my knees closed. He comes in and looks at me through gentle eyes. He has seen many private parts of many women. In a soft voice he says, "Miss Myrtle, kindly open up your legs so that I can examine your fetus." I open up and turn my head to the side, thinking that he is only going to look up my private parts with a flashlight to see the baby. He puts on his gloves and greases his fingers with Vaseline. He touches the opening of my vagina, and when he tries to insert his fingers, I feel such an intense pain that pushes a shrilling scream through my lips. Three nurses rush in, and I can see that the kind Doctor Lawrence is embarrassed. I am in pain. I never expected that he was going to put his hand up there.

"I have it under control."

I can hear the nurses saying over and over, "Complicated pregnancy, complicated pregnancy," to the other fused females that are waiting to see the good doctor.

He looks at me, with my legs spread apart and tears on my face.

"Miss Myrtle, have you been having sex during your preg-nancy?"

I shake my head no. A look of sympathy crosses his face.

"I am sorry that I have hurt you. I am going try and insert my fingers. I promise I will be gentle. Tell me if I am hurting you as I go along." And with that he inserts his fingers gently, slowly feeling around my abdomen for the two-hearted baby inside me. After finishing, he calls the nurse and tells her to prepare me for the ultrasound.

The nurse takes me to a room with a lot of equipment inside. Minutes later, Doctor Lawrence comes in, smiles, and tells me to relax. There are two other people with him, a Chinese-looking man and a black woman, both wearing doctors' jackets and carry-ing notepads.

"This is Doctor Wang and Doctor Lynn," Doctor Lawrence says. He lifts up my green robe and starts rubbing and coating my belly with oil. It feels so relaxing, not only to me but also to the two-hearted baby inside, for it has started moving around with each rub.

All three doctors smile at the movements.

Dr. Lawrence moves a square thing over my belly that is attached to a machine that looks like a television, and they all look at the screen.

"Miss Myrtle, you are going to have twins!"

"Twins! Are they attached? Are they deformed?"

"No, they are healthy twins; they are as fine as fine can be." He continues to speak to the other two doctors, but I can un-derstand very little of what he's saying. I get dressed, and when I am finished he hands me a piece of paper. "I am going to give you a prescription for supplements; you can get these at the hospital's pharmacy. It is very cheap. The nurse will make an appointment for you to come back and see me."

"Who should I pay for the ultrasound?" I ask him.

"Use the money for the ultrasound and treat yourself to lunch, as my apology for making you scream." I smile, saying "Thanks," and he smiles back.

I head for the pharmacy, thinking that he is such a kind man. Why couldn't I have been fused by someone who cares about me? Someone that I can still have sex with. Someone who would rub my belly and laugh as my belly moves. I am sad because a few moments of pleasure have given me a lot of pain.

At the gate of the hospital, there is a man selling food in a box. I can smell the food of stewed chicken and rice and peas as I near him, and this cheers me up. I take Doctor Lawrence's advice and buy myself lunch and a box of chocolate milk. I go inside the pharmacy, hand in my prescription, and take a number. I sit at the back of the almost filled room and transfer my two dumplings from the small plastic bag to my box lunch. I taste the food and it is so good. The chicken (not chicken back, for there is a leg) smells of herbs, with plenty of brown sauce. I even chew the bones. The smell of the food permeates the whole room.

"Which part you buy you food?" a woman asks me.

"From the man out by the gate." My number calls at the prescription window. I receive my supplements and head home. With money left over after buying lunch, I buy one pound of sprats from a fish vendor, a bundle of seasoning, and six limes from another vendor. On the way home I stop at the shop and buy one pound of rice, one ounce of butter, and half a pound of sugar. I cook the rice, stew the fish, and make a big jug of lemonade. I have no ice to put in the lemonade, but it doesn't matter. I eat half of the food and leave Flo's share in the pot, waiting for her to come home.

She comes home, tired and dusty with her unsold quantity of soap. I tell her that I have cooked some food and have left some for her. She looks at me. "Where you get money from fi cook?"

I can't tell her that I got the ultrasound for free because she will want the money back. So I lie. "Me find a money 'pon the street, when me was coming home." She doesn't question my story, she only digs into the food with eagerness. "The doctor say that me goin' have twins, and them healthy," I tell her. She looks up at me with her mouth full of rice and a worried expression on her face from her raised eyebrow, for instead of having another mouth to feed, she is going to have two, and she will have to buy double baby supplies.

Time passes. I am eight months and four days pregnant. My belly is now so big that I waddle like a duck from side to side with each step I take. The skin of my belly has stretched so much that it is covered with lines, deep lines, shallow lines, thin lines, and fat lines. My belly looks like a drawing entitled *Lines*.

My twins move all the time now. Sometimes they stretch inside me, and my belly stiffens up. Then I have to stop what I am doing till they relax again. Flo has lost a lot of weight; she hasn't been eating much, for when she cooks, she gives me most of the food. My stomach seems to have lost its bottom. I eat like a starving pig. As soon as I have eaten, five minutes later I am hungry again. I have gained weight. My breasts are big, and even my skinny legs have meat on them. My square face has become round, and my behind sticks out.

Cynthia had suggested, "Make we go look 'pon the body." I am part of a crowd whose eyes are focused on the ground. There is a man lying there with his head split open and his neck bent to one side. I know this man. Everyone knows him. His name is Lucky. He pushes a cart from street to street selling jelly coconut. Lucky had a dispute with a man by the name of Fisher. They came fist to fist with blows, and the fight was broken up by onlookers. Lucky went home to his room in an upstairs tenement yard. He had just cooked his dinner and went to sit against the side of the square building on a block of wood to eat his food. Fisher had climbed on top of the roof with a concrete block. As Lucky lifted the spoon to his mouth, heaped with rice, Fisher dropped the block on top of his head.

Lucky is dead. The red plastic bowl is lying beside him on the ground with the contents of stewed chicken back and rice spilled all over him. I can see the unchewed rice in his mouth. The block of wood Lucky sat on has toppled over, and near to it there is a pool of blood. The light blue shorts he is wearing are wet with urine, and his bare feet are clenched tight. A fly lands inside his open mouth.

I don't do anything much these days. I just sit around after Flo goes selling. I sit with the people who sit on the sidewalk. I chat with them about everybody's business. "Me hear say that Angela man put her out wit' the two pickney them last night," Lisa says.

"So where she goin' to go?" I ask.

"If it was me, me would not be goin' nowhere. It would be him that get put out!" Cynthia says angrily, and everyone laughs.

"Now, how do you expect Angela fi do that when she only half as big as him?"

"Wit' a big long fat stick!" says Lisa, and there is more laughter. I stand up to stretch, and Cynthia looks at my big belly. "Clara, you look ready fi put down you load."

"Yes, me tired a carrying 'round this big belly fi so long."

I see Steve occasionally on the street, always in expensive clothes and always ignoring my waddling form. He doesn't even ask me, "How are you doin'?" He just acts as if I am not there. I have gotten used to it, even though my heart hurts every time I see him. He should have graduated by now and received his exam results. The sidewalkers tell me that he has taken up with a girl that lives on Fourth Street.

Thanks to Flo, I have everything I need to give birth—

towels, nightgowns, nappies, blankets, babies' stuff, and a bag to put it all in. Flo has even saved up some money for a taxi fare. I have been seeing Doctor Lawrence regularly. He tells me that if he is available, he will deliver my twins, for deliveries are usually done by midwives. All I can think about is giving birth and seeing my twins. Will they be identical? Will they be two girls? How will I feel like to have my body free of them?

Norma, my friend that attended the center, comes to pay me a visit. She brings her little baby girl with her. She tells me to hold Tanya. I am fearful because she looks so fragile, but after a few seconds I am cooing at her.

"So, how things Norma?" I ask her, after telling her that I'm going to have twins.

"Well, me get me exam results, me only pass math. So me don't know how me goin' get a good job, for jobs askin' for at least four subjects." She looks down.

"So, Norma, why you no go back to the center and learn dressmakin'?"

"But wha' me goin' live on in the meantime? Me mother tired and sick a supporting me and me baby, and she not young anymore. So me goin' have to find some kind a work."

Norma and I have a lot in common, our babyfathers have completely abandoned us, and it's our mothers that are shouldering our pregnancy.

"So wha' 'bout your exam results?" she asks.

"You do much better than me, cause me failed all six a me subject, and me even do as bad as gettin' a GRADE V in chemistry!"

This makes her laugh, I laugh too. Here we are two teenagers laughing at how badly we did on our exams. The laugh coats our disappointment, but it doesn't matter. All that matters right now is the welfare of our children, for we need to find a way of supporting them, and at the moment it looks really difficult for both of us.

Norma leaves under the watchful eyes of the daily gossipers. She tells me she will come back and visit as soon as she is able to, meaning whenever she can find the bus fare. We promise to write to each other.

After insisting on being the godmother to my twins, Simone Baker has migrated to Florida along with her entire family. She has written to me. I have answered her, but I haven't mailed my letter yet because every time I get the money to buy the stamp, I use it to buy food.

19

NINE MONTHS HAVE NEARLY passed. Flo is having a hard time making ends meet. I am now eight months, three weeks, and two days gone. As the new day breaks, a tingle of pain is passing through my belly. Flo is just getting up. She is getting ready to go selling.

"The contractions them starting!" I don't want to go into labor without her being here.

"Lord Jesus! Hold on, me goin' get you bag!" She stumbles into everything like a drunken woman, looking for her overworn shoes and putting them on. Cynthia comes to the communal sink. "Go get one taxi fi me, Clara ready!"

"No! Wait! Me can take the bus, it cheaper!" I yell back, not wanting to waste the much-sacrificed saved money on a taxi. Flo and Cynthia look at me as if I have gone mad.

"The pain not that strong," I explain.

"Wait fi me, me goin' put on me clothes, me comin' wit' you!" says Cynthia, running toward the front of the yard. She has dropped out of high school, and quite amazingly hasn't contracted the disease of unwanted pregnancy.

Flo carries my bag. I am dressed in my only maternity dress.

We take the bus despite Flo's and Cynthia's concern that I might give birth on the bus. We reach the hospital. The nurse looks up my file, and the ward assistant takes us to the delivery section. Flo and Cynthia leave, telling me they will be back in the evening when it is visiting time.

The walls of the hospital are painted in colors that are designed to hide dirt. There aren't enough beds and many fused females are two to a single bed. Fortunately, Doctor Lawrence is on the same ward that I am wheeled to. He smiles when he sees me and finds me a bed. "Miss Myrtle, I am about to leave. You'll be seeing Doctor Mack, who is on duty now."

After Doctor Mack examines me, he says, "But Miss Myrtle, you don't seem to be in labor."

"Yes, me in labor. Me did feel a pain this morning!" I say defensively, forbidding that he should send me back home, for Flo would be very upset with me for this false alarm. He eyes me suspiciously as he helps me off the bed.

Flo and Cynthia come back in the evening with food, callaloo, and rice. They can't understand why I haven't given birth yet. I tell them, "I am having prefabricated uteral contractions." I know they don't understand a word of what I've just said, but it suffices as an explanation. When they leave, Flo says that she will come to see me in the morning.

There are two sections to this ward. There is the part where you wait for delivery symptoms, and at this point you drag your maternity bag with your belongings to the delivery section, where you give birth. This is what the other patients tell me. They are a mixture of older women and young teenagers like me. On my maternity bag I have a big padlock so that no one can steal my things; I keep the key in my brassiere. In the morning they give me eggs, cocoa, tea, and bread for breakfast. Soon I'll see the doctor.

There's another doctor, a woman with long straightened hair

and heavy lips, that examines me. She looks through my chart, and then she inserts her hand to feel the position of the fetuses. She speaks softly. "I am going to give you something to help with your contractions." She sticks a large syringe filled with liquid into the back of my left hand and tapes it down. I watch the fluid from the syringe slowly going into my hand.

That morning, Flo comes to see me again. She looks worried. She cannot understand what in heaven's name I am doing with this big syringe taped to my hand. I tell her that it is something to ease the pain. She asks me, "You need anything? They treating you a'right?"

"Yes, them treating me fine," I reply to ease her worry as she leaves for home. Life here isn't so bad, for I am getting a lot of food and I am meeting new people.

In the afternoon a woman in labor disturbs the entire ward with screams. We all waddle toward the direction of the sound. The sound is coming from a twelve-year-old girl from the country. She is lying on a bed in amniotic fluid. She writhes in pain, sweating and screaming, with her nightgown drenched and clinging to her body. Her legs are spread apart, exposing the pink fabric of her panty that is preventing the baby's head from coming out. The girl's face shows confusion, for she doesn't seem to realize what is happening to her. "Let me through!" the woman that has given birth at Jubilee Hospital six times says, and quickly pulls the panty off the girl. "Aiiieeehhh!" the girl screams as the baby comes out, along with a load of crap.

The nurse arrives and parts the crowd of pregnant women to see what all the commotion is about. She looks at the girl, the baby, and the pile of crap. "You a idiot or wha'? Don't you know that you not supposed to give birth on this section of the ward?" the nurse harshly says, but the girl couldn't care less about anything. She's lying there drenched, tired, and confused about what has just taken place. Another nurse brings a wheelchair and takes

the frightened country girl to the delivery section and closes the
door of the room. I can still hear the nurse's harsh words as they
wheel her away.

The other pregnant women say how ignorant the twelve-year-
old girl is. They say that a twelve-year-old has no business getting
pregnant. I agree with them. I am sixteen and I am going to have
twins. I should not be pregnant, but I am. So I am just like the
country girl.

Dinner is served, stew beef with rice and peas, and a
pineapple-flavored drink. I am starting to feel small contractions.
This is the purpose of the syringe taped to my hand, Doctor
Mack tells me. He says that I should give birth by morning. I am
feeling stronger cramps. I have checked my bag to see if all my
things are in order. I do not want to give birth in the waiting
ward and be subjected to the harsh words of the overworked
nurses. I lie on the bed, and now the cramps are coming more
frequently.

It's now nightfall. I can tell by the darkness at the window. I
look at the clock. The hands say 9 P.M. I need to pee, so I step
out into the hall holding my big belly and clutch the wall as
another cramp comes over me.

"Ummmehhh," I groan on the toilet.

"You a'right?" asks the voice of the woman that has been here
six times.

"No, the pain starting!"

"Don't give birth in the toilet, or else you will drown the
baby," she says jokingly. I come out of the cubicle to see her
holding her belly and laughing at her own joke. I smile at her as
I head back toward the bed.

Another pain starts, and I rub my belly in response to it. The
pain means that I am in labor. My goodness, it's happening! I
grab my bag, pulling it on the floor by the long strap toward the
delivery ward. I stop at the nurse sitting behind the desk,

and I can hear the screams and moans coming from women in labor, which makes me afraid.

"Is Doctor Lawrence on duty?"

"Nope. What's your name?"

"Clara Myrtle," I tell the nurse. "Me goin' have twins."

"How often are the contractions?"

" 'Bout every twenty minutes."

"Go into room number five. Take out two blankets, your pad, two chemise, two nappies, a clean nightie and panty for yourself. And put all of that on the table. Then take off your panty and lie down on the bed. Then as soon as you feel that the baby is coming, you just holler for the nurse."

I wish that Flo could be here with me. I find room number 5 with green sheets on the bed and a chair next to it, two tables in the corner, one with hospitals' tools, the other bare. In the other corner are two cribs, and beside the bed a fresh bottle of drip hangs from a shiny pole. I can still hear the screams of the other women as I pull my bag close to the table, laying out all the things that the nurse requested, and then pull off my panty. "Aaaiii," I groan, clenching my teeth from another pain.

"Woooeee, me vagina a burst!" yells a loud-mouthed woman. Will my vagina burst too? I wonder as I lie down on the bed, waiting for the next pain. I am starting to sweat. I feel warm. I start to cry. I hate going through this alone with all these terrifying noises coming from these other women. "Woooeee," I shudder, rubbing my belly and feeling another pain. I can't lie down any longer, but I am afraid of getting off the bed and giving birth on the floor. I stand up on the bed and wrap my arms around my crying self. I lie down again. Another pain comes and I find myself walking on the bed. I am breathing heavily and sweating. My nightgown is soaked with sweat and tears. I want to cry out like these women. I want to kill the four-eyed creature that is responsible for getting me pregnant and leaving me to go through this all alone.

While I am standing on the bed, another sharp pain grips me. I feel a flood of liquid running down my legs. It feels cool against my hot body.

"Nurse! Nurse! Come quick, me ready, me water burst!" I yell, lying down in the liquid.

A nurse comes in and asks, "Are you Clara Myrtle?" I nod my sweat-dripping head yes.

She looks at my vagina.

"You're not ready as yet!" The pain is getting stronger, and I can feel my lower body being forced out of shape. "Nurse! Nurse! Please don't leave me! Please stay with me! Nurse, me 'fraid!" I plead, but she still leaves, but only for a few seconds. She comes back and sits on the chair, watching my body wrenching in pain with each contraction. I feel like getting up! I feel like running! I desperately need to stand up. "Woooeee! Help! Me want me mother!" And on and on I yell with each pain like the other women.

"Miss Myrtle, you must breathe! Watch me!" the nurse says firmly. "Whou, whou, whou, whou!" and I mimic her.

I still feel hot, despite the coolness of the soaked sheets against my body. I look at the shiny shaft holding the drip bottle, and I begin stroking it. The nurse looks at my passage again. "In a few more minutes."

"No!" I shout at her. "Me ready right now!"

"Look! You are not ready as yet, and if you start pushin', you are goin' to be ripped apart like a tight dress on a fat woman!" I don't care about the tearing, I only want the pain to stop. "Breathe with me!" she says. "Whou, whou, whou, whou!"

She looks again. "I think that you are ready!" I feel a coarse, burning, stabbing pain. I clench my fists. "Aaahhhiiieee! Woooeee!"

I scream. The nurse looks up my vagina again. "Push! As hard as you can!" I push, and this time the force of the pain sends me reeling upward.

"Push again!"

"Me . . . can't push . . . anymore, the pain . . . killing me."

"Work with me, let's push on the count of three. One, two, three, *pushhhh!*"

I summon all the energy that I can find in my aching body and push.

"Look, you goin' have to do better than that! One, two, three, push!"

I push again, and now I feel the walls of my vagina coming apart.

"That's it! That's it! I can see the head! Come on, push again!" she screams. I cry out. I pant and clench my fists so tight that my nails cut into the flesh of my palms. I hold my breath and push again. I feel my baby sliding out of me.

"It is out! It is a beautiful baby!" the nurse yells in triumph. She sees that I am out and slaps my face with her gloved hand. She holds the baby over my face. "What kind is this?"

A human kind, I think, but somehow that doesn't seem to make any sense. Then I look again.

"It's a girl," I say in a whisper, for my voice has left me.

The nurse, after cutting her navel string, wraps her in a blanket and puts her in a crib. She tags her and puts eyedrops in her eyes.

She comes back to the bed. "I am going to insert my hand to feel the position of the other baby." She inserts her hand inside my vagina and soon after withdraws it. "I am going to have to puncture your water bag." I don't respond, for I am enjoying the wonderful feeling within me. It's like the feeling that comes with an orgasm, but more intense. I can't feel my body. I am off somewhere wonderful, so that even as the nurse catches the water in a bedpan and announces that the other baby hasn't turned like it is supposed to, and that it's going to come out footway, I don't care.

She pulls the baby out by its feet, and I still don't feel anything. She holds the baby over my face. "What kind is this?" I look at the life that came from inside me. "It is a boy."

20

"MISS MYRTLE! MISS MYRTLE, wake up! Wake up, Miss Myrtle!" I think I hear someone calling my name. It can't be possible for I am sleeping. I turn over on my side, and feel someone shaking me. "Miss Myrtle, Miss Myrtle, wake up!"

I feel a slap on my face. In my dream I search for the culprit that has dared to slap me, even though it's not a painful slap. I am going to land a mighty box on the face of the culprit that has hit me. I raise my weakened hand and aim it at my attacker. A powerful hand grabs my wrist and I feel another slap on my face. "Miss Myrtle, wake up! The twin them goin' to need milk!" What milk? What twin? My arm is still being clutched too tightly. "Let go me hand!" I say, but I am slapped again. Slap, slap, then, slap, slap again! I am becoming annoyed. "Wha' you slap me for?" I ask, struggling to free my hands so that I can fight back.

"Miss Myrtle, wake up, you are in the hospital! Get up!" The rotten intruder pulls me up. Now I am really going to beat the hell out of this persistent fool. I stare into the face of a woman who seems amused. She is wearing a little white cap on top of her straightened hair, and too much lipstick. "Miss Myrtle, are you all right?" She looks familiar. She looks like a nurse. "Um-uh," I grumble, trying to figure out why on earth this nurse is holding my hands. With tired eyes I look around the room and then at the bed. I see a bloodstain around the lower half of my body.

"Help! Help! Somebody shoot me! Me bleeding. *Help!*"

"Miss Myrtle, stop screaming! You have not been shot! It is just a little blood! You gave birth to twins last night!" the nurse yells in my face.

I realize that this is the same nurse who had told me to go to room number 5. "Oh, me God! Me remember now! Where is me twin?" I ask, suddenly feeling the need to see them.

"Calm down, Miss Myrtle. I am going to clean you up first, and then you are going to be transferred to ward six, where you will stay with your twins."

I am clean and newly padded. A well-built black man with a front tooth in gold wheels me to ward 6 to see my twins. It is early morning, and the light shines through the window.

"So how it feel, fi go one time, and have a son and a daughter in one shot," he asks me.

"It feels all right."

"Bwoy! The man that responsible fi doing that must feel proud a himself, and drink a couple a beer, fi celebrate how powerful him is!" I am now beginning to hate this warder, for he has just reminded me that I am babyfatherless. With a lump in my throat and tears forming in my eyes, I say, "Me have no babyfather! Him dead!" Before he can ask me, "How him die?" I add, "Gunman shoot him!" The warder doesn't say anything, for we have reached ward 6.

"Miss Myrtle, how are you?" comes the kind voice of Doctor Lawrence. What is he doing here? And where was he while I was giving birth? "Fine," I answer, as he pushes me along a ward filled with mothers and babies.

"I have examined your twins. I did that as soon as I came on duty in the early hours of the morning, and they are fine. In fact they are so fine, that if they were any finer, they would be doctors right now!" I smile at his silly joke, and now I am happy with the only thought of seeing my babies.

He takes me to a room along a row of other rooms, and in two side-by-side cribs, I can see my sleeping twins. There is a single bed with green sheets, a chair, a small table, and a green curtain, half drawn, that separates each cubicle. Doctor Lawrence puts my bag beside the bed. "Miss Myrtle, they will soon give you something to eat, for I bet you must be hungry."

I am starving, come to think of it.

"Thanks." I smile as the good, handsome doctor walks away with the empty wheelchair.

Through the opening in the curtain, I can see part of the body of a fat woman, lying on the bed in the next cubicle. I get up to look at my creations, and the fat woman pulls the curtain wide open, making the two cubicles into one.

"A your twin them?"

"Yes."

"But how come you so small and have twin? Twin run in you family?" My family? What family? The only family I have right now is Flo.

"No," I answer, hoping that she stops questioning me.

"Then twin must run in you babyfather side a family then?" There is that horrible word again.

"Look! Me babyfather dead! Gunman shoot him!" Tears well in my eyes, and she becomes silent. I pull the curtain closed.

"Me goin' change me clothes. Me need some privacy!"

I walk over to the two cribs, and for the first time, I take a good look at my offsprings. The little boy looks somewhat like me. He has my straight nose and my full lips. He is a bit larger than the girl, and the tag on his hand confirms it. Five pounds, eight ounces, to the girl's five pounds, four ounces. His head is perfectly round, for he didn't have to push his way into the world with it. The girl has kinky hair, skinny legs, and her face looks just like Steve's. She even has his fingers, the same fingers that once touched me. I am sad again, for here I am with two beautiful babies, all by myself, and no babyfather to share them with. Again my eyes fill with tears, and before they can flow over, I hear the fat woman's voice again.

"You done change you clothes already?" She pulls the curtain wide open.

"Me never have enough time!" I wish she would leave me alone, but instead she asks, "Me can come look 'pon you twin them?"

"Sure." I wipe my eyes as she looks at them.

"But them no identical! A two boy?"

"No! One a boy and one a girl."

"Bwoy! You so lucky, you go one time and get you son and you daughter." Luck, I am thinking, had nothing to do with it.

She sits in the chair in my compartment, with her big behind hardly fitting in the chair. I look at this bold, inquisitive woman that has taken up residence in my cubicle. She has a round face whose features have been softened by fat. Her hair needs combing, and she is clad in a yellow nightgown with pink flowers embroidered over the bosom.

"Look . . . ma'am . . . ," I stutter, trying to find a kind way of telling her to leave me alone.

"Me name Iona. Iona Calver. Wha' you name?"

"Me name Clara Myrtle. Look, Iona—" She interrupts me.

"Clara, you want see me baby, me dying fi show somebody the cute little birthmark 'pon her ankle."

I sigh.

"Not right now. Me tired. Later me will look 'pon her. Me promise. Me want take a sleep before me twins them wake up."

She still doesn't budge from the chair. I position myself on the bed, yawn, and pretend to start sleeping. She leaves, but the curtain remains open.

"Breakfast time!" says a woman in a pink uniform, who pushes a trolley with food. I sit upright. She hands me a bowl of corn porridge, bread with butter, and a cup of tea. Iona is sitting on her bed staring at me.

"Do me a favor, me have fi go to the toilet, give a eye 'pon me baby till me come back."

I nod my head, agreeing to watch her baby, as I hungrily attack the bread. When she comes back, we chat while we eat.

"Wha' time you baby them born?"

"Hold on, let me go look 'pon the tag." I go over to my twins. "Them born 10:52 P.M. and 11:20 P.M."

"Me hear say that when baby born a night, them goin' give you hell a nighttime when you want fi sleep." I have no idea if this is true. "So who goin' help you with them when you go home?"

"Me mother." The woman pushing the food trolley collects our plates.

"You ready fi come look 'pon me daughter now?"

"Yes." I walk over to her cubicle, to her baby's crib, and she stands beside me. "Don't she pretty? Look 'pon the small birthmark 'pon her ankle."

"She pretty. She almost look like you."

"No! she look like her father! Wait till you see her father; she look exactly like him." My heart tightens with the mention of that word again, and I go back to my cubicle.

It is visiting time, and in walks Flo with a black plastic bag in her hand. She looks tired and out of breath. "Me go all the way over the other ward, and them tell me say that you over ward six and me have fi walk all the way over here." I smile, for I am truly happy to see Flo's tired face. She pulls out a bowl of liver, dumplings, and boiled bananas, and hands it to me.

As if bitten by some feeling of urgency, she walks over to the cribs containing her niece and nephew. "But, Clara, you no tidy them? Look how them face and head dirty." I have no idea that I am supposed to clean them up, for I thought that all that stuff on them is part of their natural look. She goes through my bag and gets their washrags to clean them up, making several trips to the bathroom.

After cleaning them, she looks at me and asks, "You feed them yet?" Feed them? It never occurred to me that I should feed them. By the look on my face, she can tell that I haven't fed them. She gently picks up my little girl and gives her to me. I try to get her to start breast-feeding, but my little girl has no interest whatsoever in my breast. After several failed attempts, she slowly starts sucking on my breast, and Flo and I both smile in admiration as she experiences her very first taste of food. She feeds till she falls asleep, and now it's my son's turn. He has no trouble starting to feed. As soon as I put him near my breast, he starts moving his lips in search of food. After sucking for quite some time he falls asleep. Flo looks at me with awe and admiration, for it's hard to believe little me has produced twins.

In Iona's cubicle there is no voice. No sounds of any visitor. Flo collects our soiled clothes to take home to wash. She promises that she will come back to see me in the morning, leaving me with enough money to buy something to eat and two days' supply of cloth diapers. "Make sure that you feed them as soon as them wake up, and change them nappy as soon as it get wet." Then Flo finds the nurse on duty. "The girl in that cubicle with the twin them, she young and don't have any baby experience, so just lend an eye over there for me." Flo has left. The twins are asleep. Iona is asleep, and with my full belly and nothing to do I fall asleep too. I am awakened by the woman who serves food. She gives me a bowl of thick beef soup with dumplings, yam, beans, and vegetables. I tell her thanks as she goes to the next cubicle to wake Iona.

After the soup bowls are collected, Iona starts chatting away again. "Me babyfather coming to visit me this evening." Lucky her, I am thinking.

"This is me first pregnancy and me want one more child. Hopefully me will have a boy next time. Bwoy! You really blessed fi have a son and a daughter at the same time."

"Iona, give a eye 'pon me twin them, me going to bathe before them wake up." I gather a fresh change of clothes.

"All right; when you come back, then me will go bathe," she responds.

I walk into the bathroom, passing rows of sinks, and go into the first empty cubicle. I take off my nightie and hang it on the hook behind the door. I take off my brassiere, and that's when I notice my belly. The brown color of my belly skin has turned black. There are lines all over it and the loose, wrinkled flesh hangs from it like the skin of an overripe plum. I turn my head away.

Maybe it is just dirt. Maybe when I wash my belly the ugliness will disappear. Taking off my padded panty, I turn on the shower and feel the cool water. I lather my rag and wash my body, leaving my belly for last. I rinse off and put more soap on my rag and start washing my belly. I gently scrub, but the skin stays the same way, so I rub with more pressure to loosen the stubborn dirt. Nothing changes, so now I scrub really hard. The more I scrub, the more it remains the same. I scrub till my belly starts to hurt. I look at it as the water runs, and I start to cry, for the ugliness that I thought was dirt is still there. My head is now throbbing with pain, and I put it under the running water. It cools the heat in my head and washes away the streaks of my tears.

"Wha' happen to you?" Iona asks as I walk out of the bathroom, my eyes red from crying. "Me have a bad headache." I wish to be left alone.

"Ask the nurse fi two pain pill," she says and heads off to the bathroom. Dinner has been served. I have fed, cleaned, and

changed my twins. With nothing to do and not wanting to be bothered by Iona's friendly conversation, I lie down and fall asleep.

I wake to the sounds of voices. There is a distinct male voice
and the other one belongs to Iona. The curtain is drawn closed,
except for a small opening. I get up, check the twins, and through
the gap in the curtain I can see him. He's a tall man with wide
shoulders. He is wearing a blue shirt with jeans, and he is looking
into the crib of Iona's six-pound one-ounce baby girl. He is making goofy faces at the baby, and I stare at him as he gently picks
up the little bundle. He is making *coo-coo* sounds at her, and tears
flow down the side of my face. He looks so happy, cooing at his
baby. His baby! And me, I have no father for my twins to admire
their little hands and feet and coo at them! I cover my mouth to
smother my cries, for I do not want them to hear me. The more
I watch the man cuddle his baby, the more I cry. I turn my head
away, for I cannot bear to look anymore. I cry till I fall asleep.

I awake to the sounds of babies crying for the warmth and
food from their mothers. It's not morning yet. Iona lies sound
asleep and slightly snoring. My twins are quietly sleeping, but
their behinds are wet and I change them. I lie on the bed looking
up at the ceiling, which needs paint. The horrible feeling of de-
pression washes over me again. Has Steve thought about me?
Does he even care about me or his children? My eyes are tearing
again, and a single question torments me: Does he love me?

I grab my maternity bag, searching frantically for the pen that
was left over from my forgotten days of going to school. I need
a piece of paper, but I have none. I need to write. I need to
record exactly the way I am feeling. I look at the box with my
maternity pads, and within seconds I have emptied it, and now
I am tearing it apart, so that I can write on it.

I am shivering yet the temperature is warm. I am cold
deep with me. I need you to hug me and make me

warm. Where are you? Now that I need you to be with me so badly. Comfort me, cuddle me, but most of all, love me. Yes. Love me! Only your love can give me the happiness that I desperately need. Only your love can make me complete. Please love me, for now I feel like nothing.

My tears drip on the piece of carton, and I wipe them off with my hand. I put my feelings in the small pocket of my bag, check my twins, and cry myself to sleep.

A new day begins. The cry of my baby wakes me up with a jolt. I haven't heard them cry since their birth, so I rush over to the cribs and pick up my wailing son. I hold him close to me till he stops crying, and feel the wetness of his behind. I change him, and he falls asleep sucking on my breast. I gently put him in the crib, and the little girl is awake and is just lying there quietly. She looks at me through tiny eyes. Steve's eyes. And I coo at her, picking her up and holding her close to my chest. I feed and change her too, and now they are both sleeping.

Flo walks in with her black plastic bag, bringing me fried dumplings and callaloo. She stands over the crib looking happily at the sleeping babies. She can see that they are clean. "You tidy them?"

"Um-uh," I answer with my mouth full of dumplings.

Days later my twins and I have been given a clean bill of health and cans of formula by the good Doctor Lawrence. I am given the receipt of their birth, for we are going home this evening. Iona is going home too.

It has started to rain, a slow, weeping kind of rain. I am going home as a mother. I pack my bag and change back into my white maternity dress with the different-colored flowers on it. I pull my kinky hair to the back of my head in one plait. The twins are in their little hats and socks, and two new blankets are on the bed to carry them in. Iona has already left, and when we said good-bye, she told me to save my son for her daughter, and I jokingly said that I would. She left with her babyfather carrying her bag and her carrying their daughter in her arms. I almost cried after they left, but I told myself that I shouldn't cry anymore, for I must be strong for my children.

When Flo arrives, it stops raining. She carries my son and I carry my little girl, while the warder with the gold tooth carries my bag out to the road and gets us a taxi. My twins are still sleeping when the old taxi starts driving, taking us home to the slums of Greenwichtown.

21

❀

THE OLD TAXI TURNS off the main road and heads toward Fifth
Street. The whole neighborhood seems to have fallen further into
ruins while I was away, with the zinc roofs getting rustier. The same
people are sitting on the sidewalks, and as the taxi approaches our
yard, all eyes are glued to it. The driver gets outs, and Flo pays him.
When the driver takes my bag out of the car trunk, the neighbors
swarm around us. Cynthia is there too, and takes my bag from him.

As soon I can see past the crowd, my eyes stray across to the
black gate, but Steve isn't standing there. The daily gossipers
cheer me all the way to the back of my yard, for they consider
it an accomplishment that little me has produced twins. They
make me feel like a hero returning home. They are full of so
many questions, and they all want to get a good look at my
twins. I smile at the attention, but in all the faces of the crowd
there is none belonging to Steve.

Flo has already made a place for the twins on the bed. So as
soon as I enter, I lay down my sleeping daughter, and Flo lays
down my sleeping son. Cynthia puts my bag on the floor. "But
Clara, them not identical."

"No, one a boy and one a girl. Thanks fi carrying me bag fi

me." She stays for a little while, staring at the sleeping twins.

For dinner Flo cooks canned mackerel and dumplings. With no space for her on the bed, she makes a place to sleep on the floor with cardboard, old clothes, and sheets.

It is morning, and the sounds of the other tenants chatting come to my ears. As soon as Flo makes the bed and tidies the twins, they all come to the window to look at them. They give me money, for it's a bad omen to look at a new baby without giving the baby something. It isn't much, but I am nonetheless grateful. "Them is really two pretty baby."

Then the landlord's daughter, after looking, says, "The little girl look just like Steve." With all the people that come to see me, Steve isn't among them.

This is my first day home. Flo isn't going to sell today. Instead she starts cooking a pot of porridge and washes the babies' soiled clothes at the communal sink and hangs them on the clothesline. For the rest of the day we just sit around admiring the new members of our household. Flo doesn't say very much, but by her actions I can tell that she is happy.

It's been a whole month now since I have been home. The twins are doing well and are gaining weight. Flo has resumed selling her soap, and I have taken on all the chores that my twins provide. The people in my neighborhood no longer call me Clara. They call me "Twinnie" to salute me having twins, even though I have no father for them.

After a bus ride, I am at the government building where names of children are registered and birth certificates are issued. Flo and I have been calling the children Dave and Davia all along. I do not know which surname to give them for this name should reflect the last name of their father, but their father hasn't come to see them in all this time. What is the sense in acknowledging their father's name, when their father hasn't acknowledged their existence?

"What are goin' to be the names of the twins?" the naming clerk asks.

"For the girl it is Davia Donna Myrtle, and for the boy it is Dave Donald Myrtle." And so it is done.

The twins are now three months old and going to the clinic for the first time. Flo comes with me and carries Dave while I carry Davia, for I have no stroller for either of them. I have lost weight. Flo has lost even more weight, and her clothes are hanging off her. The little money that she makes can barely buy formula for the twins, much less buy food for us. Every day that she has to go somewhere with me takes a day away from her selling.

My twins are six months and can sit up on their own. I no longer breast-feed them. The squeeze of my extended family is really upon us. I consider getting a job, but my biggest worry is that I will have to pay for day care, and that will take three-quarters of my pay. I will need to pay bus fare and find money to buy work clothes and lunch at work. In order to get a good-paying job, I need C.X.C. passes, which I don't have since I failed my exams. For me there are no jobs to get. These are the thoughts I am pondering, standing behind my gate, for my twins are asleep and all my chores are done. How will I support myself and my children? I could find me a man. Someone that has a job and gets paid on Friday and brings some of it home to me. But most of the men in Greenwichtown have several girlfriends, and there aren't enough of them to go around. The men want women with big behinds and prosperity fat on them. They want light-skinned girls with firm, unmarked bellies. They will not want me for I am all bones, my hair is still in its natural kinky state, not straightened in a big hairdo, and my belly is full of stretch marks, and I am black.

It is midday, and my stomach is starting to groan. I have no food. I have to wait till Flo comes home from selling to get something to eat. I look across the street at the black gate where the father of my children lives, totally undisturbed by fatherhood.

I walk to the back of the yard, dragging my tired, dusty feet. My twins are still sleeping and I look at their plump faces. I know they are the reason why I am now all bones and have a wrinkled belly, but I cannot blame them. I lie beside them with my sullen face and the pain of hunger in my stomach, and as I fall asleep I silently pray for change.

Today is Sunday. Flo feeds Dave his porridge, while I'm feeding Davia. They make slurping sounds at each other, and their plump faces smile with the contentment of a full belly. As I spoon the last bit of porridge into Davia's mouth, I hear Cynthia yell, "Clara! Flo! Quick! Come here!" Flo and I lift up each child and quickly go outside to see what could be the cause for such urgency on this calm Sunday morning.

"Gunman shoot Steve! And him dead! Make haste, and make we go look 'pon the body before them move it!" I stare at her.

"Go look 'pon the body if you want, me will take care of the twin them," Flo says.

Cynthia barely allows me to put down Davia before dragging me by my arm, through the front yard and onto the road. We run, Cynthia in her plastic slippers, and me barefooted. There are people walking with hurried steps in the same direction. We run down the road till we come to Fourth Street, and now we have reached the spot where a large crowd surrounds a body. As we push through the crowd to get a better look, deep down inside me I'm hoping that it's not Steve, not the father of my twins.

"You steppin' on me foot!" one woman yells at me, but I say nothing, for all I want to do is see who it is. Cynthia shoves me forward, and I feel something sticky at the bottom of my bare foot. It is blood.

"Oh me God! Is Steve!" I scream.

His body lies in a pool of blood, and there are bullet holes all over him. His glasses lie broken beside him, and the plastic frame is twisted. His mouth is slightly open, showing the edges of his teeth, and there are streaks of dried blood on the side of his face. Even his well-groomed head has holes in it, and I can see pieces of his brain next to it. His name-brand sneakers have blood splattered all over them. "Him really look dead!" says one man. The tears stream down my face, for the horrible true words have pierced me.

"Wha' you crying for?" Cynthia looks at me with disbelief.

"Him was me babyfather."

"But Clara, him never even as much as give you a safety pin fi none a you twin! And him never even come look 'pon the twin them. So him better off dead anyway!" I agree with her, but I can't stop the tears from flowing. All my hopes of my twins having a father are now dead, and my heart has been craving for Steve to make amends for all the hurt that he caused me. I push through the increasing crowd to get away from the sight of the body. I sit on the sidewalk and rub my feet on the road to clean the blood off them.

"Me hear say that Steve thief drugs from somebody, and that's why them shoot him," Cynthia says. The police arrive, and I watch as they pick up Steve's body. As the crowd disperses, the meager dogs come out and lick the blood from the road.

When I return home Flo asks me if Steve is really dead, and I tell her yes. She looks pleased and says, "Serve him right! Him should have been dead a long time ago! For him is no good!" I look at my children, who are giggling and unaware that their no-good father, the boy I fell in love with, is dead.

22

STEVE HAS BEEN CREMATED, for it's cheaper than a funeral. Many months have passed, and so has my pain. Flo has gone selling soap. She leaves me some money to cook cabbage and dumplings before she goes selling. As my twins take their daily nap, I walk briskly to Miss Mumpsy's shop, hoping to quickly get back home before they wake up. I walk past the normal collection of chatting, unemployed, young black men standing at the corner of Fifth Street. "Sceet, sceet," I hear. The unmistakable sound of a male. I keep on walking. I hear the sound a second time, right behind me, so I know it is directed at me. I spin around, staring into the face of Cokee, the drug addict that everyone in Greenwichtown knows. Regardless of his reputation, I am flattered. He smiles. "Wha' happen, sexy girl?" Me, sexy? I can hardly believe what I'm hearing. "Nothin'." I walk even faster.

"Me would like fi check you, you know!" I chuckle. I don't respond to his statement, for I don't want to upset him, but on the other hand, I don't want him to think that I am in the least bit interested in him. Before I can think of what to say, he asks, "Where you going?"

"Miss Mumpsy's shop." Now he starts walking right beside me,

as if we are the closest of friends. Feeling very uncomfortable, I
ignore him for he is free to walk wherever he wants to, even if
it happens to be right next to me. He walks all the way to Miss
Mumpsy's shop beside me. "One pound a flour, one pound a
cabbage, and one ounce a butter."

Cokee is watching me. "Wha' you going to cook, cabbage and
dumplin'?" I nod yes.

"Miss Mumpsy!" he yells. "Give her a whole chicken and some
rice, and some seasonin'. Wha' else you want?" he asks, turning
toward me.

"No! Me no want you things!" I tell him, loud enough so that
Miss Mumpsy can hear and stop searching for the largest frozen
chicken in her freezer.

"Chow, man!" he says. "No worry yourself, you safe. Me no
want nothin' from you. Just take the things them, and go home
and cook some good food!"

Miss Mumpsy, even though she has heard me, is weighing her
largest chicken. She weighs rice and has started filling the plastic
bag with things that I can never afford to buy—a whole tub of
margarine, a bottle of ketchup, a whole bottle of soy sauce, and
seasoning that can last me for a month. My tongue has become
heavy in my mouth, for I do not want to take the things, but
my mouth cannot form the word "no," either. Can he afford to
pay for all these things? I wonder, halfway hoping that his inability
to pay Miss Mumpsy will be my salvation. The plastic bag is full
and looks heavy, and when she says how much everything is, I
swallow hard. Cokee takes out a wad of money from his pocket
and peels off a few bills to pay her for her goods. I stare at the
wad of money in his hand. He sees me staring at it, and he peels
off a few bills and hands them to me.

"Buy youself somethin' fi drink with the food." I look at the
money he has given me, and it can feed my family for two weeks.
I take the money although I shouldn't, but I need it. I take the

heavy bag from Miss Mumpsy, avoiding Cokee's cocaine-soaked eyes and silently praying that he will forget this whole episode as soon as his high wears off.

"You want me carry the bag?" he asks as I walk out of the shop, for the bag is indeed very heavy with all the contents. "No, man! It not heavy," I tell him, not wanting to give him any more reasons to remember the trip. So now I am walking along the streets of Greenwichtown with a cokehead beside me. He stops at the corner by the same collection of young men. "A my girl that!" I want to turn around and hand his groceries and money back to him right then and there, but my legs just keep on walking as if they have a mind of their own. It sounds nice, even if those words are coming from the lips of a coke addict.

I reach home and my twins are still asleep. I haven't had chicken in a while, and just cutting the joints gives me great joy. I fry the chicken, leaving half for tomorrow and stewing the other half with the cabbage. I have fed, changed, and burped my twins, and now I just wait for Flo to come home. When she arrives I serve her a bowl of stewed chicken with rice. Her eyes bulge at the bowl. "Which part you get money from fi buy chicken?" Flo knows Cokee from the neighborhood. "One man, meet me 'pon the road and buy me the chicken." She doesn't even wait to hear my answer, she just attacks the food, thankful to have something to eat. I guess that she couldn't care less if I take up with Cokee. To her life is very simple. If a man gives you money, then stay with him. If he doesn't give you money, then find someone else that will. She says, "You can't put love in a pot and cook it when you hungry."

Thanks to Cokee we have food, and every day when Flo comes home from selling, she has her dinner ready. It's been a whole week since I have seen Cokee, and while I am washing my babies' clothes, Cynthia comes around the back of the yard.

"Clara, somebody come to you."

"Man or woman?"

"A Cokee."

"Tell him fi come 'round a the backyard." She goes toward the front of the yard. Cokee pushes the back gate, peeping through with uncertainty, till he sees me. Now he swings it wide open and walks toward me, at the communal sink, washing clothes. "Wha' happen?"

"Nothin'," I answer.

He sits on the edge of the concrete communal sink, just watching me scrub the clothes. What else can I say to him? *How are you today? How much cocaine did you use today? Did you bring me some more no-strings-attached money?*

"You want me to go and buy a box food fi you 'round a Foodie?" Well of course I do, for Foodie's cooking is much talked about and is expensive, for he cooks only fish.

"Um-uh," I tell him, and he leaves, while I continue washing the clothes.

He comes back, just as I am hanging the last piece of laundry on the line, with a black plastic bag in his hand. Despite my eagerness to taste Foodie's cooking, I am wondering if I should really eat it, for Cokee might have put drugs in it. Nevertheless I eat the delicious stewed fish like it is my last meal.

Dave's awakening cries startle me, and I spring off the empty oil-drum seat. I dash into the room fearing that Dave's cry might wake up his sister. He stops crying as soon as he sees me, and after changing him and giving him some lukewarm porridge, I put him on the floor at the doorway. When I return from preparing a change and porridge for Davia, Cokee is playing with Dave. Dave laughs, and his chubby face is all aglow with laughter from being tickled. I smile at Cokee. "The girl no wake up yet?" I shake my head no. Like everyone else in Greenwichtown, Cokee knows the story of my twins' birth, and that they are fatherless. Cokee finishes eating Foodie's box food, and now he is tickling Dave again. Cokee lifts him up and holds him. This terrifies me, for I am not sure if a drug addict is capable of holding a baby. So I stand near to him, figuring that if he drops Dave then I will catch him. He doesn't drop Dave, and I breathe a silent breath of relief as soon as he puts him back down.

Cokee is brown like me, and a few inches taller than my five feet six inches. His hair is low-cut. His teeth are white but not perfect, as a few of them have grown out of line. His full lips accentuate his square face, and when he smiles he has a warm look about him. The white parts of his eyes are pink, probably from smoking ganja and using drugs. His eyes make him look as if he hasn't slept in a while.

When he leaves he gives me more money again, enough to last me for another week. "Me will come see you tomorrow."

I nod. "Fine with me," I say, and he leaves. I suppose he gets money from selling drugs, for I am sure that he doesn't have a decent high-paid job. Davia wakes up. I change her and give her some porridge. Then I put her on the floor beside her brother. I sit on the empty oil drum and watch them play together. I think about Cokee. Will he want something in return for all the money he has given me?

It's been more than a month since this thing has started with Cokee. He has been back several times to see me, and he continues to give me money, which I use to buy much-needed things for my twins. He has indicated that he wants to have sex with me by saying, "Every time me see you, me feel horny." I pretend not to understand, and one day he just blurts out, "Me want grine you!" I look at him wide-eyed, for I do not know what to say. My mind races with reasons why I can't sleep with him. I can't just tell him plain no, cause he has been supporting me all along. But I have no desire for him, and most certainly I don't want to get pregnant again.

"We can't grine 'pon me mother bed," I tell him, hoping he

understands that I can't have sex on Flo's bed. I am hoping that this deters him, but to my surprise he says, "Me goin' buy you a bed. You can push the table in a the corner and push the bed against the wall." The idea sounds so nice. My own bed! I do not say anything, for if he doesn't buy the bed, then I can keep using that as an excuse.

I don't see Cokee for more than two weeks. I wonder if he is in jail, or if he has been killed. Maybe he just went to live in another place, far away from me.

Boom, boom, boom! sounds a knock on our door early Saturday morning. "A who that?" Flo asks.

"A me! A Cokee!" She is not surprised, for I have told her that all these meals that she has been having all came from him.

As Flo gets up to open the door, I am wondering what the hell could he possibly want this early in the morning. "Clara wake up yet?"

"Me comin'!" I yell, getting up slowly so as not to wake my twins, and pulling on my yard dress.

"Me bring the money fi you buy the bed." He holds out a wad of bills toward me. I rub my ears and my sleepy eyes, thinking that I am not hearing and seeing properly. I am just staring at the money, so he puts it in my hand and closes my fingers over it. He doesn't let go of my hand, though; he holds it for a second and looks at me with dreary lust.

"Me will check you Monday." I wait till I hear the back gate close before stepping over Flo's bed on the floor and going into the other room.

I find Flo sitting on the edge of the bed and holding Dave. "Cokee just give me a money fi buy a bed."

"How much money?" I have no idea so I open up the wad and start counting. There is enough money to buy two beds. Flo looks shocked, but she recovers and says, "Put on you clothes.

We goin' downtown; we can even buy a chest a drawer fi put the twins them clothes in!"

A bus takes us downtown, and we go into a furniture store on King Street. Flo holds Dave as she talks to the salesclerk. "We want fi buy that bed over there. The flowers-looking one, and the small chest a drawers beside it. And me goin' be payin' cash fi them." The salesclerk is looking at Flo as one would look at someone in the early stages of madness, with confusion and sympathy. I don't blame the salesclerk, for Flo and I look like we don't have a pot to pee in.

"Have you seen the prices of the bed and the dresser?"

Flo nods her head yes.

"Do you realize that the prices do not include tax?" Again Flo nods her head yes.

"Please follow me to the office." Flo and I follow the well-dressed girl to a small room.

"When should we deliver these items?"

"As a matter a fact, me want them right now, as soon as me pay fi them." The clerk fills out the paperwork with my name and address. She keenly watches as Flo peels away the cash to pay her. We collect our receipt, and within the hour a truck bearing the furniture company's name pulls to the front of the store, loaded with our bed and chest of drawers. We are huddled into the front seat, as the truck drives toward Greenwichtown.

The sidewalkers are watching the approaching truck with devoted interest. Who has bought new furniture? When the truck comes near enough to see that Flo and I are in the front seat, their eyes speak of disbelief. They eagerly help the two men unload the bed and chest and carry them to our two small rooms at the back of the yard.

Flo's face shines with happiness at not sleeping on the floor anymore. I feel happy too, and even the twins sense that something good has happened. I walk around smiling at my accomplishment. My own bed! Flo doesn't go to sell soap today. Instead she makes a curtain from an old sheet as partition for the two rooms. Privacy, separation, and independence come to my mind as she hangs it at the doorless separation of the rooms. Today we have chicken for dinner, and we are glad, but despite that I am uneasy, for I know I will have to sleep with Cokee.

Cokee and I have been together for six months. He sleeps with me most of the week. My twins sleep all the time with Flo, making it easier. I have had sex with him. I was surprised at all the long-dead feelings he was able to revive in me. He makes love slowly, as if he has all the time in the world. He doesn't care about my stretch marks, and he says he doesn't want me to get pregnant. I use the pill, for he hates using condoms. He has a room at his mother's house and I have been there twice. His room contains a bed, a dresser, a chest, and a makeshift closet, containing expensive clothes and shoes. I have grown to care about Cokee. He is the fourth of his mother's eleven children. His real name is Kevin Keith Knight, and he has been stealing ever since he can remember. He is thirty-five years old, and he has been using cocaine for more than a year now. He gets money by stealing and selling drugs. He hasn't offered me drugs as yet, but I have seen him inhaling the white powder. He says that he had always noticed me whenever I passed him on the street. When he tells me he loves me, I smile with the appreciation of being loved. He buys things for my twins even though they are not his children, and I haven't been hungry since I met him. My life is no longer harsh, for now I have a man who cares about me, a man that says that he loves me.

Eventually Cokee introduces me to some of his friends, who are mainly thieves and who wear expensive clothes. One of them, by the name of Shaka, lives in Tivoli Gardens, a community next to Greenwichtown, and comes to my yard quite often looking for Cokee. Most times Shaka brings me spoils from his robberies, and I accept them. Since I have food, my behind is starting to show a kind of roundness. Prosperity fat is slowly gathering on my body, and more often than not I hear "Sceeet" from men as I pass them on the streets. Sometimes Cokee takes me to boom box dances that are held in the streets at nights. When we get there we eat, and he drinks Red Stripe beers while I drink soda. We dance, but no matter what we dance to, he always holds me close to him and keeps his hands on my behind. Our dancing involves mainly our hips, and sometimes he kisses my neck while we dance, and I feel his bulging desire press against me.

"Clara, me been thinkin' 'bout goin' to foreign. And been thinkin' that you should come with me, for foreign full of better opportunity." "Foreign" means any place outside of Jamaica, any place where there are jobs to support families back home. He tells me that we can go to the island of Curacao, for we do not need a visa to go there. He says that we can stay there for three months, working and saving up some money. He tells me to get my birth certificate and some passport pictures ready, for he is going to get me a passport. He says he wants us to eventually move out of Greenwichtown to a decent neighborhood.

"Clara, the police them lookin' fi me, so me figure that by goin' to foreign it will give things a chance fi cool down." He seems worried, so I hug him close to me. I tell Flo about Cokee's plans. I tell her not to worry, for Cokee knows exactly what he is doing. Besides, I tell her, doesn't he have a successful record of caring for me? I feel somewhat afraid, yet excited. The prospect of working, saving money, and giving my children a good life has really put sparkles in my eyes.

Cokee hasn't been sleeping much with me anymore. He tells me that he has to keep a low profile. He tells me that we are definitely going to foreign. He gets me my passport, and says that he only has to come up with the large sum of money for the airfare.

It is Tuesday morning. The police are in my yard looking for Cokee, and a crowd has gathered. "Cokee no live here, and no go inside me room with you big gun for me children in there!" A policeman raises his rifle to hit me, but the crowd of angry neighbors protects me by surrounding me. The police search my room; then they angrily leave, kicking the mongrel that barks at them. The look of death they had on their faces frightened me. It was their readiness to kill Cokee.

In the wee hours of the morning Cokee comes to see me, bringing me two airline tickets, his passport, and a small bag with his clothes. Cokee knows that he is being hunted. He gives me some money to leave with Flo, for she will no longer be able to go soap selling, for she will have to take care of my twins. She is happy that I am going to foreign, for going to foreign is a great accomplishment. He tells me that we are going to leave the day after tomorrow. I hug him, for I fear for him. Even if the police don't kill him, he will surely be put in prison.

The next day I am nervous wondering if Cokee is all right. Our flight is at twelve o'clock tomorrow morning. I am all packed. I know he will show up in the morning, all set to go. I tell Flo good night, and as I drift off to sleep I dream of what lies ahead, that even though I will be away from my twins, I am doing the right thing, for I am trying to make a better life for them. Knowing that Flo will take care of them helps put me at ease.

I must not have fallen asleep very long. I hear a whimpering voice and then a soft thud against the door. "Clara! Clara. . . . Clarrraaa. . . . Me . . . a . . . bleed! Clara . . . quick . . . open . . . the door!" My heart pounds as I jump off the bed. I open the door, and Cokee falls on me, covered with blood. "Oh me God! Cokee! Cokee!" Flo rushes to the door.

Cokee's blood soaks through my nightie, and his breath comes in short gasps. He groans in pain with each gasp. "Clara," he gulps.

"Please, please, don't talk, Cokee!"

Flo runs out to the street to the main road to get a vehicle to carry him to the hospital. I try to stop his bleeding with my fingers, but there are too many holes in his body to cover. My cries awaken the twins, and they start to cry too.

"Clara," he whispers between breaths. "Me . . . have . . . some money . . . in . . . me . . . pocket. . . . Go to . . . foreign . . . and make a better life . . . for . . ." The words hang in the air around me, an unfinished sentence that I can finish.

"Please, Cokee, no talk no more! You soon go to the hospital! You goin' be all right!" I cry to him, my tears dripping on his face. He takes one short gulp of air and then he stops moving.

"Cokee! Cokee, wake up! Cokee, talk to me!" I scream. He has stopped moving. I look up toward the heavens, toward the giver and taker of life. My heart burns with pain. "Nooo!" I scream at the blinking sky.

A crowd has gathered in my yard. They can see that Cokee is dead, and my stricken frame is holding and rocking him in my arms. My face twitches. They can see that my body and the floor are drenched in blood, and I can hear a voice. "Clara get up!" It sounds like Flo's voice, but I cannot figure out where she is. A hand is pulling me up, and I fight to get the hand away from me. As the strong arms pull me up, I feel Cokee's body roll away from me.

The strong arms belong to Flo, and she tightly holds me as I watch two men lift Cokee's body and take it to the waiting car on the road.

"Nooo! Bring him back! No take him from me!" I try to follow them, but Flo's strong grip prevents me from moving. "Let me go! Let go me right now!" I scream at her, but she only tightens her hold. Feeling weak and overpowered, I crumple to the ground, and Flo almost falls on top of me.

The water brings a deep chill to my body as Flo bathes me. Now my body refuses to stop shaking, and my teeth won't stop chattering. She feeds me a cup of tea and tells me to lie down and get some rest. I fight hard, but I cannot escape through the door of sleep. When I finally enter, it is almost morning.

Flo shakes me awake. "Clara, Clara, you still going a foreign?"

How can she even think about foreign when I have lost the only man that has ever loved me?

"No!" I yell at her. My eyes fill up with tears, for I know what Cokee would have wanted.

23

I FEEL HALF ALIVE. Only a part of me hugs Flo and my children good-bye, for they suddenly feel like strangers. After I hugged them, I could figure out why they would let me go. I keep waiting to hear words or any hint of uncertainty that will stop me from leaving. But there isn't any. Even my beloved twins do not cry. When I start to walk it's as if somebody else's legs are moving.

When I head toward the main road, the sidewalkers express their sympathy to me about Cokee's death. "Clara me so sorry that Cokee dead." If only they could see that I am dead too. If only they could express their sympathy about my death. As I'm walking, I try to fill my head with thoughts of the good life I will find for my family, but I can't.

My straightened hair is combed in one plait at the back of my head. I am clad in a white T-shirt, blue jeans, and black leather shoes. I take the bus to downtown Kingston. I feel a pain inside my stomach, and I cling to the faded idea that I might still be alive. If only I could hide inside the pain. My unbalanced body stumbles into a woman pushing a shopping cart, selling oranges. I look at her, and I know that I should say something. What is that word that one says when asking for pardon for an unintended action? I can't think of it so I ask.

"How much fi you orange?"

"Two dolla', them sweet, sweet. How many you want?"

She suddenly notices me. "How come you eye so red? You was crying?"

"Just one." I bite into the orange.

"Don't it sweet?"

I nod yes, even though the taste of the orange does not register, only the vague idea that I am heading somewhere. When I remember that I am supposed to be going to the airport, my legs, without any help from me, start walking.

I feel someone pulling on my blouse. I turn around and it's the orange lady. "You forget to pay me fi the orange!" The word that I was trying to remember earlier rushes to my head. "Me sorry, ma'am! Me regret it, ma'am! Me never did mean fi do it, ma'am!" I tell her, realizing that I don't know where I am going. "Where is the bus stop, fi get the bus that go to the airport?"

"Go 'cross the road, go through the park, and right in front a you, you will see them. But you have to pay me fi me orange." I pay her and when I tell her "Thanks," she only looks relieved and rushes back to her shopping cart.

"Airport! Airport bus! Ready bus a leave fi airport! Hold on, driver, take up one!" the conductor yells, looking at me.

"You sure that you goin' to airport?" I step up into the bus.

"Yeah, man," he answers, slapping the side of the bus for it to drive on.

"Final stop! Airport stop!" I have never been to the airport before.

"You sure that this is the airport?"

"You no see the airplane them? How come you so fool-fool, is country you come from? That is the airport!" I get off the bus and walk in the direction of his pointing finger.

I see signs of different airlines and people with luggage going back and forth. I have no idea where to go, so I stop at the first counter, where the sign reads AMERICAN AIRLINES. The men and women are all groomed and well dressed. I feel afraid to talk to them and show my ignorance. "Good morning, ma'am, how can I be of service to you today?" The sweet voice comes from a light brown pretty girl behind the counter. "I am going to foreign. I am going to Curacao. Where do I find the airplane?" She smiles with perfect teeth. "May I see your ticket please?" I hand her both my ticket and passport, inside the plastic bag. She looks at my ticket. "Your flight is with ALM; they are right over there." My eyes follow her fingers and, not seeing the sign, I give her a blank look.

"Come with me. I will show you where they are." She comes from behind the counter. I follow her, and when she reaches the other counter, she tells the man at the desk, "You have a passenger to check in for your twelve o'clock flight." She turns back to me.

"It was a pleasure being of service to you; do have a nice day." I feel like hugging her for being so nice to me.

"Good morning, ma'am. May I have your ticket please?" I hand the man behind the counter the plastic bag with my passport and my ticket.

"Do you have any luggage to check in?"

He sees me looking at my small bag. "You don't have to check that in; you can take it on the plane as hand luggage."

"I see that you are reserved along with a Kevin Knight. Do you know if he's still taking this flight?" I can't hold back the tears.

"Kevin died last night, so he won't be coming."

"I'm so sorry, ma'am." He hands me a tissue to wipe my eyes.

"You are all checked in. Here is your boarding pass, and you're in seat twenty-two B." I clench my teeth and take my passport and ticket from him. "Your flight leaves from gate number two, and you will have to pay a departure tax at the immigration desk."

I follow his instructions and head toward the sign that says IMMIGRATION. "Is this your first time going abroad?" the customs officer asks me, after I have paid him. I nod my head yes, for my passport is so clean and new. He stamps it. "Go straight ahead."

I continue till the pathway becomes blocked by two big machines, with four guards sitting beside them. I look at them, confused. "Put your bag on the conveyor belt and walk through." I obey, and when I reach the other side, one guard demands, "Let me see your ticket." I hand it to him. "Your flight number is fifteen-oh-two, and you will be leaving from gate two." I have no idea where gate two is, so I just stand there.

"Follow me! Look all the way down there. Do you see gate one?"

I answer, "Yes."

"Well, gate two is just beside it, and if you would like, you can go shopping in the duty-free stores in the lobby. For they will announce the boarding of your flight, when it is time."

"Thanks." I head for an empty seat. There are lots of people sitting, talking, and reading and from where I am sitting I can read one sign that says DUTY-FREE LIQUOR.

Most everybody is well dressed in nice clothes, and I feel pitiful in comparison. The clock on the wall reads 11:10 A.M., and I watch as more and more people come into the lobby.

"You takin' flight fifteen-oh-two?" I turn around to see a fat woman with several gold necklaces around her thick neck, a big hairdo, and a ball earring the size of a new pencil eraser stuck in her nose. I nod my head yes. I try to equate what all the gold around her neck can buy—a bed, a table, and maybe a fan.

"Wha' you a go a Curacao fi do, fi go shopping?"

She sits in the empty seat next to me. I shake my head.

"Me goin' there fi go to the duty-free place, fi go buy stock fi me store."

I say nothing.

"Bwoy! Me tired, me never did sure that me flight was this morning, so me rush all the way fi reach the airport."

She is wearing a short orange dress that shows most of her large legs. On her small feet is a pair of orange shoes with very large heels.

"Wha' is you seat number?" I look at my boarding pass.

"Seat twenty-two B."

"Me have seat number forty-two A."

"If you want you can sit beside me in seat twenty-two A. Cause it goin' be empty."

"How come you know that?"

"Cause me friend did fi come to foreign with me and him dead last night."

"How him dead?"

"Somebody shoot him." I hope she doesn't ask me who shot him, for I do not know.

To my relief she turns the subject to the changes in fashion, and the clothing industry. "Wha' you goin' to Curacao fi do?" she asks for the second time.

I am afraid to tell her that I am going there in search of a job and a better life, for as far as I can see life is good with her, or she wouldn't be able to buy all that gold.

"Me goin' fi visit somebody."

She digs into her orange purse, takes out a pack of bubble gum, and offers me a piece. I refuse, for I do not want to fill my stomach up with air.

"Boarding call for ALM flight fifteen-oh-two. All passengers please proceed to gate number two. This is a further boarding call for flight fifteen-oh-two, with ALM Airlines, departing from Kingston at twelve noon, and arriving in Curacao at one-thirty P.M., local time. All passengers please proceed to gate number two."

The fat woman and I get up, joining the long line of people at gate number two. We go through the gate one by one and then up a long staircase. The inside of the plane looks like a large tube, with seats that seem to go on forever. I keep walking till I find 22B. The fat woman flops down beside me in seat 22A, and when she sees me with my bag in my lap, she takes it from me and puts it in a locker over the top of my head, which I never knew existed. I watch as the plane fills up with people. Two pretty girls in uniform show us how to fasten our seat belts. If they did not show me, I would have no idea of how to do it. As the plane starts to move and gain speed, I grab the top of the seat in front of me. I am afraid, for the plane is now vibrating, and I feel my body being pushed into the seat as the plane leaves the ground. I breathe deeply, trying to calm myself, and the fat woman says, "The more often you fly, the more better you goin' feel."

I begin to relax when the voice on the speaker says we are at cruising altitude. The fat woman beside me tells me about the buying and selling business. I listen without interest, for the sounds of a Walkman playing too loudly seep into my head. I can hear the distinct sound of Bob Marley singing "No Woman No Cry." The fat woman is still chatting away, and I feel tears welling up in my eyes. I want to fight back the tears but I can't, so I clench my teeth as hard as I can, and as soon as the fat lady excuses me, I quickly follow the sign to the bathroom. As soon as I close the door I slump down on the toilet and allow the tears to flow freely. I am all alone, and I am afraid of facing the future.

I cry till my head pounds. Then I get up and wash my face with the cool water from the funny-looking tap. I stare at my reflection in the mirror, and my red swollen eyes stare back at me. I try to get rid of some of the redness by washing my face again. I return to my seat and tell the fat woman that I have a bad headache when she asks me why my eyes are so red.

"You want two aspirin?"

"Me already take two," I lie.

Two girls in airline uniforms push a trolley with food down the aisle and distribute it to the passengers. I look at all the other people eating.

"Would you prefer chicken or beef?"

"Which one is cheaper?" I ask the pretty girl. She smiles. "It's free." I am embarrassed by my lack of knowledge. "Can I have both?"

"Sure. What would you like as your beverage?"

"Milk?" She hands me the two trays of food under the unscrupulous stare of the fat woman. This time when I eat I taste the food. The boneless chicken tastes good, and I wonder if they grow chickens in foreign without any bones. When I am finished the pain in my belly has lessened. I save the beef with the vegetables for later.

The plane is about to land. It touches the runway, and I am fearful that it won't stop. Soon it slows its speed and stops completely.

"Welcome to Curacao International Airport," the voice on the intercom says. The fat woman bids me good-bye. My passport is stamped, and I walk out of the Curacao airport under the hot, bright Caribbean sun.

24

❦

MY DARK SPIRIT WALKS the streets in the blazing sun. There are
no trees anywhere. The landscape is dotted with rocks and cac-
tuses. I know I should start inquiring about work right away,
but the farther I walk, the longer the road stretches in front of
me. I can't walk anymore, so I stop on the side of the road to
rest. I scan for a shady spot, but there isn't any. My throat is
now parched. The sun has drained my energy. I am so thirsty,
and my feet ache. I wonder if somebody can give me a ride to
a town. I hold up my thumb, pleading for a ride from a passing car, as I plod along. My feet hurt harder as the day disap-
pears. I finally reach a small town. The buildings are joined
together, don't have zinc roofs, and are well painted. I see no
signs of poverty. Relieved and weary of body, I walk into a
small grocery store, my eyes staring at the different food. I ask
the white man with brown hair behind the cash register if he
needs anyone to work for him. He looks at me as if I am
crazy, or dumb, before saying no. So I ask him for a glass of
water and where I can find a cheap hotel to stay. In a funny-
sounding accent, he tells me to continue down the road and I
will see a hotel on my left. He says that it may not be very

cheap, but nothing is cheap these days. I thank him kindly and am off down the street.

By the time I reach the sign that says HOTEL, it is getting dark. I enter the lobby. A girl with a silky voice asks, "May I help you, ma'am?"

"Uh, uh, I am looking for a room for the night. How much does a small room cost here?"

"For one person?" I nod my head yes.

"That will be one hundred and twenty guilders." She sees that I am puzzled and picks up her calculator. "That will be seventy American dollars." My eyes bulge, for I have only eighty-five dollars.

"Is there a cheaper hotel near here?"

"No, the next hotel is a couple of kilometers from here." I have forgotten how many kilometers there are to a mile, but it sounds far. When I walk outside, it's getting dark. I decide to take the room, for tomorrow I will find work, and seventy dollars won't mean anything. I go back inside. "I am going to take it."

"How will you be paying, with cash or a credit card?"

"With cash." I do not know what a credit card is.

She gives me a receipt, and smiles as she hands me a key.

"Your room is number seven; go upstairs, and it's the first door on your left." I follow her directions, and as soon as I open the door, I fall on the bed with fatigue.

The walls inside the room are painted white; the bedspread is covered with different-colored flowers that match the curtain. There are a dresser, a closet, a small television, and a table with a chair inside the room. Over the bed is a painting of a funny-looking shell. The bathroom has a bathtub, and fresh white towels hang on the towel rack. I eat my beef dinner from the airplane and wash it down with water from the bathroom sink. With my aching and tired body, I fall asleep, hoping tomorrow I will find some work.

I feel rested as I stretch, getting out of the bed, glad that a new day has arrived. I bathe myself and then pack my bag. I want to steal at least one of the white towels, but the fear of getting caught prevents me. When I return the key to the room, I ask the girl behind the desk if she knows of anyplace where I can get a job. She says no. As I leave I feel my belly yearn for food. With my last fifteen dollars in my pocket, I walk down the road.

I walk all day, among the narrow streets of the pastel-painted buildings. I ask everyone I see about finding work. I tell them that I can do anything, but now the sunlight softens as evening approaches, and still I have no job, and only ten dollars left after buying something to eat. Though my legs hurt from walking and my arm tires from carrying my bag, I continue.

It is nearly dark. I find myself near a cemetery. There are graves as far as my eyes can see. My legs stop moving and my voice yells, "No!" for a small voice inside my head suggests that I should sleep here.

Then where the hell you goin' sleep? it asks again.

"Me no know!" I yell, so loudly that I startle myself. I walk into the cemetery with nicely kept graves, cautiously stepping with light steps as if I might wake someone. I walk past rows of graves with flowers on them, continuing to the far end of the cemetery till I come to a recent grave. I make the best bed possible out of my clothes. My eyes begin to twitch with nervousness. Soon I am engulfed by darkness. I lie down on my bed and tell myself to think that I am lying in a beautiful garden where I can smell the flowers. I can't fall asleep, for my brain magnifies every small sound, and with each sound I open my eyes searching the darkness. There is something moving on my face. It feels as if someone is stroking the petal of a flower across my skin. In my sleep I brush the flower away, only to feel something crawling across my face! I jolt upright just in time to see a large cockroach run down the side of the gravestone I am sleeping on. My chest heaves with fright. It is now morning.

The sun hasn't risen yet, and with hurried hands I put the clothes I made my bed with back in my bag. I rub the sleep out of my eyes. I cannot believe I have slept inside a graveyard. Suddenly I need to pee. Instead of pulling down my panty, I pull the crotch away to one side and watch as the yellow liquid soaks into the ground. I must find work, is all I am thinking as I leave the cemetery and head down the street once more.

I have been in Curacao for eight days. My spirit is sinking. All my money is gone, and I haven't found any work yet. I am still sleeping in the cemetery, and I have been cleaning myself in the bathrooms of restaurants. I am now desperately hungry.

I find myself inside a park with a few trees and a few benches. I don't know how many, for I am too hungry and too dizzy to count. I am alone in the park. No, I am not alone. There is a white woman with dark hair sitting on a bench with her little girl, who looks the same age as my twins. They are eating something that looks like ice cream. I am sitting on the far end of the park, being kept from falling over by the good grace of the backrest of the bench. The sun is high in the sky, and I watch them with weary, hungry eyes. They look so happy. The little girl giggles to something her mother says. How can they be so happy, when I am so hungry and miserable? Ah, hunger! My eyes follow the spoon as it goes from the plastic container to the little girl's mouth. I watch as she licks the plastic spoon with her little pink tongue.

I could walk over there and beg them some. No, I am too weak to walk. I could crawl over there and beg them some. No, they won't give me any. I could crawl over there and stick them up with my plastic knife and demand that they give me the ice cream or else I am going to kill them. They won't be happy anymore. They will hate me for robbing their food just as much as I hate them for having it. I am still watching them as the little girl hands the container to her mother, who then throws both containers into the garbage can. She holds the little girl's hand as they both leave the park.

With renewed hope my strength comes back, and I wait till they are out of sight before going over to the garbage can. I look inside, and I can see the two containers. My heart is beating fast, for I am praying that they haven't eaten all the ice cream. The outsides of the containers look wet, so I know there is something inside them.

"Oh, oh," I breathe in relief as I open up the containers and see some melting ice cream in them. I dig my dirty fingers into the soft cream, shoveling it into my mouth, and my whole body trembles with gratitude. I wipe the containers clean with my fingers, and feel sad that my meal has ended. Maybe there is more food in the garbage. With frantic fingers I rummage through the garbage, but there is only rubbish.

On the bench where I have left my bag there is an old man sitting with a walking stick beside him. He has a box next to him that says "Kentucky Fried Chicken." I didn't notice him enter the park. Did he see me going through the garbage? I stare at him, and he stares back. Should I just run and forget about my bag? Should I rob this old man of his chicken?

He holds out a piece of chicken from his old hand toward me. Is he giving it to me before calling the authorities? I am still standing there, just staring at him. He beckons for me to take the piece of chicken by moving his hand and head. Maybe I can grab the chicken and my bag at the same time, and then run. I walk toward the old man, my eyes fixed on the piece of chicken. As soon as I am close enough, I grab the chicken from his hand and hungrily begin to eat it, forgetting that I am supposed to run. He watches me. The chicken is so good that I chew and swallow the bones. I turn around to see the old man's small, squinting blue eyes staring at me as he holds the whole box of chicken in my direction. I immediately attack more meat. He is wearing a washed-out pair of jeans, a light blue short-sleeved dress shirt, and canvas shoes. On his wrist is a small digital watch, and his eyes are behind brown-rimmed glasses.

"*De donde Usted? Vous êtes de quel pays?* Where are you from?"

"Jamaica," I answer, my mouth full of chicken.

"Ah, so you do speak English. I had no idea where you were from, but I do know that you are not from Curacao, for we have no people going through the garbage for food." He did see me going through the garbage. Maybe I should run before he calls the authorities. My mouth is so full of chicken, and my mind is being burdened with too many thoughts, that I begin to choke. "Take it easy. Here, drink some of this." He hands me a bottle of drink from a paper bag.

"Ehhh, eahhehhhh eaahhh," I cough, knocking my chest so that the food goes down.

After several sips from his drink my cough subsides.

"What is your name?"

"Clara." I don't want to tell him my full name, in case he calls the authorities.

"My name is Hans. Hans van Dogen." He holds out his withered hand for me to shake it. I grasp his frail hand briefly, not holding it tightly lest it should break.

I am about to eat the last piece of chicken in the box.

"What about me? I need to eat too."

I hand him the box and watch as he delicately eats the last piece.

"So, how did you end up in Curacao?" I don't want to tell him the truth. "I came to visit somebody."

"Where does the person live, in Willemstad, Punda, Otra Banda?" I don't know what to tell him.

"Do you want back the rest of your Pepsi?"

"Yes, if you would be so kind. Are you trying not to answer my question?" He is inquisitive.

"Yes, I am."

"Ah, I see. I can bet that you didn't come here to visit somebody, for I saw you eating from the garbage. How did you end up here?" He looks at me and sees that I still do not want to answer.

"Tell you what. If you tell me how you ended up here, then I will tell you how I ended up here."

I turn my head to look at the feeble old man with little white hair left on his balding head. I look into his tiny blue eyes, under thinning eyebrows, for any display of trickery, but there is nothing, no emotion, no hints of his feelings.

"I came here to find a job. I came here looking for work. But I haven't found any as yet."

"Who told you that you could find work here?" Tears roll down my face. "Cokee told me so."

"You don't have to cry. Here, take this." He hands me a folded white handkerchief.

"It's okay." I refuse his handkerchief and wipe my face with the edge of my skirt.

"Why are you crying?"

"Because Cokee is dead." Now the tears are flowing faster. We are sitting side by side on the bench. The old man puts his withered hand around my shoulder. "Don't cry," he says. "I will help you find a job."

"Thanks," I mumble and wipe my tears with the back of my hand.

He tells me that he comes to the park every Friday to eat his chicken. He laughs as he speaks. "I am not supposed to eat fast food." I have no idea what fast food is. He says that after he eats his chicken he goes to visit his wife.

"Where is your wife?"

"In the cemetery," he replies.

"She takes care of the flowers in the cemetery?"

"No. No, she is dead; she is buried in the cemetery." I swallow hard.

We leave the park. He tells me that he will take me with him to visit her, and we get into his cream-colored car. He says that her name is Hanna and she died a year ago. My eyes flutter. He says that he goes to her grave every Friday just to talk to her. "So how long ago did Cokee die?"

"It's been eight days." He doesn't ask me any more questions, and we drive in silence.

We reach the cemetery, the same one that I sleep in. I follow behind his slow steps. He stops right in front of the grave that I have been sleeping on. "Hanna Emily van Dogen, 1924–1994, Rest in Peace," says the stone. There is a dove engraved above the word "Peace."

"Hanna, I want you to meet Clara. I just met her in the park, so I feel that you should meet her too."

"Come closer," he urges. "I don't think that she can get a good look at you from where you are standing." I walk closer to the grave that has been my bed for several nights, and feel that Hanna already knows me.

We leave the cemetery. "First I will take you to my house so that you can get yourself cleaned up. Then we can try to find you a job."

I feel so grateful for his kindness. "Thank you." He drives for a while and then stops in front of a row of houses. The houses are all painted in light blues, pinks, and greens. They have red-tile roofs, and all the front doors open up onto the street.

Hans parks his cream-colored car in front of a door. "This is my home."

I get out of the car and watch as he gets out with the help of his walking stick. From the set of keys, he selects the house key

and begins opening the light-yellow-painted door. He holds the
door open while I enter the hallway. A table in the shape of a
half circle stands against the off-white wall, and a mirror with a
carved frame hangs above it. On the floor by the door is a tall
basket with a large umbrella and two more walking sticks. The
floor is covered with brown tiles. I stand in the hallway waiting
for him.

"Go ahead, go inside, and welcome to my home!"

I walk into the living room. There is a long brown leather sofa
sitting against the wall. On the other side of the sofa is a brown
chair with an end table beside it, while on the other side sits a
chair matching the sofa, and another end table with a lamp on
it. In the middle of the floor is a large white rug with a beautiful
pattern of red, blue, yellow, and brown done in squares, and on
top of it sits a coffee table. In the corner of the room there is a
shelf filled with books, pictures, little statues, and a bouquet of
dried flowers. Quite a few paintings hang on the walls. The most
obvious is the one behind the sofa, a painting of a man with a
beard, which I stare at.

"Do you know who that is?" Hans points to the painting.

"Your father."

"Ah, ah, ahhh, ah," Hans laughs, holding his stomach as if
laughing might kill him.

"That's the funniest thing I have heard in a long time," he says.

Feeling somewhat silly, I try again. "It is your brother." He
shakes his head no, while still laughing. "Then it's your son or
your uncle," I insist, but he still laughs.

"That's Vincent van Gogh's self-portrait, eighteen eighty-nine."
I look at him blankly. "You don't know about van Gogh, do
you?" I shake my head no.

"Don't worry, it is not important. Put your bag down, and I
will show you the house."

There are two bedrooms, a kitchen, two bathrooms, and a

laundry room. The dining table is inside the kitchen, while the bedrooms are nicely decorated with matching bedspreads and curtains. There is a small backyard with green grass. All around the house are photographs, and I see a younger version of Hans and a woman, smiling happily, with blond hair, blue eyes, and bright red lipstick.

"That's Hanna." He strokes the face of the photograph. "Go get yourself cleaned up." I head off to the bathroom. After showering and changing into my last change of clean clothes, I walk out into the living room, where Hans sits reading.

"Ah! You look so much cleaner," he comments. "Are you hungry?"

I nod my head.

"Would you like a sandwich?" I have no idea what he means.

"Could I have some bread and butter, please, if not too much trouble?"

"Well, of course you can." I follow him to the kitchen. He makes himself a sandwich with lettuce, tomatoes, a white-looking thing from a jar that he says is mayonnaise, and some flat round meat. I eat my bread and butter, and he offers me tea which I gladly accept. After we have finished eating, I volunteer to wash the two plates and two cups in the sink, but Hans strongly objects and says he will wash them.

"So, Clara, what kind of job are you looking for?"

I ponder for a moment. "Any kind a job, for I can do anything."

"Such as what?"

I hesitate. "Well . . . uh . . . I can cook, I can clean, I can wash clothes, I can look after children, and I can . . . uh . . ."

"I see. But jobs like those don't pay that much money."

"How much is not that much money?" I ask eagerly.

"I think they pay the guilder equivalent of three hundred American dollars per month."

My mind quickly converts it to Jamaican dollars, and as far as I am concerned that is a good salary. I could never earn that much money in Jamaica for doing the same thing. My eyes shine.

"How well can you cook?"

I can cook stew beef, stew chicken, steamed cabbage, rice and peas, soups, and great porridge.

"I can cook very well," I tell him.

"Tell you what, Clara, I have a job for you. I will pay you three hundred American dollars monthly and you will wash, cook, clean, and run errands for me."

"Thank you! Thank you!" I grab his withered old hand and shake it briskly.

"Well, you can start today. Now you can wash those two plates in the sink if you want to. And then you can familiarize yourself with the house. There is plenty of food, and you can cook whatever you feel like for dinner, as long as it's not too greasy." I smile, and he smiles back at me. I want to cry from gratitude, for now I can send money home to Flo and my twins. I can save up some money, buy a piece of land, build a house, and take my family out of Greenwichtown.

I make dinner while Hans naps. Stew chicken and rice, with sliced tomatoes sprinkled with salt. He says it tastes good. As night falls I sort out my small wardrobe.

"Good night. And thanks for everything," I tell Hans. "Sleep well."

My body welcomes the soft bed in comparison with Hanna's grave. As I drift off to sleep I think of Flo, my twins, and what I have left behind in Greenwichtown.

25

It is daylight. I jump out of bed with energy. I tiptoe past Hans's bedroom, and his door is slightly open. I can see his face; his mouth is wide open and he is sleeping. After changing into the worst of my clothes, I start to clean. I sweep the whole house, wipe the tile floor with disinfectant, clean the kitchen and bathrooms, and dust all the furniture. Having finished with the cleaning, I make rice porridge for breakfast. I hope Hans will like it. He sleeps till about eleven o'clock. While I am washing my clothes by hand, I hear a loud, heavy thud. I drop the wet clothes and rush into Hans's bedroom, where I find him on the floor trying to get up.

"Hans, are you all right?" I help him sit on the bed.

"I am all right, it is only old age syndrome. Can you help me to the bathroom?" I support him to the bathroom. Soon he walks out with slow, dragging steps, dressed in yesterday's clothes. He goes into the kitchen, and I cheerfully announce, "I made breakfast."

"What did you make?"

"Porridge, rice porridge."

"Tell you what. Why don't you make me a cup of tea and cut

up some bananas, and I promise that I will eat the porridge for lunch."

I make him his tea and bananas. I ask him if there is anything else that he would like. "Only my walking stick." After giving him his stick, I clean his room and change his sheets. Finishing my laundry, I put the sheets into the square thing that Hans says is a washing machine. Fortunately the directions are on the lid, and I read them four times before turning it on.

When I am finished, I find him sitting on the sofa in the living room reading a book.

"Hans, can I have your address, so that I can write my family? For they don't know where I am."

"Well, of course. There is some paper and envelopes over there, and I have pens inside the drawer of the end table."

I get a sheet of paper.

> Dear Flo, I hope that this letter finds you and the twins in good health. I am happy to tell you that I have found a job, as a domestic helper. It's a good job, and I am being paid, $200U.S. per month, so as soon as I get paid, I will be sending you some money. The man that I am working for his name is Hans van Dogen. He is a very kind man. Kiss the twins for me. Love Clara. My address is Clara Myrtle % Hans van Dogen, Bonaire Street 25, Curaçao, Netherlands Antilles.

I address the envelope to Flo in Greenwichtown. I lie about my salary so that someday I can buy a house for my family from my savings. As soon as I finish my letter, Hans says, "I will take you to the post office."

We get into the car.

"Can you drive?"

I shake my head no.

"You will have to learn, for sometimes I am unable to."

We arrive at the post office, and soon it's our turn at the counter. "*Ik wil drie postzegels van dertig cent, en vier een gulden, alstublieft,*" Hans says.

"What did you say?" I am puzzled by the sounds he made.

"Oh, I just told the girl that I want three thirty-cent stamps, and four one-guilder stamps."

I give him an uncomprehending look.

"I was speaking Dutch."

On the way back to the house, Hans tells me more about Curacao. "In Curacao we speak four languages: Dutch, English, Spanish, and the dialect of Papiamento. I think that you should learn some of the languages if you are going to stay here for a while. I have a friend who is a lawyer, I will ask him to help me straighten out your paperwork." I tell him that my real name is Fay Myrtle.

Weeks pass. I have told Hans about my twins and Flo, and hesitantly I told him about Cokee. He absorbed it without any reaction, he only offered me his handkerchief when I started crying while telling him about Cokee's death.

Today when all my chores are done, he tells me that he will begin to teach me Dutch and Spanish. Papiamento, he says, will seep into me from contact with the local people, like osmosis.

"Get a pen and paper; we can do some work before lunch."

"Hans, how many languages do you speak?"

"Well, let's see. Spanish, English, German, Dutch, Flemish, and I can get by with Italian."

"Who speaks Flemish?"

"Belgians."

"I did French in high school," I say because I feel ignorant in comparison with Hans.

"*Alors, tu parles français?*" Most everything that I have learned in school has left my head. Finally I translate and answer the sentence.

"No, I do not speak French," I reply.

"Tell you what, why don't we start with some French, for Spanish is relatively easy, and then we will do Dutch." I nod my head in agreement.

Hans's teaching has become part of our daily routine. He teaches me after breakfast, and then between lunch and dinner after I have finished my chores. There is a television, hidden by doors in the bookcase, and he has a sound system with lots of cassettes. Sometimes while he is teaching me, he'll play music, mainly without words.

"What is that?"

Of course I have no idea what it is, and he says. "Tchaikovsky, Eighteen Twelve Overture." I memorize each sound with a name.

I have been with Hans more than a month, and he has paid me three hundred dollars. I open up my own savings account, and I send Flo two hundred dollars. Flo sends a letter back to me, telling me how glad she is that I am working. She mentions that Cokee was cremated.

I am now in Curacao for six months, and Hans has gotten my papers straightened out, allowing me to stay here longer. I am now able to make simple sentences in Spanish, Dutch, and French, and as Hans said, I am picking up Papiamento. I have learned to drive, and when I pass my driving test, Hans hugs me and says "Well done, *mon élève*." He no longer calls me Clara or Fay Myrtle; he now calls me "my pupil," in French. I tell him that we should celebrate.

"Come on, Hans, I will buy you dinner."

"No! *Mon élève,* save your money. I'll buy *you* dinner."

"No, I am buying you dinner, and there is nothing more to say about it." I drive us to a Chinese restaurant in Willemstad. This is my first time eating Chinese food. When our orders arrive, I watch as Hans starts eating with two pieces of sticks. I eat with a fork, and we have tea with our meal. When the waitress brings us the bill with our fortune cookies, we start arguing again about who will pay for dinner.

"Tell you what," says the Chinese girl, in a funny-sounding accent. "Why don't you both pay the bill?"

We both start laughing, and Hans allows me happily to pay for dinner.

Many more weeks have passed, and I have gotten to know some of the neighbors. Olga is a white woman and she looks about fifty. Her bones are short and she is fat. She lives with her husband, John, and sometimes they invite us to dinner. The other neighbor is a Spanish family by the name of Alvarez, a couple in their mid-thirties who have a five-year-old daughter named Maria.

Flo still writes to me. I send her money every month, and even though I miss my children terribly and long to hold them, I tell myself that I am doing the right thing by being so far away. If I was still in Greenwichtown, I know we would have little food. And even though it hurts me, I remember what Flo said, that you can't put love into a pot and cook it when you're hungry.

Today is Monday. Hans doesn't feel very well, so I tell him that I will take him to a doctor. "No!" he says, so firmly that I am almost offended. "I will go myself," he adds in a softer tone. He comes back from the hospital looking very sad. I press him to tell me what is wrong but he simply says. "*C'est rien!* It's old age syndrome." He says it is nothing, even though he brings home a whole batch of pills that I must ensure that he takes on time.

———

After a year I have saved up one thousand American dollars. I receive a letter from Flo, and I open it.

> Dear Clara. Good day to you and Hans. Dave Davia and me is fine. Thanks for the money. I use some of it to buy things for them birtday, and me goin make them take photograff, down town in the parke. By the way. Donna daughter dead. car kill her. me go look pon her little body, and the whole a her head just splash out in the middle of the road. Donna, bawl the whole day. She goin bury sunday. rite soon. from Flo Higgins.

I answer Flo's letter, telling her all the grammatical mistakes that she has made. I tell her about my life, about my studies with Hans, and about him not feeling too well. I head to the post office. It is my turn at the counter. *"Quiero que mandar por correro esta carta a Jamaica."* I hand her my letter, feeling proud that I can communicate in Spanish.

It's been eighteen months. My savings total one thousand, six hundred dollars. I am fluent in French, Dutch, Spanish, and Papiamento. Sometimes Hans takes me to the library and shows me paintings by famous artists such as Rembrandt, Picasso, and his favorite, van Gogh. "Hans, there is your painting," I tell him.

"Yes," he says. "My painting is a lithograph; it's a copy of the original."

Almost two years have passed. Today is Saturday. It is time for Hans to take his medicine.

"Hans, wake up. It's time for your medicine." I shake him gently. He doesn't move, so I shake him harder. "Hans, wake up!" He still doesn't move. "Hans! Hans! Get up! Hans, wake up!"

"Oh, my God! Oh, my God!" With tears running down my face, I frantically dial the emergency number, give them the address, and tell them that Hans isn't moving. I rush back to the bedroom, and I shake him again, but he still doesn't wake up. I run to the house next door and start banging on the front door. "Olga! Olga! Come quick! Hans is not moving!" Her face comes into view. She is not surprised by what I have said.

"Hurry up, Olga! Hurry up!" I rush back into Hans's bedroom and shake him again. Finally she reaches the bedroom. She gently touches his face.

"Clara, I am sorry. He is gone."

"Are you mad?! Are you crazy? He is not dead, he is only sleeping!" I yell at her. I shake him so hard that his stiffened head lifts up from the pillow. "No! Noo! Nooo!" I collapsed on his withered old body.

The ambulance arrives, and as the two men try to take away Hans's body, I start fighting them. "No! No! You can't take him. No! He is not dead. He's only sleeping! Please don't take him." Olga grabs my waist with her fat, strong, white arms and holds me as the ambulance drives away. As soon as it goes out of sight, I flop down on the street.

Olga pulls me up off the road and takes me inside. "Clara, come stay with me at my house. I promised Hans that I would make sure that you were all right when this happened."

"You knew that he was going to die?" I ask in disbelief.

"Yes," she says calmly.

"Why didn't you do something? Why didn't you tell me? I could have done something! I could have taken him to the hospital!"

"There was nothing that anyone could do."

"How can you stand there and say that? I could have done something!" I yell at her.

"No, Clara, there is nothing that you could have done; he had cancer, prostate cancer, and I am surprised that he lasted this long. For the cancer had spread through his whole body." The thought that Hans had cancer all this time makes me cry even harder and numbs my body with grief.

Olga takes me to her house and makes me soup, chicken soup, but I have no need for food. She gives me beef and potato stew for dinner. I don't eat it either. I just sit there thinking about Hans. I remember the time when he said that he wanted to cook and made sausage and sauerkraut. I remember how he laughed at me when I said, "That's not sauerkraut! That's cabbage!" I remember the times that I went with him to Hanna's grave. I think about Hanna and feel good that they are together. "I am going to miss you," I say out loud. I swear that I hear Hans saying, "I am going to miss you, too." I stop crying and tell Olga that I am going home.

It's been two days since Hans's death. A knock on the door gets me up from the sofa to open the door. It's the postman. He hands me a large envelope addressed to me. *"Danke,"* I tell him, heading inside. I open the envelope, and sheets of paper fall out. On top of the pile is a letter in Hans's handwriting. "My dear *élève*," it begins.

> I am writing you this letter to tell you that you should not cry about my death even though you will miss me. I am at peace now from all the pains that I have been having for so long. Many nights, I had to cover my mouth and cry so that you couldn't hear me. I know that I should have told you, but then it would

have made you sad. You see, I was diagnosed with prostate cancer the same year that Hanna died. By the time the cancer was found, it had already spread to my lymph nodes and lungs. It was only a matter of time before it killed me. I will be happy now. I will be with my dear Hanna.

The first day I saw you in the park, you made me feel so sad, for here was a human being eating from the garbage. I felt sad because it reminded me of the Second World War. It was such a terrible time. I was a soldier then. I was so young and full of life. When my parents moved to England, I gladly enrolled in the army because I was going to stop all the injustices in the world.

That was when I met my beautiful Hanna. We got married after the war, and we went to live in Holland. I wanted children. Hanna did, too, but soon after our marriage, she developed ovarian cancer. They removed her womb, and I loved her even more. But she always felt bad that she couldn't give me children.

I spent my whole life as a carpenter. Hanna at the time was a schoolteacher. She loved being around children. When I got too old to work and my body got fed up with the weather, I told Hanna that we should move to someplace warm. She chose Curacao. She said that it reminded her of Holland, but much better because the sun shines all the time.

Over the years she developed cancer in her bowels, and by the time it was discovered it was too late. I cried the whole day. I knew if Hanna died, I would be all alone. I took care of her the whole time, and when she died I wanted to die too.

The same year that Hanna died, I began having

terrible pain and urination problems. I went to the
hospital and was diagnosed with prostate cancer. The
cancer had spread too much to do anything about. I
told the doctor that I couldn't care less about treat-
ment, for I wanted to die and be with Hanna. The
doctor told me that I had at most a year to live. Well,
that was almost three years ago, and now I know that
I am really dying as I sit here in my lawyer's office
writing this letter to you.

As far as my burial is concerned, most of it has
been taken care of. I am to be buried in the spot next
to Hanna. By the way, I want to be buried in something decent. My black suit will be fine. I have left
you my house. It has been converted to your name,
with the few dollars that I have managed to save over
the years.

I have enclosed the name and address of my dear
friend and attorney, Yous. He is still my attorney after
I'm dead. He is a good man. We have been friends
for a long time. He will help you with any problems
that you might have. I will miss you. With all my
love, Hans van Dogen.

I put the letter on the bed, wet with tears. I look at the papers.
The house has been converted to my name. There are bank papers, and altogether there is the sum of twenty thousand guilders,
more than ten thousand U.S. dollars, in my name. I flop back
on the bed, shocked.

I call the morgue and the funeral parlor to make sure that
Hans's wishes are carried out. I go to the morgue and dress Hans
in his black suit. I brush his whole head, even though there is
little hair there, for Hans always brushed the balded part of his

head. The funeral is this afternoon, and I buy myself a black dress and pair of black shoes.

The funeral service takes place inside an old stone church. People who knew Hans fill the benches. Everyone sniffles while the pastor prays. Olga is dressed in a black dress done in lace that goes all the way down to her ankles.

We are at the cemetery where I once slept. The spot next to Hanna's grave has been prepared for Hans's coffin. After the pastor says the last prayer, the coffin is lowered inside the hole. The pastor beckons for me to throw the first handful of dirt on the coffin. Seeing my discomfort, Olga holds my hand and walks with me toward the hole. She directs my hand to pick up some dirt and, with her hand guiding mine, I release the dirt on top of the coffin. I hear the pitter-patter of the dirt against the wood.

26

"WOULD YOU LIKE SOME orange juice?" The pretty stewardess serves me breakfast. "No, just a cup of tea with milk, please." I watch as she delicately pours the hot water into the cup. I sweeten the tea, stirring it slowly, and stare at the rising steam. It's been more than two years since I have seen my twins and Flo. What will it feel like to hold them in my arms again after such a long time?

After eating an omelette I feel nauseous and head for the bathroom. I throw up in the toilet. My mouth reeks of a bitter taste; my eyes tear, but I feel better. I wash my face and stare back at myself in the mirror. A terrible pain invades me, and I cannot fight it. My lips quiver, my eyes twitch, tears flow down my cheeks and drip on the metal basin. I shudder as the feeling intensifies. "Aaahhhiiieeeiii," I murmur as my body convulses. I am going home to where Cokee died in my arms. I am going home to where the no-good father of my twins was gunned down. The burden of life is heavier, for the survival of my family lies entirely upon my shoulders, and death continues to claim its part. I look at myself more closely. I know that my body hasn't changed much, and my face is still the same, but I feel different.

Living with Hans has changed me; made me aware that there's
a world outside Greenwichtown that I am only a small part of.
My existence is so small that except for Flo and my twins, no
one will know the difference if I no longer exist. The knowledge
that our lives can change in a heartbeat without our acknowledg-
ment or approval saddens me. My head throbs like the beat of a
pulsating drum. I breathe deeply to quell the pounding pain inside
my head. I splash my warm face with the cool water, and after
washing my face for the fifth time, I return to seat number 34G.

"Ladies and gentlemen, this is Captain Burke speaking. Please
fasten your seat belts and observe the no-smoking sign. We are
about to land at Norman Manley International Airport, Kingston,
Jamaica. We hope you have enjoyed your flight, and on behalf of
the entire crew, I would like to thank you for flying with ALM."
The captain repeats the same message in Spanish and Dutch.

After the plane lands, I see the anticipation of the other passengers as their eyes scan around for their hand luggage. I have only a
small bag, tucked under the seat. Soon I join the line of people getting off the airplane. My hair is combed to the back of my head and
held together by a clip in the shape of a butterfly. On my feet are
cheap sneakers below my faded pair of jeans. My light blue T-shirt
reads CURACAO over the silhouette of a man on a surfboard. As I
get out of the doorway and onto the stairs, the hot Jamaican sun
and the cool breeze coming off the Caribbean Sea caress my face. A
slight smile crosses my lips as the familiar sounds of people speaking patois wash over me, for I am home.

After going through customs, I walk out of the airport, where
all the taxi drivers are busy hustling potential customers.

"Where you goin', nice girl?"

"Me goin' downtown. But me goin' take the bus." The eager
driver's face droops to a scowl as I head toward the bus stop.

I arrive downtown squeezed among the standing passengers on
the bus. As soon as the bus slows, the sellers swarm around it

like hungry bees. They jog to keep up with the bus as they push
their merchandise through the windows. "Bag juice! Popcorn!
Biscuits! Banana chips! Three rag fi five dolla'!" The passengers
ignore them despite their loud cries as the bus empties out. As
I stand on the sidewalk, my eyes scan the familiar sights that
depict the day-to-day hustle and bustle of downtown Kingston:
sellers with their merchandise, carts selling syrup on crushed ice
in plastic bags, hoards of people, and noise. Thirst leads me to
the cart man that sells jelly coconuts. "Sell me a jelly," I tell the
cart man.

"You goin' wash off you stomach? You want one that was on
ice?" I nod yes to both questions, and watch as he skillfully chops
an opening in the coconut with his machete.

"Me want the meat too," I tell him after drinking the liquid,
and he splits the coconut in two halves with one chop of his
machete, then chops me a spoon from the husk of the coconut.
I eagerly eat the soft jelly.

I walk to where the buses that go by Greenwichtown are
parked. Immediately two conductors grab my wrist and try to
drag me in the direction of their buses.

"You goin' to Bridgeport?" "You a go a Waterford?"

"Let go me hand!" I shake myself free from their grips.

"Me only going as far as Greenwichtown!" Another conductor
appears. "Come with me, lady, see the bus here that have seat."
I follow him, ignoring the irritated look of the other conductors.

"Ready bus a leave! Waterford!" There are only two seats
inside the bus, and I take the one with a window.

"You comin', sweet girl?" the conductor asks a woman who
looks old enough to be his mother.

"But, boy, you bright and presumptuous! You no see that me
is big woman?"

"All right, Mother." The bus is finally loaded with passengers and drives off, taking me to my family in the ghetto of Green-wichtown.

As the bus drives on, a storm builds within me. My palms sweat, my bowels rumble, and my heart pounds faster than normal. What do my twins look like? Has Davia outgrown the looks of her father? Does Dave still have those deep dimples? Will they still remember me as their mother? Has Flo changed? My head spins with a million questions as the bus drives on, along Marcus Garvey Drive. The next stop is mine.

"Next stop, driver!"

The conductor hears me and slaps the side of the bus, signaling for the driver to stop. When I see the old broken-down homes, rusty zinc fences, dusty streets, and people sitting on the sidewalk, a heavy feeling of gloom hangs over me like a dark cloud. I exhale deeply. I could have been stuck here, never knowing anything else. I could have melted into the hopelessness that is so much a part of the air the people breathe here.

People who know me wave to me sadly, for they know that I have been in foreign. My jeans are faded, my sneakers are cheap, and most notably, I have no gold hanging from my body to signify my wealth. My hair is in its natural kinky state, and I walk along the street instead of driving in a taxi. I wave back to them and force a smile, for their eyes express what they are thinking: *She came back from foreign without any money!*

As I reach the corner of Fifth Street, I think of Flo. I am sure that my letter has not reached her yet, and she doesn't know that I am coming. I walk up the road, and my eyes stray toward the black gate. It looks different now. The black paint has peeled off, revealing the rusty iron. There is no one standing there. Memories of passing through that black gate filled with love, happiness, and sadness drift through my head like vapors from the depth of my soul. A tear develops in my right eye, and I brush it away for I should look happy when I see my children.

"Clara, is good fi see you come back from foreign," the sidewalk gossipers tell me when I reach my yard. At the same time their eyes acknowledge my lack of prosperity. A part of me thinks that they are somewhat happy that I am not well-to-do, for now I can rejoin them on the sidewalk. Cynthia is sitting with a baby in her lap.

"A your baby that?"

"Um-uh. Him name Byran, after him father."

"The same Byran that dead?" Flo had written to me about Byran, who died after his cousin stabbed him during a fight.

"Um-uh." She smiles. I swallow hard. I had always admired Cynthia's ability to escape the disease of unwanted fatherless pregnancy.

I open the front gate, and a mangy, malnourished dog that probably doesn't have the strength to bite me, even if it wants to, approaches me.

"Flo! Flo!" I push open the back gate that is missing a hinge at the bottom, causing it to drag along the ground. A black face pushes out from the room's window. Flo rushes to hug me.

"Jesus Christ! Clara! Lord, me so glad fi see you!" I drop my bag to embrace her. Her eyes flood with happy tears. My twins appear at the doorway, wearing only their tops and underwear. "Clara!" they scream, and it is the most beautiful sound that I have heard in my entire life. All my questions have been answered. I rush to them, collapsing on my knees to hug their plump little bodies tightly and feel the warmth of their soft faces against my neck. They clasp my shoulders and for a moment we just stay that way. Finally I release them.

"Clara, you know that me miss you!" Dave says, and now tears flow freely down my face.

"Me missed you too."

"You want some a me porridge?" Davia asks me, as they wipe away my tears with their small hands.

"Yes," I whisper, as I follow them inside the room where three plastic bowls lie on the old table.

"Bwoy! Me *so* glad fi see you!" Flo enters the room. For the first time, I notice that she has gained weight, a sign that life is not all that bad with her. The rooms haven't changed, but the green paint is dirty and starting to peel from the walls. The door frame is now rotten from the invasion of termites. One of the windowpanes is cracked, and pieces of masking tape prevent the entire pane of glass from collapsing.

"Sit down! Sit down, and rest you feet!" Flo pulls out a chair for me to sit on. "Why make you never tell me that you was comin'?"

"Me did send you a letter, but me reach here before it."

"So, Clara, how things in foreign?" The thought of Hans comes to my mind. "Hans dead, Flo, him bury not too long ago. Him leave me him house, and some money," I add, watching Flo's face.

"How much money?" she asks.

" 'Bout a couple thousand U.S.," I tell her.

"Bwoy, me sorry fi hear say that Hans dead. For him was such a good man. You know, Clara, me save up some a the money that you been sendin' me. For me was hopin' to save up enough to buy a house and move out a Greenwichtown."

I hug her. I know the money I sent her was just enough for them to get by on, and the thought of her scrimping to save pains me. I have been saving for the same reasons: to buy a house in a place far away from Greenwichtown.

"Flo, me have enough fi we buy a house."

She smiles.

The thought I have buried in my head for all these years surfaces.

"Flo, don't you think that is time that we go visit Ma?"

"Um-uh!" she says. "But me was waiting till me buy the house, so that she can live with we."

"Make we go look fi her anyhow. Me sure that she long fi see we."

"All right. Make we go tomorrow." I nod my head, agreeing with her.

Flo rushes to the shop to buy things for dinner. She is going to cook stewed chicken with rice and peas.

As night falls, my eyelids droop with the weight of sleep. My twins snuggle close to me in bed, holding on to me as if I am some dream they fear will disappear when they awake.

27

DAYLIGHT FINDS FLO AND the twins smiling. Flo goes to the shop early, and we have eggs, canned sausage, and bread for breakfast before our trip. We all shower and change into our best clothes. We head for the bus stop. While waiting for the bus, I ask Flo, "Which part Ma live?"

"She live someplace near High Gate." She pats her short hair, as if the quick trip to the bus stop has ruined her hairdo.

"How come you never had any children?" I dreaded asking her this question all these years. Hesitantly she looks at me, and for a moment I feel she won't answer me.

"Me leave Ma house when me was thirteen, and me been on me own ever since. Me never did have any money. So when a man say to me him give me some money if me let him touch me, me said yes. So till me was fourteen that was how me live, with all them man touchin' me. Then all of a sudden me belly start growin'. So me figure that somethin' wrong. But me never did pay it any mind. So then me move into this small room with this man, name Junior. And him was always beatin' me fi every little thing! And all that him want me fi do is wash him dirty clothes. And in that yard the pipe was all the way next door. So

one day, when me was carryin' this big bucket a water on me
head, me fall down and start to bleed. When them carry me to
hospital, the doctor put me to sleep. And when me wake up him
tell me that me was pregnant, and that me won't be able to get
pregnant again." She smiles and pats her short hair again. "When
the doctor tell me that, it was the happiest day a me life. Till
me start living with Finger, and him start naggin' me 'bout havin'
baby." She stops talking and looks out into the distance, but then
her lips start quivering and her shoulders heave.

"One night after Junior beat me, me stab him with the kitchen
knife, and bury him in the back a the yard. Then me get on a
bus and never went back!"

I hug her to comfort her, and after crying on my shoulder for
a while, she breathes a sigh of relief as if a heavy burden has been
lifted. "Me happy that you have the twin them," she says, wiping
her eyes.

Soon we are in downtown Kingston, looking for a country bus
that goes to High Gate. The twins want something to eat, so we
buy them biscuits from a vendor on the sidewalk. The bus to
High Gate waits to fill up with passengers as the conductor helps
us into the bus. People appear with boxes, bags, and bundles of
merchandise that the conductor piles high on the top of the bus.
There isn't enough space on the bus top for everything, so the
aisle of the bus is packed with goods as well. We hold the twins
in our laps, and the old country bus jerks as it drives on toward
the country, taking us to Ma.

As the bus drives on I see small towns, country people, barefooted children, goats, cows, a man on his donkey, lush green
trees, and open fields along the side of the road. This is what I
have been longing for, to run barefooted along the side of the
road and know nothing else, to listen to stories that Ma used to
tell us by the fireside while she cooked, and to have food and
Ma was enough.

The bus reaches another town, and sellers swarm around it. I buy banana chips for all of us. "Buy a juice from me no, nice lady?" a boy with a bag-juice bucket pleads. "We no want no bag juice," Flo tells him. We wait and wait for passengers to get off and new ones to get on. I watch a woman sitting on a stool that was intended for a small child, with a white bucket in front of her. She is skinny, and her gray apron hangs loosely between her legs. Sitting beside her on a piece of cardboard is a little girl with large eyes, in an old brown dress. Her small feet are dirty from dust despite her plastic slippers. Clips hang from her two plaits on the side of her cheek. One hand rests on her lap while the other touches her face, where her thumb is buried inside her mouth. She smiles at me with her thumb still in her mouth, and I smile back. I dig into my pocket and pull out some money and wave it at her through the bus window. She springs from the cardboard and rushes toward the bus.

"How many bag juice you want, ma'am?"

"Four." I watch as she runs back to her mother who opens up the bucket and hands her the bag juices. She takes them to me, and my eyes follow her as she goes back to sitting on her cardboard. I smile as her mother pats her on her head. "Good work, Denise. Keep lookin' out fi more customers."

The twins try to count trees that the bus speeds by, while I suck on my bag juice. I am almost twenty years old, and the last time I saw Ma I was about four. Do Mavis, Clive, and Julie still live with her? Will she remember me? What will I say to her when I see her? Is she still poor and selling tobacco? Does she still live in the same little house with all those beautiful flowers?

The bus reaches Linstead, and again the sellers swarm, preventing the passengers from getting off. I buy peanuts for all of us. When the bus reaches Bogwalk, many passengers get off. The conductor unloads the goods on top of the bus. The driver gets out of the bus: "Me goin' piss." Minutes later we are driving again.

"Clara, we almost reach!" I am starting to see things that are familiar, an old tree stump by the side of the road that Clive and I rested on on our way from the shop.

"Driver, give me a stop a the next corner!" The conductor slaps the side of the bus and yells, "Corner stop! Corner stop, driver!"

We get off, and the old country bus rambles on, leaving a trail of black smoke behind it. From the road I can see the small shack that had once been my home. The zinc sheets on the roof are completely rusty. One side of the shack is cardboard instead of wood. The flowers with the rows of stones around them are the only beautiful thing about the shack. Holding the hands of the twins, I swallow hard, following behind Flo down the path.

The ground is slightly wet from last night's patter of rain, and the small blades of grass tickle my ankles. We reach the shack.

"Miss Voy! Miss Voooy! Miss Voooy!" Flo yells. Unconsciously she leans against the side of the shack with her right hand, and her hand goes right through the cardboard, allowing sunlight to enter the shack.

A meager old woman wobbles to the door. Her lips part and show her toothless gums. "A who that?" She rubs her withered hand over her sooty old dress as if she is trying to get the wrinkles out of it.

"A me Miss Voy! A Flo!"

"Jesus Savior! Me so glad you come look fi me! Come closer, me can't see too good, me eye them get dark!" Tears form in my eyes, for I remembered Ma as a strong woman, and I expected to find her that way. Her eyes must be really dark, for she doesn't even see me and my twins, her grandchildren. "Miss Voy, Fay come too, and we bring her twin them." Flo looks back at me.

The old woman smiles, showing her gums. Streaks of tears run down her bony face and glisten in the sunlight.

"Fay, where you is? Come closer! Me never think that me would see you again!" I run to her open arms. Her arms have aged in my absence. I embrace her and feel the pain of needing her, which I have kept inside me for so long, release its grip. I wipe away the tears from her bony, wrinkled face. "No cry, Ma," I tell her, even though I am crying too. Flo hugs us, and now Flo is crying too. The cries of the twins get us to pull apart, for we had forgotten about them. I fall to my knees hugging them.

"Hush ya. Sheee! Don't cry. Sheee!" Flo and I lift the twins up, bringing them close to Ma's face so she can meet them.

"Is two girl?" Ma feels the faces of the twins.

"No, Ma, one a girl and one a boy."

"Where is them father?"

"Him dead, Ma."

"Come inside, come inside!" she urges us.

The shack is still the same. The old table from Missy's yard is still there. The big pillow stuffed with banana leaves lies on the dirt floor. The kitchen no longer exists, for Ma now cooks inside the house. As a result of all the wood fires, everything is covered with black soot.

"So, Ma, wha' happen to Julie, Mavis, and Clive?" I sit on the old rickety chair.

"Them get big and gone live on them own."

"Where them live?" Flo asks.

"Me no know. Me no have no idea at all."

"Ma, wha' ever did happen to Stumpy?"

"Stumpy live over Mass T property. Mass T dead. Stumpy marry one nice girl, name Dimples, and them have one little boy. But Dimples dead couple years after that. Me hear that she did have a lump inside her head, and it burst and kill her."

"Me sorry fi hear that," I tell her.

"You know, Fay, all them years Stumpy been asking me where you is. And me keep tellin' him that me don't know. I think that him feel that me been lyin' to him. You should go over there and tell him."

"But, Ma, me just arrive."

"Is a'right child. Me will still be right here when you come back."

"Flo, keep the twin them, me goin' to look fi Stumpy." I head toward Mass T's property. The more I walk, the more I think about the past.

"That bush is called search-me-heart." I can almost taste the tea that Ma used to make with it. I pick a piece of bush and hold it to my nose. I inhale deeply, closing my eyes and opening them toward the cloudless blue sky.

I reach Mass T's property, and I can see a house, a rough-looking house. There is a field alongside the house, growing yams, cabbage, and tomatoes. I can see the outlines of an outhouse and a kitchen. A tan-colored cow grazes in the pasture. On the shaded doorstep of the house sit a little boy in a red shirt and a man with a beard and wide shoulders.

"Stumpy! Stumpy! Stumpyyy!" Across the field the man gets up from the doorstep, and looks at me. He runs toward me with his black plastic field boots raising dust behind his heels.

"Fay!" His hug lifts me off the ground.

He puts me down on the ground. "Fay, wha' ever did happen to you?" He looks just like I had pictured him in the cane field. "Fay, all them years I wait fi you come back. And when me ask Miss Voy where you is, she say she no know. Then when me ask her when you comin' back, she say she no know. Which part you was, Fay?"

"Me was in Kingston, Stumpy. Me was livin' with me sister Flo."

"Fay! You have no idea how much me miss you." He wipes the tears from my face.

"Me miss you too Stumpy." He hugs me again tightly, and his beard tickles my neck. He holds my face in his large hands and asks, "Fay, you remember wha' me did tell you at we dollyhouse the last day that me see you?" He looks into my eyes. "Um-uh," I mutter.

"Me did tell you say that when me get big, me was goin' marry you and build a big, big field. And you laugh and say how me goin' marry you when you taller than me?" How could I have forgotten that?

"Fay? You remember that? You really, really remember that?" he asks.

"Yes, Stumpy, me remember."

"Fay, me did mean every single word of it!" He searches my face for hope.

"But Stumpy, me all grown up now, and me life is different now, and me even have twins."

"Chow, man! That no matter, Fay. You still live with them father?" he asks.

"No. Them father dead."

"Come meet me son." He holds my hand and leads me to his little boy. "Fay, this is me son, Wayne." I drop to my knees in the dirt to hug the child, for I know how it feels to miss a mother. To my surprise he hugs me back and doesn't want to let go of my neck. I stand up, holding the child in my arms. I tell Stumpy that Flo and my twins are at Miss Voy's yard and I want him to meet my children. He closes the door to his house without locking it. "You not goin' lock the door?"

"Me no have to lock the door, for everybody know everybody." I have forgotten how life is in the country. I carry Wayne all the way to Ma's yard, and as soon as I reach it my twins run toward me, asking me where I got this little boy from.

"Stumpy, this is me twins," I tell him.

"A who this?" Davia looks up at Stumpy.

"Dave, Davia, this is Stumpy, and this is him son Wayne." I put Wayne on the ground.

Ma and Flo are at the doorway, watching the three children play as if they have known each other all their lives.

"Wha' happen, Miss Voy?"

"Flo, this is Stumpy," I say, before Ma can answer. Flo looks at Stumpy. "Nice fi meet you."

"Nice fi meet you too." Stumpy looks at me.

"You people must be hungry, is about time we cook some food," Ma says.

"Me will find some wood," Stumpy offers.

"Me will go to the shop." Flo goes off with the three children running behind her with the promise of sweet biscuits.

"Me goin' fi some wood over me yard." I volunteer to help Stumpy carry the wood. I follow him to his yard. He asks if I would like a drink of cool water. I answer yes. I walk behind him into the kitchen. He pours me some water from a plastic pitcher. He watches when I drink it as bits of water escape down my chin. I hand him the glass, and when he takes it, he grasps my hand. He looks at me and pulls me toward him. He presses his lips against mine and slowly parts my lips while his beard tickles my face. His strong arms encircle my waist, holding me against him. He kisses me slowly. He lets go of me. "Come make we go get the firewood." I float behind him.

Flo cooks soup with chicken, beans, yams, dumplings, carrots, potatoes, scallions, pumpkin, and everything else that is available. We sit on the floor to drink our soup. When night falls, the full moon shines and lights up the whole village. The twins yawn, their faces yearning for sleep. Stumpy picks up Wayne and says that Flo, the twins, and I can sleep in his house if we want to, for he can sleep in the kitchen. Flo says no. I would have said yes. He leaves, and I walk him to the road. I bid him good-bye.

"Fay, dream about wha' me tell you."

"Me will, Stumpy."

I go back to find Ma fluffing the banana-leaves mattress on the ground. Flo is already lying in the other room, with the twins beside her. I hug Ma again.

"Fay, you remember that you use to sleep on top a me, when the bed was too lumpy?"

"Me remember, Ma."

I help her to lie on the noisy bed. I lie beside her, and she holds me close to her. I smell the smoky scent of her clothes, and the night creatures play their music. I fall asleep, snuggling up to the warmth and comfort of Ma's body.